WEREWOLF

Matthew Pritchard

SAPERE BOOKS

WEREWOLF

Published by Sapere Books.

11 Bank Chambers, Hornsey, London, N8 7NN,
United Kingdom

saperebooks.com

ISBN: 978-1-913028-73-2

'Do not rejoice in his defeat, you men. For though the world has stood up and stopped the bastard, the bitch that bore him is in heat again.'

— BERTOLT BRECHT

Acknowledgements

I would like to thank the following people:

Chris, Jen, Linda and Jim from Salt Publishing for their continuing support.

Peter and Rosie from Ampersand for believing in me.

My family and friends for … everything, really.

Ian Wickes and Domyan Shalloy, who both read early drafts of the book and helped sharpen the storyline.

Hugh 'Basset' Winter, who served in occupied Germany after the war and was the first person of my acquaintance to mention the word 'werewolf' in connection with German soldiers. Although I am certain most of the stories he told me were either wildly exaggerated or entirely apocryphal, they did pique my interest enough that in later life I began to investigate the subject further.

The historian, Dr Christopher Knowles. Not only did his blog provide me with fascinating details of day-to-day life in the British Zone of Occupation, he was also deeply generous in giving me both his time and opinions as I sought to make the book as historically accurate as possible.

PART ONE

1

August 1945
Occupied Germany; British Zone

Safe now within the shadows of the trees, Little Otto pulled the mask from his face and peered back towards the house.

British soldiers in berets and leather jerkins lounged by the wrecked kitchen door, smoking cigarettes and chatting as a shaven-headed sergeant dragged Little Otto's suitcases out of the kitchen and smashed the locks from them with a rifle butt. One by one, the soldiers yanked articles of clothing from the suitcases and began comparing and trying them against themselves.

'Blasphemous pricks,' Little Otto hissed, as he saw his trophies defiled. That clothing was his. It was meant to be savoured and enjoyed. Caressed. Touched. Smelt.

Little Otto's fingertips fluttered across the surface of his Mask of Many, seeking reassurance in the rasp of its leathery surface. He buried his face in the mask's rigid folds, sucking in its soothing aroma — glue and the tang of cured flesh. His breathing slowed and his heart stilled; anger and hatred faded. He ran his fingers across the loops of twine that bound the mask's lips as he considered his position.

The soldiers would head down into the cellar soon. That was when the real fun would begin: he'd left all his tools down there. But it was what he'd left at the top of the house that most concerned him. His eyes went towards the garret window, the room he'd been in when the soldiers had arrived and begun bashing at the door with their boots. Otto had had to escape through the hole in the roof.

He fingered the heavy key in his pocket. Should he move his treasures? No. There were too many of them. Where would he put them all? He would just have to wait it out.

A cry sounded within the bowels of the house, followed by shouts and sudden flustered activity. A young soldier ran outside, rested his rifle against the side of the house and sprinted in the direction of the town, his face pale.

Little Otto watched the soldier go then tucked the Mask of Many inside his coat and loped towards the deeper dark at the centre of the wood.

A small matter. He had been interrupted before. He knew what to expect.

But he wouldn't let anyone stop him this time, though.

2

Detective Inspector Silas Payne took the Brunswick road north-east out of Eichenrode. He followed the pitted strip of tarmac for a half-mile then turned his utility onto a dirt road. A soldier in British uniform appeared from between the trees and waved for him to stop.

'Are you the gentleman from Scotland Yard, sir?' the young private said, as he bent beside the car window. 'HQ said you were coming.'

Payne handed him his identity papers. As the private turned to examine them, Payne noticed the man seemed to have an article of clothing stuffed down the front of his battle blouse: the end of a white woollen sleeve was dangling above the private's belt buckle.

'How many bodies are there?' Payne said, taking back his identity papers.

'Two. Least that's what I heard.'

'You've not seen them?'

The private adjusted the strap of his rifle and shook his head. 'I've seen enough of dead bodies for one life, sir, what with all the fighting I've done. The house is just around the corner. Ask for Sergeant Beagley.'

Payne drove away, thinking how glad he was that the war was finally won; the private looked barely old enough to vote.

The house was set back from the road behind a row of oaks. It would have been an impressive dwelling once — three stories of half-timber built in the rural German style with bay windows on the lower floor — but the walls were peppered with bullet holes and a mortar had ripped a massive hole in the crow-stepped roof. The shell had obviously exploded inside the house, as the unkempt garden was strewn with glass and household items.

A group of soldiers stood beneath the shade of an oak. When Payne pulled up next to them, they waved for him to go round to the back where a burly sergeant with close-cropped hair stood leaning against the jamb of the back door, hands in the pockets of his leather jerkin.

'Who wants to know?' he said when Payne asked if he was Sergeant Beagley.

'Detective Inspector Payne, Scotland Yard. Major Norris of Public Safety Branch has asked me to look into this matter.'

The sergeant looked him up and down, as if to check Payne was real. Then, he said, 'You're a bit off your usual beat, aren't you, Detective Inspector?'

Payne smiled politely. He'd been in Germany only four days, but he'd already heard that particular quip more times than he cared to remember.

Beagley led him inside.

'The corpses are in the cellar,' he said, indicating a low door in the wall beside the fireplace. He crossed the kitchen and started down the cellar steps, but paused when Payne did not follow him.

The crime scene was a shambles from a procedural point of view, but nineteen years' service with the Metropolitan police had taught Payne the benefit of taking the time to notice the small things. He stood in the centre of the room and slowly turned a full circle.

There were no chairs or tables in the kitchen, but there was a sink in the far corner and the shelves above it were lined with tins of British army rations. Payne turned back towards the door. The wood on the inside of the frame was splintered. He crossed the room and bent to examine the door handle.

The wood around the latch bolt was cracked and the escutcheon plate was crumpled inwards. It looked like the door had been kicked open from outside. The damage looked recent, too. Had Beagley stood in the doorway to hide that fact? Payne decided that he had: Payne's examination of the door had caused Beagley to frown.

Payne straightened and traced his finger over the words chalked on the exterior face of the door: '*Requisitioned by 21st Army Group*'. Those hadn't been written recently, though, the chalk was too faded and smudged. That meant the house had likely been requisitioned by combat troops when they occupied the area back in May. The occupation force was called the BAOR now, the British Army of the Rhine.

'Are British personnel billeted here?' Payne said.

Beagley motioned towards the tins on the shelf. 'Looks that way, doesn't it?'

Payne picked up a tin of bully beef and wiped a fingertip through the light covering of dust on its top. There was dust on nearly all the horizontal surfaces in the kitchen, now that he came to look. No, Payne thought, no-one had lived there for at least a month, maybe longer.

The air in the cellar was moist and cool. Cobwebs dangled from the rough-hewn beams in the ceiling and the wooden steps creaked as Silas Payne followed Beagley's torch-light down into the darkness.

The male corpse lay on a heavy table in the centre of the cellar. The woman lay on the earth floor. Both were naked but for pieces of sacking that covered the woman's breasts and both their groins.

'Did you put that sacking there, Sergeant?' Payne said.

Beagley shook his head. 'That's how we found them. My boys didn't touch a thing.'

Payne turned on his own torch and touched the back of his fingers to the man's naked arm. The corpse was ice cold and rigid, the skin a whitish-blue colour. The woman's was the same. Blood had pooled in the lower half of both corpses, in the buttocks and the backs of the calves. That told Payne they'd been lying like that when they died, or had been placed in that position soon afterwards.

Payne shone his torch on the horizontal bruise that circled the man's neck just below the Adam's Apple. It looked like someone had wrapped a ligature around his neck then twisted it tight, but there were no other injuries on the man's body: no cuts, bruises or scrapes; no damage to the fingernails. That was uncommon in a strangling: the violence of the victim's death throes was normally terrible.

The woman's body had the same horizontal bruise across the neck. However, unlike the man, she seemed to have struggled. Two of her fingernails were broken and she had a bruise on the side of her face. Her upper lip was slightly swollen, too.

That still wasn't much damage if she'd been strangled, though, Payne thought. Perhaps the killer had knocked her unconscious first.

'That's the creepy bit,' Beagley said, motioning towards a small table at the far end of the cellar.

The table was covered with surgical instruments. There were four scalpels, a hacksaw and a length of serrated wire ending in wooden handles. Beside them were a long, curved sewing needle and a roll of catgut; beyond those, various glass vials filled with liquid and a syringe. A leather apron hung from a hook in the wall and Payne saw there was a bundled tarpaulin beneath it.

'That there's a surgeon's needle,' Beagley said. 'I've seen medics stitch wounds with 'em.'

Payne crossed the uneven soil floor to take a closer look. A neat rectangle of felt covered the table top and the scalpels and hacksaw were set out upon it perfectly parallel to one another.

Payne studied the labels on the vials. Avahxim. Goloqta. They sounded like brand names. The list of chemical compounds was written in German. Payne could understand the words, but they meant nothing to him.

'Do you think someone was going to operate on 'em?' Beagley said. 'Before they were strangled, I mean.'

'I've no idea,' Payne said, as the beam of his torch glinted on scalpel blades and curved glass. The same thought had occurred to him, but operate for what?

'What were your men doing out here?' Payne said. 'It's quite a long way from the town.'

'We were doing a sweep through this area. We still do them even though the war's over. Keeps the lads sharp. We'd not patrolled this area before and … well, we saw this house had been requisitioned so we came to see if we could scrounge a cuppa. Nobody was home, so we came inside and this is what we found.'

Payne nodded. Beagley wasn't lying, but he hadn't told Payne the whole truth, either: the sergeant's answers had been preceded by momentary pauses, as if assessing how best to answer to his own advantage. You didn't get far in the Met without learning to spot that.

Payne returned to the bodies. The dead man looked to be about Payne's own age, early forties, but the woman was younger, perhaps as young as twenty-five.

'What's this tattoo here, sergeant?' Payne said, indicating small Gothic letters tattooed on the inside of the man's upper arm.

'Lord, I didn't notice that,' Beagley said, bending to examine it. He blew air. 'It's his blood group. That means he was Waffen SS. We've been briefed to watch for that among the refugees. Some of these bastards are trying to skip the country now they're facing trials for war crimes.'

Payne pushed the brim of his hat upwards. That complicated things. He needed to speak to Major Norris.

'Looks like the bastard got what he deserved, anyway,' Beagley said with a sneer.

Payne ignored the comment. From what he'd seen of conditions in the British Zone of Occupation, the line between proper justice and arbitrary vengeance had become badly blurred.

'Men from the RAMC should be coming here soon to take the bodies away for an autopsy,' Payne said. 'Can you and your men guard the house until then?'

Beagley agreed. The two men went back upstairs to the kitchen. Payne began to examine the rest of the house.

Some of the ground floor rooms were furnished, but the air in them smelt stale. Payne's shoes stirred dust as he walked across the rugs.

There was nothing of any worth in the rooms upstairs. The furniture had all been broken up and burnt; charred scraps of chair legs and bed frames littered the fireplaces. It confirmed the impression Payne had formed in the kitchen: no-one had lived there for weeks.

At the rear of the first storey was a small staircase that led to the second storey garret. Payne climbed the steep, uneven steps with a wary eye on the ceiling above him: the mortar blast had cracked the roof beams and they sagged in a downward V directly above his head.

The door at the top of the stairs was heavy and old. Payne turned the handle. The door wouldn't budge, but Payne couldn't decide whether it was simply locked or blocked by rubble on the other side. He tried shoving the door with his shoulder but stopped when the roof beams creaked and dust and rubble poured onto the brim of his hat.

He went downstairs and out into the back garden. Cushions, scraps of paper and fabric lay mouldering in the unkempt grass. The sun was below the horizon now and the shadows between the trees were deepening into darkness. Thick clouds raced westwards, like puffs of dirty smoke.

The branches of a tall oak shaded a bower at the back of the garden. The bower held a broken child's swing and a circular well-head made of red brick that rose a yard or so above the ground. Moss grew between the pitted bricks of the well and its wooden cover was gnarled with age.

Two hessian sacks rested against the bole of the oak. Payne toed the sacks and sniffed the air. Just for a moment, he fancied the wind carried with it a faint chemical tang. He tried to lift the cover from the well, but it was held in place by shiny padlocks, one on either side. He bent to examine the padlocks, but paused when a dull explosion sounded somewhere to the west of him. Payne took his binoculars and walked through the trees to where he could look out across the whole valley.

Engineers were clearing anti-personnel mines from the western approaches to Eichenrode; the fields around the town were still strewn with thousands of the wretched things. From here, Payne could see the sandbag revetments of the German trenches that the mines had been placed to defend. He watched as a plume of dirt rose briefly against the horizon and another dull pop sounded.

He went back to the front of the house and saw the RAMC ambulance had arrived. Payne put on his gloves and went downstairs to collect the surgical tools and vials as evidence. Then he took a camera from his utility and photographed the dead bodies.

'All set, Inspector?' Sergeant Beagley said when he'd finished.

'Just a few more questions before I go, if I may. How would I find out which unit requisitioned this building? And whether anyone is billeted here now?'

Beagley shrugged. 'The first units through here, back in May, requisitioned practically every building that was standing. Normal procedure was to give the German owners a chit and eight hours to sling their hooks. But a lot of those troops have gone back home, now. I suppose you could try Housing Branch, see if they've got records, though I doubt it. They were drowning in requisition chits and receipts last time I went there.'

Payne nodded, made a note of it. Then he looked Beagley full in the face.

'Do you know where the victims' clothes are, Sergeant?'

'Clothes?'

'Both bodies are naked. I presume they were clothed when they came here.'

Beagley's frown returned. 'They might have been killed somewhere else and brought here.'

'Not according to the marks left by livor mortis. You see, when the heart stops pumping, the blood sinks in a downward direction. In this case, the blood has pooled in the back, buttocks and calves, which means they died in a horizontal position, lying face upwards — most likely right where they are now. So, tell me, Sergeant, did your men find any clothing inside the house?'

Beagley's big face had become hard and aggressive. Payne thought he was seeing the real man for the first time.

'No.'

'Are you sure? Because I fancied that young private out by the road had a white jumper shoved down his battle blouse. And that kitchen door has been recently kicked in, which means your men were likely hoping to find more than a cup of tea inside. So, I'll ask one last time: Did your men —'

'Questions, questions,' Beagley said, dropping his voice. 'It's always the same with coppers, isn't it? Well, I've got news for you. Whether that door was kicked in or not ain't your concern, and I'll tell you why: me and my lads were out here spilling our blood and guts while you were back home checking blackout curtains. So you can take your questions and shove 'em where the sun don't shine. If I'm going to be questioned by anyone, it'll be the redcaps. Clear?'

Payne held Beagley's eyes. Then he turned and walked back to his utility.

'You're way off your turf, copper,' Beagley called, as Payne drove away. The other soldiers laughed.

Payne thought about what Beagley had said as he headed back to town. He'd been chancing his arm, trying to strong arm a man like Beagley. After all, Payne had no jurisdiction over army personnel out here. Truth be told, he wasn't sure he had jurisdiction over anyone.

But he was damn sure about one thing: Sergeant Beagley was hiding something.

3

The next day dawned, overcast and grey. As was his habit, Captain James Booth rose early and took a walk through the streets of Eichenrode.

The fighting in this part of town had been especially fierce and hardly anything man-made was left standing: the odd chimney stack, a brick facade. They reminded Booth of the monastery ruins in the dell beyond his old school's rugby field. *Perhaps this is how history's footfalls always look*, he decided, *scraps of architecture rising from mounds of pulverized stone.*

The Germans queuing beside the standpipe at the end of the road looked as bleak and broken as their town. Opposite the standpipe, the trunk of a huge oak formed an unofficial noticeboard for the German populace. Hundreds of papers fluttered from the tree's bullet-scarred bark, and all began with the same words, *Ich suche*, and then the name of the missing family member that was sought.

Booth paused in his customary spot opposite the oak and lit a cigarette. Six months ago, the thought of standing on German soil and looking out over biblical desolation would have thrilled him, but now that victory had arrived it didn't seem quite as pristine as he'd always imagined it. One of Booth's friends in Bomber Command had assured him that by the end of the war the RAF could deliver more tonnage of bombs in a single weekend than the Germans dropped on London during the whole of the Blitz. Booth had assumed the man was exaggerating. Now he wasn't so sure. The bombed areas of London were mere purgatories compared to the hell of some of Germany's urban areas. The scale of the destruction was beyond imagining.

When Booth returned to the billets of his field intelligence unit, the duty sergeant gestured towards a man in a cheap grey flannel suit standing opposite the door to Booth's office.

'My name is Detective Inspector Silas Payne,' the man said, shaking Booth's hand. 'I hear you're the man to speak to about werewolves.'

Booth closed the door to his office, checking his watch as he did so. 'So, you've been seconded to the Control Council for Germany, Detective Inspector? Should I call you that, by the way, or just Mr Payne? Or should I use your CCG rank?'

'I'd prefer Detective Inspector. But it's your decision.'

Yes, you would prefer that, wouldn't you? Booth thought. You could tell this Silas Payne was a policeman. It was the way he stood, with his hands thrust in his pockets, rocking on the balls of his feet as he took everything in. And that long, bony nose of his, it was just right for sniffing around in other people's affairs.

'What brings you to our part of Germany, then, Detective Inspector?' Booth said, inviting Payne to sit.

'I'm to run a training centre for German policemen here in Eichenrode.'

'A training centre? I wasn't aware there was one.'

'There isn't. That's the problem.'

'Oh, dear. Been a bit of a stuff up back in Blighty has there?'

'I've got the building. What I don't have are students. They've all been interned.'

'I'm afraid I'm partly to blame for that,' Booth said, wondering why Payne's thin, austere face seemed so familiar.

'The Colonel in charge of this area ordered us to arrest all the German policemen a few weeks back.'

'Was that wise?'

'Colonel Bassett — that's our commanding officer — is typical of these Blimp types the military government are wrenching out of retirement and turning into ad hoc proconsuls: still wet with the mud of Flanders fields, and with no interest in seeking *rapprochement* with the "damned Jerries", if you catch my drift. The good colonel has a tendency to conflate all Germans with Nazis, and once he got his hands on a list of names and addresses, he had us round all the local police up. I think he's convinced they're all ex-Gestapo agents. But do tell, Detective Inspector, what is your interest in the werewolf insurgency?'

'There was a double murder here yesterday. The dead man was Waffen SS. Major Norris of Public Safety Branch has asked me to look into things. It's been suggested these Nazi partisans, the werewolves, were involved.'

'I say, this isn't something to do with that clandestine field hospital they found out by the Brunswick road, is it?'

Payne frowned. 'Who told you it was a field hospital?'

'Well, that was the rumour doing the rounds in the officers' mess last night. I presume the soldiers that found your dead bodies must have reported it that way. But I can see from your face you don't agree.'

Payne shrugged. 'I found surgical tools and vials of medicine there. But I still think it was something else.'

'Something else ... how?'

'That's the problem. I don't know. It's just a feeling. But I know a murder scene when I see one.'

Booth sighed. 'Well, I'm afraid supposition and hunches won't get you very far with Colonel Bassett. If it's been reported to him as a field hospital, that is what it will be *in perpetuum*, no matter how eloquently you argue the contrary.'

Payne had a notebook out now. 'What can you tell me about the werewolves, captain?'

'It seems they were the brainchild of Himmler, back in late '44, but the whole thing was always very hush-hush, for obvious reasons. The fact that the Nazi hierarchy were preparing partisan-style resistance in areas the Allies were poised to conquer constituted an open admission that the war wasn't going quite as well as the propaganda ministry would have had people believe.

'The German code name for it was *Operation Werwolf.* According to a training manual I translated in October, these partisan cells were to have access to arms dumps and explosives and were to "*fall upon the Allied lines of communication like werewolves.*" That said, we've not had many problems with them in this sector: just the odd cut telephone wire, pit traps, that sort of thing. I think the werewolves' main impact has been psychological, principally due to the name. It's so terribly evocative, isn't it?'

'I've heard the British advance guard found bodies strung up from lampposts when they moved into Eichenrode. I've been told they were Germans executed by the werewolves.'

'Ah, yes. Didn't actually see it myself so I can't say. But it's more probable that those people were killed by SS or Wehrmacht units engaging in a last minute spasm of hate.'

'Wasn't there one of those elite Napola boarding schools in this region? The children at those were bred to be fanatics.'

'Agreed. But it's important to realise that children are what they still are, even now. Or, rather, young adolescents.'

Payne tapped pencil against notepad for a moment, then took a cardboard file from his satchel. 'Do you think adolescents did this?' he said, handing Booth a series of photographs.

In the first, a naked male body lay on a wooden table. The second showed a woman lying on a dirt floor, her breasts and crotch covered with sackcloth. Thick bruises ringed each of their necks. A third photo showed surgical implements on a table. *No, he's right*, Booth thought as he looked at the photos, *this was not carried out by a teenager.*

'In each case, the victim was strangled,' Payne said. 'As you can see in the photos, there is a furrow in the flesh of the neck that indicates a ligature of some sort was used. An army medical officer performed an autopsy last night and he suggested that, given the bruises found on the backs of the necks, some form of tourniquet was applied and used to gradually tighten the ligature until strangulation occurred.' Payne gestured towards the photos. 'Have you seen anything like this before, Captain?'

'Well, if it were something to do with the werewolf insurgency, it would suggest a level of organisation we've not seen before. But anything's possible, I suppose. It does look like some type of medical operation was about to be carried out, doesn't it?'

'What about British soldiers murdering Germans? Have there been many incidents?'

Booth shifted in his seat. He blew air and gestured towards the photos. 'Surely you're not suggesting British soldiers did this?'

'I'm not suggesting anything, Captain. But I can't discount the possibility at the moment. And it seems to me that blaming it on werewolves could be a convenient smoke screen. Have there been any incidents of British troops committing murder?'

'Murder is such an emotive word, isn't it? But if you're talking about summary justice being dispensed, well, yes, I'm afraid there have been some incidents, mainly involving combat troops. Some of the fellows we had here at the beginning of the occupation were real tough old 30 Corps veterans. They'd seen more fighting than you or I could imagine, and they'd all lost someone dear to them. You never know how a chap will react when he's put under that sort of pressure. Suffice it to say that 99 per cent of those incidents were limited to the weeks directly following the German collapse. It was all a bit chaotic back then. But I really don't think this —' he motioned towards the photos of the corpses — 'could have had anything to do with British soldiers.'

Payne made notes then said, 'You mentioned that you used a list to arrest the local Nazis. How come this Waffen SS man hadn't been caught and interned already?'

The faint note of reproach made Booth look up from the paperwork he was sorting, but Payne's expression was neutral. *I know who you look like*, Booth thought: Old Crippley, a schoolmaster he'd had, a former cleric; Payne had that same air about him, horsehair shirts and self-denial.

'Arresting Nazis is not a clear-cut business, Detective Inspector. Men hide out in the woods. They lie about who they are, mix themselves in with the DPs, the displaced persons. Don't forget, a lot of these chaps will be facing prosecution for war crimes. The prospect of the hangman's noose does tend to give a chap pause before handing himself in.'

If Payne noted the irritation in Booth's voice, he chose to ignore it, so Booth went over to the attack. 'Actually, talking of Germans, I suppose you'll need to interview some sooner or later. I don't mean to be rude, but do you actually speak any German?'

Booth repeated the question in German for good measure, but the smile on his lips faltered when Payne replied in rapid and flawless German, saying that, yes, he thought he knew enough to manage.

Booth needed a moment to overcome his surprise.

'Well, I must congratulate you on your German, Detective Inspector. It's as good as mine, I'd say, and I was top of my class at Oxford.'

'I've been told you have access to files on SS men,' Payne said, ignoring the compliment. The policeman possessed a deep inner calm that was really quite annoying, Booth thought.

'Yes. A unit of our advance guard captured a load of files from *RuSha*.'

'And what is that?'

'*RuSha*? The SS Race and Settlement Main Office. It was originally established to safeguard the racial purity of the SS, but it ended up organising most of the mass deportations that occurred in the conquered territories.'

'What do the files consist of?'

'Before joining the SS, a man had to obtain a licence from *RuSha* to prove the purity of his bloodline — a little like a pedigree for a dog, really. Part of that process involved supplying lots of photographs — something which has proved very useful to chaps like myself who are trying to find former Nazis.'

Payne nodded towards the photo of the dead man's face. 'Is there any way we could use the files to find out who this man was? I can't really move my investigation forward until I know who the victims were.'

Booth laughed when he saw that Payne was serious. 'Detective Inspector, there are tens of thousands of files. It would take weeks — months — to check every single photo.'

'We have his blood group, though. I checked with the surgeon, he's AB negative. Less than one person in a hundred has that type of blood. Surely that should whittle it down?'

'It's impossible, Detective Inspector. Absolutely impossible,' Booth said, rising to show Payne the conversation was over. 'Now, unfortunately, I've got to head off somewhere. Call me if you need anything else, though. Always happy to help.'

And even happier to refuse you, again, Booth thought as he closed the door on the policeman, then wondered why he'd taken against the man so. *Must be the resemblance to Old Crippley,* he decided.

4

This really is too much, Ilse Drechsler thought, as she hovered beside the bed.

Cousin Ursula's breathing was deep and regular now and the irritating mucus-rattle barely audible, but it had taken four hours to get her to sleep.

Four *hours*.

Each time Ursula seemed on the verge of drifting off, she had begun to writhe and fight with unseen attackers, gritting her teeth so hard it seemed the tendons in her neck would snap. Part of Ilse had longed to go downstairs and leave Ursula to it, but she couldn't risk her cousin crying out and attracting attention.

No-one must know Ursula was there.

Ilse took a corner of the bed sheet and lifted the covers to inspect Ursula's injuries. The whole of her lower half, from the breasts down, was covered in bruises, and the sheets beneath Ursula's posterior were damp with blood.

That was the problem: whatever wounds she had were *inside*. Ilse had tried to examine the damage, but whenever she went to part Ursula's thighs, the woman became hysterical. Whatever it was, the wound smelt bad now. It smelt of rot. Ilse should call a doctor, but there were so few left in Eichenrode and those that had stayed couldn't be trusted; they all worked for the Tommies now.

There was no way round it, she realised, Cousin Ursula must stay hidden until she got better and then she must go somewhere else: there couldn't be *two* women called Ursula Drechsler living in Eichenrode…

Ilse's troubles had begun months earlier, out east in the Warthegau. The Russian breakthrough had come so suddenly. In the morning, the radio had said the front was stable; by lunchtime, the Russians were everywhere, like a ravening swarm of rats, biblical in their savagery. When a friend in the German High Command had phoned to warn Ilse, she had barely had time to bundle together a bag of possessions before the shells began to fall. There'd been no time to warn anyone else. Cousin Ursula had been away shopping in the town at the time. Ilse had taken Ursula's identity papers, hoping to find her cousin on the road later.

But when Ilse stopped running that first evening, the horizon in the east was a solid mass of smoke and flame, and the rumble of tanks and artillery was all that could be heard.

Weeks of hell followed.

Ilse went to her Berlin house first, thinking she would be safe there, and then managed to escape the capital before the Russians encircled it. After that, what was left? Her parents' house in Eichenrode was the only place she had to go.

It took a week to drive there, each day more chaotic than the last as the Reich fell apart. When German soldiers took the car from her at gunpoint, she had to walk the last leg of her odyssey, more than thirty-six hours across country, dragging her suitcases behind her.

She didn't glimpse her conquerors until the third day of peace, when English soldiers knocked at the house and asked to see her papers.

And that was when Ursula's identity documents had become so useful.

Dear dizzy, dim little Cousin Ursula, with her plaited hair and dirndl skirts. Oh, she'd danced with her share of SS officers and rattled collection tins for the *Winterhilfswerk* fund — but she'd never joined the Party. That fact was worth its weight in gold, now. The Tommies were arresting Party members and locking them up. Torturing them, some said. Ilse was damned if she would go to prison just because she'd done what millions of other Germans had done and hitched her horse to the Nazi wagon.

After pretending to be Cousin Ursula a number of times, it was relatively simple to actually *become* her. There was a man in the town who had attached Ilse's photographs to Ursula's documents and the switch was made.

Ilse had wondered at first whether posing as her cousin might be too obvious, but she was glad of her decision when she came to fill in the *Fragebogen*, the huge questionnaire the Tommies were making all Germans complete. There were more than a hundred sections, detailing membership of political parties and churches and Nazi organisations ranging from the SS and the Gestapo to the Kameradschaft USA; other sections enquired about speeches given, articles written, rallies and parades attended and all sorts of other personal questions about scars and census results and relatives who belonged to the Party. You couldn't possibly hope to invent an identity; the questions were far too complex.

But Cousin Ursula had spent so much time wittering on about her life that Ilse actually found it easy to think herself into Ursula's shoes and the Tommies had swallowed her story. As far as they were concerned, she was Ursula Drechsler, aged thirty-four and unmarried. The fact that Ilse hadn't returned to Eichenrode since her parents had died meant that the chances of anyone from the town recognising her were minimal. The set up was perfect ... until two days ago, when the old man in the cart had arrived, calling out at the door, speaking with a thick Prussian accent. Ilse had told him to leave without opening it, but then the old man had pulled back the covers of the cart and Ilse had realised that the bloodied, bruised thing that lay within was her cousin.

'Men at the frontier,' the old man had said, as if that explained everything.

The only words Ursula had spoken in all the days that had followed were to ask for a bundle of letters from her bag. When Ilse fetched them she'd managed to read only the first line of the top one — 'My darling Ursula' — before Ursula had snatched them away and clutched them to her bosom. They were still there now, a crumpled mass tied together with blue ribbon, rising and falling softly as Ursula slept.

Ilse rose, tiptoed away from the bed and went downstairs, taking the crooked steps one at a time. The farmhouse was a ruin. A heavy explosion had reduced the front rooms to a pile of rubble and soldiers had slept in the still habitable part at the rear: soldiers from both sides, to judge by the cans and ammunition crates dumped around the place. That wasn't all they'd left, either: the pigs had pissed and shat all over.

She stopped by the kitchen window to examine her reflection in the cracked glass, then looked down at the dowdy frock she wore, the woollen stockings, the heavy shoes. *God, I look like an old washerwoman*, Ilse thought. Small wonder people found no difficulty in mistaking her for Cousin Ursula. *Still, I must possess something men want*, Ilse thought with a faint smile, thinking now of the Englishman she had taken as her lover at the end of May.

Ilse's Tommy had arranged things with the military government so that the farmhouse would not be requisitioned. That was something at least. Half a roof over her head was better than nothing. After all, where else could she go? Since the Tommies invaded, there was no running water, no electricity, no post, no buses or trains, no coal or milk. In the town, people queued at a standpipe for hours to get water and they lived like troglodytes, crowded together in cellars.

Besides, even if she had had somewhere else to go, how would she have got there? Germans weren't allowed to go anywhere unless they had permits from the military authorities or the Red Cross — and it was damned risky even then. It was not a good time for Germans to be wandering the roads. Ilse had already been set upon once by a vengeful horde. That was how she had met the Tommy. He'd fired his pistol in the air and scared the bastards away. If it hadn't been for him, she would probably have been killed. Or, worse, they could have left her like Cousin Ursula.

No, this shattered hovel was the best she could hope for at the moment. She couldn't imagine how other people were managing. Even with the food the Tommy brought her, she was still famished. The hunger was always there, in the pit of her stomach, sucking at her wellbeing from within. And at least her arrangement with the Tommy had the semblance of a relationship. She had seen the way many German women were surviving now, whoring themselves in bombed-out buildings for tins of peaches and cigarettes.

The floorboards above creaked and Cousin Ursula cried out; her groans echoed through the cracks in the house. She was having another of her attacks. Ilse rose wearily. She needed medicine, but where could she get it? And what sort of medicine? She had no idea what Cousin Ursula needed.

She was about to go upstairs when she heard a vehicle coming towards the house. She peered through the window, ducking back when she saw her Tommy parking his jeep.

She mustn't let him inside: he might hear Cousin Ursula's moans. It would raise too many questions.

Ilse took a moment to arrange her hair in her reflection in the window, then slipped through the kitchen door and went round to meet the Tommy at the front of the house.

'*Liebling*, what a lovely surprise,' Ilse said, throwing her arms wide and beaming at him.

'Hello, my darling Ursula,' Captain James Booth said.

5

Silas Payne parked his utility outside the *Rathaus*, the town hall building which was now home to the British military government in Eichenrode.

He wasn't overly fond of young Captain Booth, Payne decided. Perhaps it was the big words he had used: rapprochement, conflate. Payne had always mistrusted men who felt the need to show their learning so obviously. Or perhaps it was because Payne had met so many Captain Booths back in London, earnest young men fresh from university for whom 'The War' had been little more than an extended jolly.

Look at the street names in Eichenrode. The first thing the Military Government had done on occupying the town was to remove all the street names with connections to the Nazi regime, but a competition had then begun among the junior officers to see who could find the replacement that would prove most irksome to the Germans: Churchill Platz, Eisenhower Straße; the former high street was now 'El Allee Main'.

But then Silas Payne had always disliked the Army, disliked anything that encouraged people to subsume themselves in a greater whole. No good ever came of mass emotion. He'd learned the truth of that when policing football matches as a young copper. Wasn't the current state of the world proof that he was right?

The *Rathaus* building was still dressed for war, with sandbags piled against the exterior wall and crosses of tape on the windows. Payne showed his ID to the guard at the door, then headed upstairs to Major Norris's office.

Norris led the CCG's Public Safety Branch for the administrative district to the west of the city of Brunswick. As such, his duties and responsibilities were many and arduous; too arduous, to judge from the harassed, sleepless look of the man.

Norris was in his early fifties, but had the air of a man with whom old age had caught up quickly and unexpectedly. When Payne walked upstairs to his office, he found the major trying to unravel some dispute between German civilians — not an easy task, given that Norris obviously spoke no German. He was followed wherever he went by an officious young German woman with a clipboard and pencil who translated for him. If it weren't for Norris's uniform, a casual observer would have thought the translator had been the person in charge.

As Payne listened he realised that most of the time what she translated was not precisely what Norris had said; sometimes she would even add her own information. When Norris mentioned that Payne spoke German, though, she looked at him sharply and blushed. Her translations were scrupulously correct afterwards.

How these men were supposed to govern the country without speaking German was beyond Payne, but that seemed to be the story of the occupation so far. If the war had demonstrated one thing about the British, it was the immense depth of their trust in muddling through somehow.

It was twenty minutes before Norris had finished with the German civilians. Late afternoon sun filled the room as he invited Payne into his office.

'Here we are, Detective Inspector, take a seat and tell me what you've managed to ascertain about this wretched business out by the Brunswick Road. They're saying in the officers' mess it was some sort of ad hoc field hospital.'

Norris frowned when Payne failed to reply, then realised that the policeman was looking at his translator. 'We shan't be needing you for this, thank you, Fraülein Seiler.'

The woman's eyes met Payne's for the briefest of moments. Then she smiled and left the room.

'Indispensable,' Norris said when she'd left. 'And her father, too.'

'What does he do?'

'Doctor. He's taken charge of the medical care at the civilian internment camp near town. We can't have the chaps we lock up falling ill, can we? That wouldn't be very civilised, would it? No, we've got to work on rebuilding the world, now, get things back to how they were before all this bloody mess started.'

Norris sucked a Bismuth tablet as he listened to Payne's report, one hand on his stomach.

'So, Captain Booth agreed with your assessment?' he said when Payne had finished.

'Yes. He seemed to think the field hospital theory very unlikely. He thought the same about the involvement of werewolves.'

'But what were the drugs you found?'

'I'm still trying to ascertain that.'

'Surely that lends credence to the field hospital theory?'

'It's a strange kind of hospital that strangles its patients.'

Norris thought about that, staring at the window. 'Do you think this Beagley chap and his boys might have been dispensing a bit of summary justice? Found out this chap was SS and did him in?'

Payne shook his head. 'Beagley seemed genuinely surprised when I spotted the SS tattoo. And, if they had killed them, why would they report it? But I can't rule out the possibility that other British personnel were involved. And I'm certain that

Sergeant Beagley was hiding something — the theft of the victims' belongings, most likely. That's why I asked if you could speak to Beagley's commanding officer.'

'Yes, I got your message about that and we're in luck. Turns out the CO is a friend of my bridge partner.'

'And?'

'Well, as you can understand, I couldn't very well just weigh in and start accusing people of theft — Sergeant Beagley has an impeccable war record, after all. But I did mention the matter and the CO applied some pressure in the right quarters.'

Norris rose, walked to a corner cupboard and withdrew a large brown paper parcel tied with string, which he placed on the desk.

'It seems some of the victims' clothing had gone walkabout. This is what has been sent over.'

Payne cut the string with his penknife and unfolded the paper. Inside was a selection of sturdy, practical clothing, both male and female: trousers, vests, skirts. The only remarkable item was a long ebony dress in a tailor's box. As Payne opened the tissue paper in which the dress was wrapped, a waft of apples and pears rose to greet him. The dress was made of silk; silver embroidered butterflies fluttered down from one shoulder strap and across the bodice.

'Is this all of it?' Payne said. 'It doesn't seem very much. And this clothing must have been inside something. Were there any bags or suitcases?'

The pained look returned to Norris's face; he cradled his belly protectively. 'It's all we're going to get. I've stepped on enough toes as it is getting you that.'

'With all due respect, Major, two people have been murdered. And if the world is ever going to "get back to normal", the concept of murder has to start meaning something again sooner or later.'

Norris looked at Payne as if trying to decide whether he were serious. When he realised he was, he said, 'Oh yes, well of course, you're perfectly right. Couldn't agree more. What was it Churchill said at the beginning of the war? You know, the thing about us having to win the war so the world could move forward into *something-or-other.*'

'Broad uplit sunlands.'

'Precisely, Detective Inspector. Broad uplit sunlands. Let's go forward and find them, eh? Show the world the efficiency of British justice. But let's do so without upsetting any applecarts. No murky diversions. No fuss.'

'Fuss?'

Norris winced, as if Payne's failure to understand caused him genuine pain. 'What I mean, to put it into words of one syllable, is that if you intimate that British soldiers have been murdering Germans, you're going to get yourself into hot water. And when the *supposed* murder victim is ex-Waffen SS, then said water is going to get very hot, very, very quickly. Do I make myself clear? You're not going to make yourself any friends out here if you're seen to be taking the Germans' side.'

'Police work is not conducive to popularity as a rule, Major.'

'Well, just tread easily. These regular army chaps are already looking down their noses at the CCG. Let's not give them anything to crow about, eh?'

When Payne reached the door, Norris said suddenly, 'I'm not going to regret putting you in charge of this, am I, Detective Inspector Payne?' — as if he'd spent the whole conversation putting off asking that one question.

Payne paused in the doorway. 'That depends on whether you want to know the truth or not, sir.'

Norris reached for another Bismuth tablet. That did not seem to be the answer he'd hoped for.

Payne took the package of clothing and went downstairs. On his way out of the *Rathaus*, he passed a room where three women in ATS uniforms were working. Payne paused as he listened to the clack of their typewriters. Then he went back and knocked on the door.

'Excuse me, ladies. I don't suppose you could spare me a minute, could you?'

The three women crowded round when Payne put the tailor's box on the table and withdrew the long silk dress.

'Lord, look at that, Angie,' the youngest of the ATS women said. 'What an absolute beauty. Look at the embroidery. I haven't seen anything like this since before the war.'

'And even then, it was only with your nose pressed up against a shop window.'

'Too right. I'll bet this cost 10 guineas. Where on earth did you find it, Detective Inspector? Is it for sale?'

Payne smiled and shook his head. 'It's part of an investigation actually. I'd just like a woman's opinion on it, if you ladies wouldn't mind. I'm a bit out of my depth when it comes to dresses.'

'Well, for starters, this isn't a dress, it's an evening gown.'

'Where might you buy it?'

'You wouldn't buy it; you'd have it made especially.'

'Do you mean to say this is a one-off?'

'Of course, it is,' Angie said. 'You don't think any woman able to afford something like this would risk having someone else turn up wearing the same dress, do you? This will be the fellow who made it, I imagine,' she said, pointing to an address on the inside of the box lid for which Payne had not even thought to look. 'Maurice Petiot, Rue La Salle, Paris. Ooh, doesn't that sound posh?'

Payne thanked the women and went back upstairs to Norris's office, feeling pleased with himself. It was one of the basic rules of good police investigation: if you knew nothing about a subject, always ask someone who did.

'Do you have a French dictionary and a telephone I can borrow?' he said to Norris.

'What on earth for?'

'I need to call someone in Paris.'

It took Payne an hour to get the Paris telephone number for the tailor and another hour to get connected. Payne's French was of schoolboy standard, but he had a French-speaking intelligence officer provide him with a detailed description of the dress and the other vocabulary he would need.

The line crackled as the phone rang, then a man's voice answered.

'Yes, I am Monsieur Petiot,' the tobacco-hoarse voice said in response to Payne's query.

Payne began to explain who he was in faltering French, but Petiot said, 'Yes, yes, but what do you want?'

'An evening gown you made. If I describe it to you, might you remember it?'

'*Might* I remember it, Monsieur? Each article of clothing I produce is unique. I burn the patterns once each one is completed.'

Payne had ten lines of French describing the material and style of the dress. Petiot interrupted him halfway through the third.

'A full-length evening gown in black silk with a halter neck and a bow brooch at the back? Butterflies in silver lace? I began to make it April 3rd, 1943. I finished it on the evening of the 5th. And that was only because a supplier failed to get me the taffeta I needed.'

'Do you remember who you made it for?'

'Of course.'

Payne waited but Petiot began a muffled argument with someone beside him.

'I will not shut up, woman.' The line became louder. 'I made it for a German SS officer. Konrad Jaeger. He was a Haupt-something or other. He said it was for his wife but I didn't believe him. No man buys such a dress for a wife.' Payne went to ask more but the line became muffled again. He heard Petiot's voice rise in irritation. 'Take your hand from my arm. What I say is true. I'm not ashamed of whom I do business with. The Germans have gone but what do we have now instead? Communists and social —' The phone went dead.

Afterwards, Payne phoned to Corps HQ, where the captured SS personnel files Booth had mentioned were kept.

'This must be him, sir,' the clerk said an hour later by telephone, reading from the *RuSha* file. 'Konrad Jaeger, from Hamburg. Joined the Nazi party in 1929, the SS in 1934. Rose to the rank of *SS-Hauptscharführer*. That's the equivalent of Battalion Sergeant Major. Saw service in France, Yugoslavia and Italy, then transferred back to France. Of good solid Aryan stock and … oh, look at this,' the clerk said. 'He's got a pink chit in with his file.'

'What does that mean?' Payne said.

'It means the lawyers in Nuremburg are looking for him, sir. It seems your *SS-Hauptscharführer* Konrad Jaeger is a war criminal.

6

Captain James Booth was in a foul mood. What the hell was Ursula playing at?

He'd been to her farmhouse three times in the last two days, and on each occasion Ursula had found some excuse not to invite him inside. He'd convinced himself he was imagining things after the first two visits, but now he was not so sure. It was especially galling because without Booth Ursula wouldn't even have a damned house: if he hadn't sorted things with Housing Branch — at a great deal of personal risk and expense — the house would have been requisitioned long ago and she'd have been left to fend for herself. Didn't she realise he'd risked his bloody commission doing that?

For the umpteenth time that morning, Booth found himself on the verge of becoming genuinely angry; then he remembered who it was he was thinking about and the emotion faded. He could never get truly angry with his dear little Ursula.

He had met her back in May, when his detachment first arrived in Eichenrode. Booth had been driving back along the Brunswick road when he'd seen a group of ragged men pointing and prodding a young woman. Christ, he went cold when he thought about how close he'd come to driving past. Ursula had been holding her ground, but there was no doubt it would have ended badly: physical violence, almost certainly, rape or murder quite possibly. In those early days of peace, German civilians were fair game and most British troops did little to prevent the Nazis' former slaves from venting their anger.

But Booth *had* stopped and set himself between Ursula and the vengeful horde with only his uniform and sidearm to deter them. It had been enough.

Just.

Afterwards, he'd meant to drive Ursula to a safe distance further down the road, then ask her to get out. After all, the non-fraternisation order was rigidly enforced back then; he wasn't even supposed to talk to Germans, let alone give them lifts. But as they drove and chatted and Ursula calmed and began to smile, he found himself inventing excuses to keep her with him while they drove through the summer evening. When she shivered, he let her wrap his greatcoat around her shoulders, and suddenly it seemed that the evening air had never smelt so fresh or clear…

Part of him knew it was foolish to get so dippy over *any* woman, let alone a German one, but when it came to his feelings for Ursula, the voice of reason was shouting into the wind. One heard about this love-at-first-sight rot, but nothing had prepared him for how overwhelming it would be when it came. Like a flash flood, within minutes of setting eyes on her he was trapped upon a strip of high land staring down at a world consumed by surging torrents.

Of course, he'd been scrupulous about checking her background. He'd had a patrol drop one of the *Fragebogen* questionnaires into her house the day after he'd realised he had feelings for her. The one hundred and twenty-four questions were designed to pinpoint how deeply a person had been involved with the Nazi party, and were so baffling in their depth and complexity it was very difficult for that person to lie without being caught out. The answers were then checked against the German records the Allies had seized and the person was graded from I to V, with I being a known war criminal and V an ordinary civilian.

Ursula Drechsler was a category V, which meant she was considered to be almost completely innocent. The only blots on her copybook were a cousin in the Waffen-SS and her former role as a leader in the *League of German Maidens*. That wasn't really anything to worry about in the greater scheme of things. After twelve years of dictatorship, there were few Germans who didn't have some connection with the Nazi regime. Besides, the idea of Ursula teaching German girls to cook and sew was risible: the poor thing could barely peel a potato.

No, Booth felt no compunction about his romance with her. Quite the opposite, in fact. If the Allies were ever going to get Germany back on its feet, they would need people like Ursula. In some ways, it was his *duty* to protect the decent Germans. And part of Booth felt he was owed some happiness. He was tired of obeying orders. He'd done nothing else now for years — years when he should have been living it up at university. The constant bustle and activity of the war had hidden the fact that life had become an enervated, sterile thing, more of an existence than a life, really. It was time to feel human again and that was precisely what Ursula had given to him. God, the last two months had been bliss. It was as if before meeting her he'd been emotionally colour blind.

So, why won't she let me in her bloody house?

The thought came to him in a sudden jag of petulance and he found himself drifting towards anger again. He lit a cigarette from the butt of the one he'd just smoked and brooded.

Had he done something wrong?

That was the most likely explanation, but he was damned if he could think of what it was he might have done. But then women were always so difficult to read…

Although Booth would have been loath to admit it, he'd not had much experience with the fairer sex. When had there been time? He was only twenty when the war began and he'd been called up in '42. He'd walked out with girls, naturally, but girls were all they had been. Ursula was thirty-four. She was a fully-fledged woman of the world. He'd realised that the first time their relationship became physical: unlike for him, it obviously hadn't been Ursula's first time.

He chewed his lip. That thought did nothing to improve his mood, so he went back to considering why she would not allow him inside.

Was it the state of the house? Did she feel ashamed of living in a ruin?

No, it couldn't be that, either. She'd let him inside dozens of times before without any problem. Besides, after all the cleaning and repairs Booth had done around the place, it was a palace in comparison to how it had been when he first met her. No, this problem was recent. It had only really cropped up in the last two or three days.

He smoked his cigarette and calmed himself. Anger faded again and was replaced by a deep yearning to see her, but Booth knew that wouldn't be possible until the evening: Ursula had to work at the transit camp today. Booth had considered trying to wangle her an exemption from that — God knows, she'd dropped enough hints — but he'd decided it was best not to tempt fate. Besides, after the business with her house, he couldn't really afford another bribe.

He would get Ursula a present, he decided, a crate of victuals. That always got him into her good books — like most of the Germans in the town, Ursula found decent food hard to come by. Booth finished his cigarette and drove across town to the supply depot, where he asked to speak to the regimental quartermaster sergeant, Suttpen.

Jacob Suttpen had first come to Booth's attention when their division had crossed the Rhine and the really serious looting began. Legend had it that one of the combat units spent a whole morning fighting their way into a German town, only to find that Suttpen and his helpers had already been there an hour and had filled two lorries with furniture, paintings and mirrors. Booth had no idea whether the story was true, but he could well believe it. Since then, Suttpen had established himself as the nexus for every shady deal that happened within a dozen miles of Eichenrode.

It was Suttpen that had ensured Ursula's farmhouse was kept off the requisition list. Apparently, he had a contact in Housing Branch that could arrange things like that. Booth was not surprised. Suttpen seemed to possess the innate ability of divining which palms needed greasing and of determining exactly how much it would cost.

A storeman carrying a wooden crate told Booth that Suttpen was at the back of the depot. When Booth got there, he found Suttpen talking with a short, ferrety German man in civilian clothes whom Booth recognised from somewhere. The German was frowning as he listened to Suttpen and he occasionally cupped a hand to his mouth to whisper something in the quartermaster sergeant's ear. The two men carried on talking, but when Suttpen saw Booth, he hissed something and the little German bolted.

'Not interrupting anything, am I?' Booth said.

'What? Oh, that? That was nothing, sir.'

'That man seemed quite worried about something.'

'Nothing I can't handle, sir.'

'Isn't that fellow the German doctor that treats Colonel Bassett?' Booth said, realising where he'd seen the man before. 'Doctor Seiler, isn't it?'

Quartermaster Sergeant Suttpen forced his spiv's smile even wider than usual. 'That's right, sir.'

'You know you're not supposed to speak with German civilians, don't you? The non-fraternisation order is still in effect.'

'That was business, though, sir. I slip Doctor Seiler some supplies when I can. Medicine, bandages, that sort of thing.'

'Well, don't let the other ranks see you chatting with him out in the open. It gives the wrong impression.'

They walked as they talked, Suttpen leading Booth into his office at the rear of the building. When they were inside with the door closed, some of Suttpen's servile manner disappeared as he reached below his desk and pulled out a box covered with a cloth. This he lifted to allow Booth to examine the merchandise within: onions, potatoes and leeks on one side, apples and pears on the other, with an assortment of tins and jars down the centre.

Booth nodded. 'How much do I owe you for this? The usual?'

Suttpen's smile became especially oily and complicit. 'Oh, you can have these on the house, this week, sir.'

Booth frowned. 'That's suspiciously generous of you. Why do I get the feeling you're going to ask me for a favour?'

Suttpen beamed. 'You're a sharp one, sir. You really are.'

'Go on then.'

'This business with the house out by the Brunswick road. They say some policeman chap's been looking into it. Is that right, sir?'

‘Yes. His name is Detective Inspector Payne. Of Scotland Yard, no less.’

For a moment, Suttpen’s smile faltered and was replaced by a hard, thoughtful look. Booth lifted the box of vegetables. ‘I’m afraid I can’t say anything more than that, though,’ he said, enjoying the disappointment on Suttpen’s face. ‘It’s all a bit hush-hush. But thanks for the victuals. I’ll make sure they find a good home.’

Suttpen didn’t seem to hear him, though. Outside, Booth fell to chatting with a lieutenant from the signals. He was still there talking when Suttpen left his office carrying a bottle of whiskey, a loaf of bread and a length of sausage.

It took Booth a moment to realise what it was about Suttpen’s appearance that had drawn his attention. It wasn’t the food he was carrying: it was the holstered sidearm he now wore at his belt.

7

Ilse had to do three days' work for the Tommies each week.

She'd had no say in the matter. Back in May, English soldiers had simply turned up at her house one day, kicked at the door and manhandled her into a lorry, along with a dozen other terrified German women. At first, she'd thought that someone had denounced her and she was being taken away to prison, but no, they'd simply wanted her to work.

For the first two weeks, she was made to clear rubble from streets in the centre of Eichenrode; once that was done, they put her to work at a transit camp the International Red Cross had set up at the local fertilizer factory.

She woke early and checked on Cousin Ursula. Ilse was taking a chance by leaving Ursula alone all day, but what choice did she have? She put an apple, two slices of stale bread and a glass of water on the table beside Ursula's bed, then explained where she was going and when she would be back. Ursula just stared at the ceiling and clutched her letters.

It was a forty-minute walk to the transit camp. Ilse hated the place.

O'Donnell, the Irishman that ran the camp administration, was a drunkard and a gambler. Rumour had it he had lost a fortune at poker to an English soldier, the one who ran the supply depot. Worse than that, though, he was a lecher. Only just the other day he had tried to grope her, but Ilse had scraped her booted foot down the front of his shin and left the leering jackass writhing and cursing on the floor.

Then there were the actual inhabitants of the camp: Poles, Ukrainians, Greeks, Czechs, Italians, Yugoslavs. God, the way they looked at Germans, nowadays, it was like being locked up with a bunch of wild animals. Ilse had lost count of how many times they had insulted or spat at her.

Still, she should give thanks for small mercies. The first week in July, a Polish man had accused another of being a Gestapo informer. Within seconds, a crowd had started kicking and punching the man as he rolled in the dust. Then men and women came with sticks and beat the man to death while the Tommy soldiers just watched. The man's body had lain there for an hour afterwards, the blood leaking from his cracked head.

A Tommy officer had come to the camp after that and bawled at the inmates. They mostly left the Germans alone, now, and that suited Ilse fine. She didn't want to go near those shabby, tattered, lice-ridden people anyway. The first thing the Red Cross nurses had to do each morning was line the camp's inhabitants up and pump clouds of white powder up their shirt sleeves and down the front of their trousers and skirts to stop typhus from spreading. That said everything you needed to know about the quality of the people in the camp.

The German women Ilse worked with were not much better. Most of them were peasants that spent all their time bemoaning the fate of the sons and brothers and husbands they'd lost in the war. And they were all so craven. That irritated Ilse more than anything else.

When the Tommies first came to Eichenrode, they had set up boards in the square outside the *Rathaus* and forced the Germans to walk in single file past them. The photographs pinned to the boards supposedly showed what had been happening in concentration camps in Germany — the words YOUR FAULT! were written at the top of each board — but Ilse didn't pay them much attention. The English and

Americans had their propaganda, the same as anyone else. She felt no guilt. Why should she? She'd never hurt anyone. That was why Ilse always made a point of walking with her head held high. She was not ashamed of being German and she wouldn't let anyone bully her into feeling that way. Besides, the English had no claim to the moral high ground, not after the way they had firebombed Germany's cities.

It was mid-morning now and Ilse was making her way through the centre of the camp towards the brick outhouse where the camp's supplies were kept. She knew there were medical kits inside, little bundles with bandages and plasters and syrettes of morphine. She had no idea what she would do with the kit once she had it, but she had to do something for Cousin Ursula. Ilse needed to make her well and then get rid of her. She couldn't keep turning Booth away when he came to her house.

The soldier guarding the hut recognised Ilse and waved her inside. The medical supplies were stacked in wooden crates next to huge tins of the white typhus powder. Ilse fished inside one of the crates and removed a canvas package. It was a little larger than a bag of sugar and had the words *Field Medical Kit* printed across the top of it in English.

Should she take the whole thing? Or would it be better to open it and take what she needed?

As she debated the matter, she realised the soldier outside was talking to someone. Ilse hurried to the opposite side of the room, stuffing the medical kit down the front of her dress as she did so.

'And what are you doing in here, might I ask, Fraülein?' a man said in broken German.

Ilse turned and felt her heart plunge when she recognised the figure in the doorway: it was O'Donnell, the one that had tried to grope her.

He was a slender man with a ready smile, although close up you noticed that his eyes were small and dark and his cheeks patched with rosacea. He seemed to shave only every other day and he smelled like he slept in his clothes.

O'Donnell passed a hand through his lank hair and smiled as he walked towards her.

'If you touch me, I'll claw your eyes out,' Ilse said in English.

He held a hand up in mollification. 'Don't worry. I just want to talk.' He reached behind him, brought out a bottle of whisky, some bread and a length of cured sausage. Ilse's stomach did a queasy flip at the sight of so much food.

O'Donnell laid them atop a crate then backed away, hands still raised. He motioned for her to take them.

'Where did you get it?' she said.

'I've got friends in the army. Same as you.'

'What's that supposed to mean?'

O'Donnell said nothing, but he smiled now, showing his yellowed teeth.

'What do you want in exchange?' she said, fighting the temptation to throw herself on the food.

'There's a policeman here,' O'Donnell said, his voice low but clear, as if he were used to speaking in half-tones. 'His name is Detective Inspector Payne. I need to know why he's so interested in that house out by the Brunswick road.'

'What could I possibly know about that?' she said.

'Your captain knows something. I want you to find out from him.'

Ilse's hand froze an inch from the food. 'Captain? What captain?'

O'Donnell's wide mouth twisted into a lecherous smile.

'Captain James Booth. The same Captain Booth that recently paid to keep a certain ruined farmhouse off the list of requisitioned properties. Christ, you don't think I don't know, do you? Eoin O'Donnell don't miss a trick, remember that. Not a single one.'

Ilse's hand hovered above the food. O'Donnell knew about Booth; there was no point in denying it. What mattered now was what he would do with the information.

Ilse scooped up the food. Then she said, 'I'll take this for now. But you must bring me more when I find something out. Cheese. And some eggs.'

O'Donnell folded his arms. 'Quite the little business woman, ain't ya? How's about this? You take that lot there and I won't mention the medical kit you've got stuffed down the front of your dress.'

He laughed when he saw the panic on Ilse's face.

'Go on, get out of here,' he said. 'And I'll want some answers soon.'

As Ilse passed him, he said, 'Course, you're way too much woman for the young captain, aren't you, Ursula? But I guess he'll find that out the hard way.'

Then he pinched her bottom.

'Pig!' she said and slapped his hand away.

O'Donnell's laughter followed her as she hurried from the building.

8

Silas Payne was billeted in Eichenrode's police station. Since he'd taken residence there, Germans had knocked at the door on a number of occasions. Was he the new face of authority, they had asked. Did they report crimes to him now? He'd even had one comical exchange with a heavily disguised woman offering to denounce her neighbours 'as she used to do' in exchange for food and tobacco.

He was standing in the window of the police station now, still in his pyjamas, enjoying the bright morning sunlight and watching German children playing football in the street with a tin can.

The file on the Waffen SS man, Konrad Jaeger, lay on the table behind him. He'd had the clerk at Corps HQ send it over to him by courier the previous evening. The file contained two photos of Jaeger. Payne had compared the photos with those he'd taken of the murder victim and there was no doubt it was the same man. The clerk had also included a handwritten note on the war crimes for which Jaeger was wanted: *It seems Herr Jaeger had a predilection for shooting French civilians. He's wanted on four counts of that. He's also accused of torturing two women suspected of resistance involvement.*

Payne had considered what that might mean. The French Zone of Occupation was in the south-west of Germany, but there were plenty of French soldiers and personnel passing through this area all the time. Could that have something to do with Jaeger's murder? It was possible, he decided, but unlikely. An act of random violence still seemed the most likely explanation — and yet nothing about the crime seemed random to Payne.

He sipped coffee and wondered what it was about the killings that had given him the hair-at-the-back-of-the-throat sensation he always got when he was missing something. It was the surgical instruments. It wasn't just their presence, it was the way they had been set out: it went beyond the mere orderliness of the professional. Their arrangement had the fussy precision associated with a ritual or obsession. That was it, Payne realised. It wasn't what had happened that had bothered him, it was what had been *about* to happen. The killing of the man and woman had been only the first stage in something larger and more sinister — Beagley and his men had *interrupted* something, he was sure of it.

Payne had converted his bedroom from a small office at the back of the police station. He went there now and put on a clean suit. Returning to the front of the police station, he heard the clatter of horses' hooves on the asphalt of the street outside.

Colonel Bassett's adjutant, Captain Fredrickson, had been out hunting with some of the other officers. A pair of bloodied fox tails hung from the pommel of Fredrickson's saddle. A private soldier walked behind the mounted men, holding the leashes of five beagles. Rumour had it Fredrickson's father was something big in the city and that the hounds had been shipped out to Germany especially.

When Fredrickson reached the German children and their tin can he rode his horse straight at them, causing them to scatter. Fredrickson said something over his shoulder as he rode past and the officers behind him laughed.

Payne finished his coffee, thinking about something Major Norris had said the day before, something about getting the world back to normal. Norris was wrong: the world would never be the same again. Not now. Buildings and bodies weren't the only things the war had damaged. It had skewed men's morals, too, and let the wilder side of human nature run free. Some of the British soldiers Payne had seen in Germany wore expressions you normally only saw in the hard, lawless parts of the East End, and three months of occupation had shown that the members of Eisenhower's Great Crusade were prone to succumb to their baser instincts, too. Payne had heard stories about the wild days at the end of the war — the shootings, the beatings, the rapes. And now there were stories of lorries full of loot being bussed out to Holland and of cargo planes taking off loaded with antique German furniture.

When he had been a young copper, Payne's first sergeant had summed up good police-work for him. 'When a crime's been committed, there's only two types of people, Silas: victims and villains. Comfort the former, catch the latter and don't pay no heed to whether you likes or dislikes either one of 'em. Remember that and you'll do all right.'

Payne *had* remembered it; had made it the cornerstone of his whole career, in fact. That was what this murder case represented to Payne. Britain had fought the war for a cause higher than the individual and it was time to put the morality underpinning that cause into practice, to stop basking in the VE-day sunshine. If the war was going to have meant anything at all, then all this lawlessness had to stop. The British people owed it to themselves to govern Germany well.

At nine o'clock, Payne took his utility and drove across town to what was left of the local hospital. This was the place where the Royal Army Medical Corps had set itself up. The soldiers on guard outside recognised Payne and waved him through.

He crossed the waiting room and headed downstairs to the laboratory.

Captain Shelley was the GDMO — General Duties Medical Officer — for Eichenrode. He was a cheery, good-natured sort who had performed the autopsy on Jaeger's body and had offered to take a look at the vials of medicine Payne had found at the murder house.

When Payne knocked at the lab door, Shelley answered it, wearing a white lab coat over his uniform and drying his hands on a towel.

'I'm glad you came over, Detective Inspector,' he said scratching at his long nose. 'You've saved me a trip.'

'Have you found something?'

Inside the laboratory, a small German man was removing the lab coat he wore. Test tubes containing coloured liquids stood in racks on the table.

'This is Doctor Seiler,' Shelley said, introducing the man. 'His daughter works as an interpreter over at the *Rathaus*. He's been helping me out. He's a far better chemist than I am.'

'Oh, you're embarrassing me, Captain,' Seiler said brightly, extending his soft, moist hand for Payne to shake. 'But I'm always glad to help the British. You can't imagine what a relief it is to be finally free of that Austrian monster and his Brownshirts.'

So far, Silas Payne had met three types of German: the first were those that were too tired and broken even to notice the occupation; the second resented it bitterly and were suspicious and surly; the third were like Doctor Seiler, Germans that had recognised which way the wind now blew and were determined to fill their wings with it.

Payne shook the proffered hand, thinking that Seiler reminded him of a theatrical agent he'd interrogated once: the easy smile, weak chin and unctuous manner were all uncannily similar. Like his daughter, Seiler spoke good English and, like his daughter, Seiler seemed intent on lingering to hear what Payne had to say.

'Yes, Detective Inspector, a truly fascinating case,' he said, turning to the test tubes on the table. 'But, as I said to Captain Shelley, I might be able to provide more information were I to know specifically where these items were found and what the case entails…'

Seiler's raised eyebrows invited Payne to comment. Payne said nothing.

'Oh, well, I'll be going,' Seiler said, once the silence had become uncomfortable. Still, Payne said nothing. Seiler gave a weak smile and headed towards the door.

'Close it behind you,' Payne said.

'We could have talked in front of Doctor Seiler,' Shelley said when the German had gone. 'Most of what I'm about to tell you is his information, anyway.'

'Better safe than sorry. Besides, I have managed to identify the male victim and I'd rather Seiler didn't know.'

Payne explained who Konrad Jaeger was, then asked Shelley what he had found.

Shelley indicated the vials on the table, the ones Payne had taken from the cellar of the murder house.

'These are all fairly standard vaccines. According to Seiler, these particular brands were used by the Wehrmacht for troops who were fighting abroad. North Africa, places like that.'

'Are they difficult to get hold of?'

Shelley shrugged. 'Under normal circumstances I would say yes, but who can say nowadays, with so much military equipment left lying around everywhere? Someone could easily have stumbled across a crate of medical supplies.'

'What are they vaccines for?'

Shelley indicated each of the vials in turn. 'Hepatitis A. Tetanus. Tuberculosis. Typhus. But, as I mentioned last night, this is the one that interested me,' he said, tapping one of the vials with a pencil. 'I've used this myself, before the war, and I've never seen it that colour. So we ran some tests.'

'And it's not a vaccine?'

'Far from it. It's some form of barbiturate.'

'What effect would that have if it was injected? Could it be used to kill?'

'Depends on the dose. At this level of concentration, I would say it was more likely to induce unconsciousness.'

'Why would someone store a potentially lethal drug in a wrongly-labelled vial?'

Shelley shrugged. 'Human error. Or perhaps the original receptacle was broken and they were trying to salvage what they could.'

'Or someone was pretending to inject a vaccine when in fact they wanted to render the person unconscious before strangling them.'

Shelley smiled. 'That's the policemen in you talking, Detective Inspector. But, yes, it's perfectly possible. And it would explain why Jaeger's body does not bear any cuts or scratches, despite his having been strangled. He could have been sedated first.'

'How quickly would this barbiturate take effect if it was injected?'

‘In a matter of seconds. Why?’

‘I think it explains the minor injuries the woman suffered, too. I think the killer injected Jaeger first. But as Jaeger wilted, the woman smelt a rat and panicked, forcing the killer to subdue her physically before he could inject her and put her out of the picture, too. Can you check the bodies for needle marks?’

Shelley shook his head. ‘I’m afraid the bodies have been burnt. Colonel Bassett’s orders. We have only limited capacity for storing bodies here.’

‘What about the scalpels and the knives? Do you have any theories about them?’

‘That was the other thing I wanted to talk to you about,’ Shelley said, his face serious now. He led Payne across the room to a table where the tools found in the cellar had been laid out.

‘You were quite correct in assuming that these are surgical tools. Of course, the scalpels and the saw could theoretically be used for other purposes, but this is the real clincher,’ he said, indicating the length of serrated wire with the wooden handles. ‘In the trade, this is known as a Gigli wire saw. It’s used in surgery for bone-cutting — amputations, that sort of thing. It’s such a specialist tool, I can’t really imagine it being used for anything else.’

‘What are you saying? That the killer *was* intending to operate on the victims at some point?’

Shelley shook his head. ‘Not an operation, Detective Inspector. I think he was planning on performing a dissection.’

At midday Payne drove to the centre of town and parked outside the offices of Housing Branch, the administrative organisation that dealt with the requisition and allocation of housing in the area. Shelley's information worried him. That was why he wanted to know precisely who had requisitioned the murder house and which unit had been billeted there.

The Housing Branch clerk rolled his eyes when he saw Payne and said, no, he still hadn't had time to determine which British unit had requisitioned the house by the Brunswick Road. Nor would he find it any time soon, to judge by the man's languid tone of voice.

'It's imperative you find the details,' Payne said. 'Can't you have a look now? Or at least show me where to look?'

'Listen, chummy,' the clerk said, putting his pencil down, 'nearly thirty per cent of the thousand or so addresses on the German records in this town don't exist anymore. And most of what *is* left has been requisitioned by us. We've got boxes and boxes of ruddy chits and receipts.' By way of illustration, he pointed towards a pile of cardboard boxes that leaked paperwork. 'There's only four of us work here, you know. And if you think I'm going to let you loose on them, you've another thing coming. It's taken me weeks to sort that lot out.'

'Isn't there some central office that keeps copies of the requisition chits?'

'That would be in Brunswick. You'd have to fill in a form. Or you could go to Brunswick.'

Payne asked who was in charge.

'That'll be Mr Lockwood.'

'Let me speak to him, then, please.'

Mr Lockwood was a nervy little mole of a man with the face of a born bureaucrat, small and pinched beneath hair that was lacquered and swept severely across his forehead. The belt of his CCG uniform served only to accentuate the extent to which his belly protruded beneath it. He emerged from the gloom of his back office and peered at Payne through thick glasses.

'Yes. Yes. What is it? Do I know you?'

He blinked three times very quickly when Payne told him he was a British policeman. When Payne explained a double murder had occurred in a requisitioned house, Lockwood said, 'What house? It's nothing to do with me. I mean us. Whatever it is.'

'It's a house on the Brunswick Road, about half-a-mile beyond the town. Big one, three stories, with a hole in the roof. Perhaps you know it?'

Lockwood did. As Payne described the house, the colour drained from the man's face and, for a moment, he seemed somewhere else entirely, his myopic eyes unblinking now.

'Dead bodies?' he said, making a visible effort to hide his distress. 'Nasty business. Very nasty.'

'You can appreciate why it's so important to know who requisitioned the house, then. And who is currently billeted there.'

'Well, you'll have to fill out a form requesting the information,' Lockwood said and bolted for the safety of his office, but Payne called out his name before he could close the door.

'It really is very important. There could be very serious repercussions for anyone involved. Especially if they try to keep information from the police.'

Lockwood's face was the colour of wet ashes now.

Payne filled in a form requesting the name of the unit that had been billeted at the murder house. Then he went outside and walked to a point across the square from which he could see the steps of the Housing Branch office. Lockwood knew something about the murder house, Payne would stake his pension on it.

The question now was whether Lockwood would sit and stew or run to someone else for advice. Payne's bet was on the latter. Experience had taught him to spot that certain light in a man's eye that preceded panicked flight.

The morning wind was sharp, a reminder that September was just around the corner. Silas Payne pulled the collar of his coat up and leant against the wall, his eyes fixed on the door of Housing Branch. He would wait as long as it took.

When the European war had ended back in May, the invading armies had simply stopped wherever they were and established military governments. Germany was divided into four zones: British, Russian, American and French. Now, in August, members of the Control Council for Germany — the CCG for short — were moving in to take over local administration in the British zone.

It was a vast and complex task. The policy of denazification — by which all trace of Nazism would be purged from the country — meant Germany's entire bureaucratic structure had to be rebuilt from the bottom up. The task for the British was especially difficult, as their north-western zone contained most of Germany's big cities — cities the Allies had spent years systematically destroying. Payne had heard Major Norris comment on it: 'The Yanks got the scenery, the French the wine. All we got were bloody ruins.'

It wasn't an exaggeration. The situation in the British Zone was chaotic: no water, no electricity, no gas, no schools, no doctors. Roads and bridges had been bombed, train tracks destroyed. Millions were homeless, millions starving.

From what Payne had seen, the arrival of hordes of CCG bureaucrats would do nothing to alleviate the problem. Payne had rubbed shoulders with all sorts of misfits at the 'training' session they'd been given before being sent out to Germany: drain inspectors, retired officers, failed businessmen and civil servants from every far flung corner of the Empire. Some Army wags were already saying CCG stood for Charlie Chaplin's Grenadiers or Complete Chaos Guaranteed.

As a fluent German speaker, Payne had been seconded from Scotland Yard to come and run a training school for German policemen, but the most productive thing he'd done during his first seventy-two hours in Germany was to sweep the floor of the police station. It was bloody frustrating, given the state of the country. That was why he'd jumped at the chance to look into this murder. The one thing Silas Payne truly feared was inactivity and he would do —

The door to Housing Branch opened and Payne withdrew to a spot around the corner that was out of view, but only the clerk taking paperwork over to the *Rathaus* emerged. Payne resumed his vigil.

He wondered how the German police would have handled a situation like this and decided he knew the answer. He'd seen the windowless cell deep in the basement of Eichenrode's police station, the cell with the metal chair bolted to the ground and porcelain tiles on floor, walls and ceiling.

Tiles: they were easier to sponge down afterwards. Look carefully and you could still see the brown-red stains on the grouting.

That was no way to police a country and that was the whole point of his coming to Eichenrode. Germany's national police force had been more or less forged by the Nazis and German policemen needed to learn what it meant to police society within a democracy. No more midnight knocks. No more *Nacht und Nebel.* No more tiled cells. The German police were to be public servants, nothing more. It was important the new Germany got that part right. How a society chose to police itself was a measure of how civilised it was. From what Payne had seen of Germany so far it had a long, long way to go.

A few minutes later, the clerk returned. Payne withdrew around the corner again and watched as the man headed up the stairs, opened the door … and Lockwood pushed past him down the stairs and set off along the road, walking with small, rapid strides.

Payne gave him a twenty-yard head start, then set off after him.

Wherever he was going, Lockwood was in a hurry. He didn't want to be recognised, either: the little man wore a civilian coat over his CCG uniform and he walked with the brim of his hat pulled down.

They crossed town for half-a-mile, heading towards Eichenrode's eastern edge. The damage here was less severe and many of the British personnel had been stationed in houses there. Payne wondered whether Lockwood was headed back to his billet, but when he saw the man turn left and stop at a sandbag revetment manned by British soldiers, Payne realised Lockwood was making for the supply depot.

The depot was the centre of life in Eichenrode, the only place you could get anything at the moment: food, clothing, blankets, chocolate, cigarettes, alcohol. During the war, Payne had heard soldiers laugh about the quality of the goods at the army stores, but, in the bleak economy of post-war Germany, with its boarded-up, bombed-out shops, the depot seemed a veritable Aladdin's cave of wonders.

The supply depot in Eichenrode occupied three warehouses. The canteen and kitchens were situated in the largest of the buildings, while the two other buildings held the stores. The whole area had been surrounded with barbed wire fences. Guards with rifles and Bren guns patrolled the perimeter.

Lockwood headed for the larger of the two stores.

Payne waited before following him inside the building, considering what to do. It was possible Lockwood was only here on some trivial errand. If he followed him inside, Lockwood would be alerted — something Payne wanted to avoid doing until he had some idea of what it was he was on to. However, it was also possible that Lockwood had come here because he wanted to speak to someone.

He would take a chance and follow Lockwood inside, Payne decided. The little man's attitude had been so hurried and furtive that Payne was convinced that his visit to the depot had some connection with the questions Payne had been asking about the murder house.

Payne showed his ID papers to the guard on the door and walked inside, to a small room with a wooden counter. Half-a-dozen people in CCG uniforms were queuing before the counter, waiting to hand their requisition chits to the storemen. Long green curtains hung behind the counter and obscured the stores from view.

Mr Lockwood was nowhere to be seen.

Payne walked to the head of the queue, ignoring the grumbles behind him, and said to the storeman on duty: 'A little man with glasses just came in. Did you see where he went?'

The storeman pointed behind him with his thumb. 'He's round the back with the quartermaster sergeant. You can't come through this way, though,' he said when Payne went to lift a section of the wooden counter. 'That's for authorised personnel. Go outside and walk round the back.'

Payne went outside and walked to the back of the building, wondering how it was that Mr Lockwood of Housing Branch had come to be considered 'authorised personnel' at an army supply depot.

The ground at the back of the warehouse had been churned into thick mud by the passing of hundreds of vehicles. It was here that the lorries, trucks and utilities of the British Army came to collect their provisions. A dozen storemen in green shirts and braces carried boxes and crates out onto a ramp. Here soldiers loaded the goods into the back of their vehicles.

Payne asked a storeman where the quartermaster sergeant was and the soldier pointed away to the left, towards a concrete outhouse. Payne walked between two of the lorries queuing to receive supplies, and followed the blind side of the vehicles to get closer to the outhouse.

The regimental quartermaster sergeant was a stocky man with slicked back hair; he was about Payne's age. He was listening to Lockwood speak, and, as he did so, a sneer appeared on his face. Lockwood was speaking with rapid, nervous hand movements, but he froze when the quartermaster sergeant stepped closer and grabbed his forearm.

The man was trouble, Payne realised. He'd crossed swords with far too many cheap thugs and conmen in his life not to recognise the expression on the quartermaster sergeant's face as he wagged a finger at Lockwood. Bullying came easily to him; violence, too, most likely. Payne frowned when he noticed that the backs of the quartermaster sergeant's trousers were stained with soot-like black marks.

He watched as the two men continued to talk and Lockwood's air of perturbation increased. Then the driver of the lorry which shielded Payne gave a long toot on the horn and shouted something at Payne from the cab. Both Lockwood and the quartermaster sergeant looked up, but Payne had already withdrawn. Payne crossed behind the vehicle's tailgate and saw Lockwood hurrying away.

Payne headed towards the front of the supply depot, thinking about the expression on Lockwood's pale face. Payne recognised that, too: whatever it was that Lockwood had gotten into, he was in way over his head.

9

When Captain James Booth looked at his wristwatch for the third time in as many minutes, Chaplain Clifford said, 'Am I keeping you from something, Captain?'

Booth smiled and pulled the sleeve of his battle-blouse down. He'd been hoping to slip out and see Ursula this evening, but the chaplain's visit had scotched that: curfew would begin in an hour and Booth couldn't keep inventing excuses about why he needed to pass through checkpoints and sentry posts after dark. Besides, he didn't want the chaplain to think him rude. Ursula's present would have to wait until tomorrow.

They chatted while the Polish boy, Piotr, prepared them tea. When Piotr leant over to pour, the chaplain tried not to stare at the boy's face, but it was difficult not to: the upward twist of Piotr's hare lip nearly reached his nose, revealing snaggled teeth and a moist patch of pinky-coloured gum.

Piotr set the teapot on the table and extended a grimy hand. Booth handed him a packet of cigarettes.

'He's a trifle young to smoke, isn't he?' the chaplain said, when Piotr had left the room.

'The cigarettes aren't for him. Tobacco is the currency around here now. He uses them to buy food and firewood.'

'How old is he?'

'I've never been able to establish that. About thirteen, I would guess, from the looks of him, though I'm not sure what his mental age would be. Truth be told, I don't think he's really all there, but you won't meet a simpler, more helpful soul.'

'Where on earth did you find him?'

'I took him under my wing in Holland and he's been with me ever since. The Nazis had him working in a factory there.'

'He sounds fortunate to be alive.'

'Yes. But the luck didn't extend to his family. From what I've been able to ascertain, they're all dead. But Piotr's my good luck charm. I made a sort of covenant when I found him. I promised God I'd look after Piotr, no matter what, as long as nothing bad happened to me. Rather selfish, I know, but Piotr delivered admirably on his end of the bargain.'

'Your concern for his welfare is admirable, captain, very admirable indeed.' The chaplain blew on his tea and rested the cup in the saucer. 'Actually, Piotr's welfare is the reason I stopped by.'

'Really?'

'One of my congregation mentioned you were looking after a Polish orphan. It just so happens, a friend of mine back in Hampshire has established a home for Polish children in a little Hampshire town called Fleet. I could speak to her if you liked, see if she had room for Piotr.'

Booth shifted in his seat. 'I don't know if I'd want to send him off with strangers, padre.'

'I understand that completely, but you have my personal assurance of the quality of this woman's credentials. She is half-Polish herself, on her father's side.' He sipped his tea. 'Also, there is the question of the suitability of the boy's current environment: no schools, no family, the somewhat lax moral atmosphere that unfortunately prevails in Germany at the moment. It would be easy to imagine the boy falling in with a bad crowd, given the amount of time you are forced to dedicate to your duties.'

Yes, there is that, Booth thought as he offered the chaplain a cigarette. 'Can you tell me a bit more about this woman?'

Ten minutes later, Chaplain Clifford finished his tea and rose. 'I see I have piqued your interest, captain. Please feel free to consider the matter for a few days and let me know your decision.'

Booth showed the chaplain to the front door and smoked a cigarette on the steps, looking out across the ruins of Eichenrode. Across the street, Piotr was playing some form of tag with a group of German children.

Booth was only half joking about the covenant he'd made. When Booth had found Piotr, the boy had been little more than a tangle of pale skin and protuberant bones, sleeping beneath the machine he tended in a filthy Dutch factory — and yet, when Booth had wept at the boy's pitiable condition, Piotr had smiled and hugged him and tried to wipe the tears from Booth's face. That was the thing about Piotr, Booth had realised: despite all the horrors that had befallen him, he had never lost hope. That was why Booth had taken it upon himself to care for him. There was something pure and essential about the boy. If anything happened to Piotr, the world would be a worse place for it.

His cigarette finished, Booth jumped into his jeep and drove west through the town. If he couldn't see Ursula tonight, he might as well get on with some work and he had a new batch of information films to sort. They were making lots of these back in England now, short films and documentaries designed to be played to the occupation troops. The general idea was to outline what the purpose of the British occupation of north-west Germany was going to be, but no-one back home seemed to be controlling the output and the films often contradicted each other. When you watched the films back-to-back, as Booth did, it gave a depressingly composite view of the lack of direction behind the occupation: rather like a man groping his way through a darkened room trying not to bump into things.

A church in the centre of Eichenrode had been rigged as a makeshift cinema, although the structure was less than perfect: the exterior walls were cracked and pitted and there were numerous holes in the roof. The evening air in this part of town was still heavy with the smells of war, gasoline, brick-dust, cooking fires and damp tarpaulin. Booth parked outside the cinema and headed towards the back door, but paused as a sudden peal of laughter drifted from within the building, the sort of laughter men make when they tell each other dirty jokes.

The door to the cinema was locked. Booth rattled the handle then rapped loudly on it. The sound of hurried, furtive movements came from the other side. Then the bolt was drawn and Sergeant Hoyle's face appeared in the crack.

Hoyle was regular army and had a particular way of snapping out a parade-perfect salute when he had something to hide. Booth did not bother to return the salute. He pushed straight past Hoyle and said, 'What the devil are you up to in here, sergeant?'

A group of men was gathered inside. All stood to attention when they saw Booth's insignia. Although the men were older than Booth, there was a curiously schoolboy air to them as they exchanged glances and hung their heads. They looked guilty as hell.

Booth saw that the projector was set up with a roll of film and the huge white blanket that served as a screen was unrolled.

'What are you watching? Don't bother denying it; you've obviously just turned the projector off.'

'Begging your pardon, sir, but it won't be of any interest to…'

'I'll be the judge of that, sergeant. Now show me the damned film.'

Hoyle looked sheepishly at the other men, then put the film on.

The projector whirred and the film flickered into life, showing a black and white image of a bedroom. It took Booth's eyes a moment to separate the grainy black and white images into two naked bodies copulating, the woman's pale buttocks raised high as she knelt forward on the satin sheets, the man crouched behind her. Booth's jaw dropped as he took in further details — the candles beside the bed, the huge mirror on the wall — then he said, 'What the devil is this filth? Turn it off, sergeant. Turn it off, now.'

Hoyle hurried to remove the film from the projector. Booth told the other men to leave.

'Well, sergeant, you've some explaining to do,' he said when they were alone.

Hoyle was standing rigidly to attention again. He said nothing.

'Where did you get this from?'

'A patrol brought some canisters of film in when we were first billeted here.'

'How many canisters of film are there?'

'Four, sir.'

'You'd better let me see them.'

Hoyle took a box from under the table. Inside, there were four circular metal film canisters. In the centre of each lid was a piece of paper. TO BE USED WITH was printed on it in German, followed by a vertical list of German surnames. Nearly all of the surnames had been crossed through, although

Booth noticed some of the surnames were repeated on different canisters.

Booth opened one of the tins. The circular label stuck to the inside had a strange oval shaped design on it — a vertical sword circled by a loop of ribbon, the whole surrounded by runic designs — and the words *Wehrwissenschaftliche Zweckforschung* printed below it. Booth frowned when he saw that: it meant Military Scientific Research.

'How long have these private viewings been going on, sergeant?'

'Not long, sir.'

Booth gestured towards the film canisters.

'Is the content of all four films sexual in nature?'

'That one is. The other two are something different.' Hoyle's face clouded. 'It's not very pleasant stuff, sir.'

'Let's take a look.'

Each film ran for about two minutes. The films were all silent, the images blurred and grainy.

The first film showed groups of five men in civilian clothes being made to run from a point behind the camera down into a gully. Away to the right and left of the image, German soldiers stood with rifles, chatting amongst themselves and smoking. At a signal, they lifted their rifles and fired down into the pit. Another five men were then run forward and the process was repeated. A German soldier chewing a hunk of bread walked in front of the camera and smiled. The image faded.

In the second film, naked women stood in single file, arms wrapped around sagging breasts in an attempt at modesty. Some stared at the ground, others had their mouths open, as if wailing. One among them stared openly towards the camera, shouting at the cameraman.

'Oh Lord, don't you dare!' Booth said when a German soldier appeared from the left of the image, threw the woman to the ground and shot her twice in the head with a pistol. The camera lingered on the blood pooling beneath her hair; then the image flickered and faded to be replaced by a vast tangle of limbs.

Hundreds of dead bodies were piled on top of each other in a concrete chamber. Men wearing leather aprons and equipped with metal tie tongs dragged the bodies on to carts. The floor was covered in a dark pool of effluent.

The film finished. The loose end of the reel whickered within the projector as Booth and Hoyle stared towards the now empty screen. Booth could say nothing. His mouth hung open.

'I said it wasn't very pleasant viewing, sir.'

'You know what this is, don't you, sergeant? This is evidence of war crimes. When the hell were you planning on showing this to me?'

Hoyle said nothing. He clearly hadn't been planning on showing Booth anything.

'Box those films up and bring them to my office. And don't tell anyone else about this.'

It was evening, now. Booth walked outside, enjoying the sensation of cleanliness the limpid air imparted. The sunset tinged the horizon red and backlit the town's ragged skyline. When Sergeant Hoyle came out with the box of films, Booth said: 'Now, sergeant, I think you'd better tell me exactly how these films came into your possession.'

10

Ilse spent the afternoon working in the transit camp's laundry.

She normally tried to avoid this duty, as it was hard work, but there was a particular German woman, a bony old hag with a witchy nose and warts, who never took her eyes from Ilse. When the Tommies divided the women into working parties, Ilse always made sure she wasn't in the hag's group. The woman wasn't mentally stable.

The laundry was set up in a large concrete chamber to one side of the main body of the camp. Ilse was one of six German women working there today, but they were forbidden from talking among themselves. A Tommy with a rifle and a Red Cross nurse watched over them as they stirred huge cauldrons of boiling clothes and hefted sopping baskets through to the drying room.

Ilse thought about Captain Booth as she worked.

Poor Booth had fallen head over heels in love with her, but there was nothing Ilse could do about that. She'd felt a little sorry at having to turn him away *again* the previous evening. She had come to enjoy his company. It was nice to have at least one Englishman look at her with something other than contempt or indifference, even if he did think her name was Ursula. Physically, Booth was young and fit, two words that could never have been applied to Rüdiger towards the end of their marriage.

But O'Donnell knew about Booth. Would that be a problem? No, Ilse decided, not as long as she did what O'Donnell wanted. But who was this policeman he'd mentioned? And why was O'Donnell so worried about him?

Ilse had heard rumours about the two dead bodies that had been found in the cellar of a house out by the Brunswick Road. Lots of Germans were whispering about it. Rumour had it they'd been murdered by the Tommies. Did O'Donnell have something to do with that? It wouldn't have surprised Ilse if he did. O'Donnell had that look about him, the look of a man who would smile as he picked your pocket. *Say what you like about the Nazis, they knew how to deal with people like that*, she thought.

How the hell had O'Donnell found out about her and Booth, though? Ilse thought about this and decided the Tommy soldier called Suttpen must have told O'Donnell. Everyone knew Suttpen and O'Donnell played cards together; and Booth had had to bribe Suttpen to stop Ilse's farmhouse from being requisitioned.

By late afternoon, the soldier that watched over the laundry had begun to chat with the Red Cross nurse. When he invited her outside for a smoke, Ilse hissed at the woman next to her, a big-hipped Bavarian with ruddy cheeks and her hair sweat-plastered to her forehead.

'What is it?' the woman said when Ilse hissed again. 'We're not supposed to talk.'

Ilse stole a glance over her shoulder then moved closer.

'Have you heard about the murders on the Brunswick Road?'

Murder: it was strange the power that word had. Millions had been 'killed' in the last five years and nobody seemed to pay a blind bit of notice. But use that word, murder, and the world still caught its breath.

'They say it was the Tommies,' the Bavarian woman said, dropping her voice to a whisper, 'and I believe them. My neighbour works at the *Rathaus* and she says the man they killed was in the SS.'

'What about this English policeman who is investigating?'

The woman waved her hand dismissively. 'I don't believe they *are* investigating. What do the Tommies care if Germans die?'

Ilse went to say more but the Red Cross woman shouted something at them and the Bavarian woman blushed and hurried away.

Ilse had to fight not to lose her temper. She wasn't a schoolgirl to be shushed like that. What the hell were they punishing her for, anyway? What had Ilse ever done? She'd never killed anyone. She'd always been very fair to the Polish girls that served her in the Warthegau. This was so humiliating, being forced to soak and scrub other people's filthy clothing. *But that's the whole point, isn't it?* she thought. It wasn't enough that the Tommies had won the war: they wanted the German people to *know* they'd been beaten. They were going to rub their noses in it. Still, it could be worse, she thought. God, if things were like this with the English in control, what the hell must things be like under the Russians? Then she remembered Cousin Ursula. *That* was how things were under the Russians.

The sun was sinking low in the sky when the Red Cross woman let them leave. Ilse hurried across the camp to the place where she'd hidden the medical kit and the food O'Donnell had given her. She almost cried with relief when she saw that they were still there. She took a nibble of the bread and sausage after making sure she wasn't watched, then stuffed the whole lot down the front of her dress and headed for the gates.

As always, there was a huge queue outside the factory's admin building. This was where people queued to obtain the identity documents and travel permits they needed to get home. It always made Ilse happy to see how crowded it was.

That was good. The more of them received their wretched documents, the more of them would leave and the faster Germany could get back to normal again.

Close to the gate now, she heard the rumble of a lorry behind her and the tooting of its horn. When she turned and saw the Red Cross symbol painted on the roof, she stole away into the bushes by the side of the road.

So, he was back, was he?

The man who drove the lorry was named Joost. He was a strange fellow, practically the only man in the camp that didn't ogle the women. In fact, he didn't really seem to notice anyone; he seemed to look through people. He said he was South African, but Ilse had discovered he wasn't actually one of the official Red Cross workers. Still, the war had thrown up all types of refugees. There were hundreds like Joost in every transit camp, people willing to help out in order to improve their own status a little. Joost was often gone for days at a time, picking up supplies and dropping people off at different transit camps. He'd given Ilse a lift, once, but he'd begun to take a very roundabout way to get to her house. When she'd asked him where he was going, he wouldn't reply. In the end, a British patrol had stopped them and made Ilse get out because she didn't have the right documents. Ilse remembered feeling quite relieved.

When the lorry had passed, Ilse emerged from the bushes. She was nearly at the gates when someone in front of her called her name.

It was the hag woman, the mad one, standing by the gates. Ilse tried to hurry past, but the woman blocked her path, hissing at Ilse as she did so.

'Who are you?' Ilse said, pushing the woman away and quickening her step. 'Leave me alone.'

Ilse ran now, heart racing, but when she reached the bend in the road, she could not resist looking behind her.

The hag stood in the middle of the road, staring straight towards her.

Ilse continued to run. Panic gripped her, but it wasn't until she was halfway home that she realised why: the hag had called her by name — but not Ursula, the one everyone in the camp knew her by.

She had called her Ilse.

11

Silas Payne woke early and busied himself preparing coffee and bacon over the potbellied stove in the police station. As he ate, he considered how to move his investigation forward. He had spoken to Major Norris the previous evening and told him that he thought Mr Lockwood and Quartermaster Sergeant Suttpen knew something about the murder house.

'Lockwood?' Norris had said. 'Little fellow with jam jar specs? You can't surely think he's capable of killing someone?'

'Experience has taught me that anyone is capable of anything, given the right circumstances, major,' Payne had replied. 'But I didn't say I necessarily thought they were responsible for the murders. They know something, though, I'm sure of it.'

Norris sighed. 'Well, Quartermaster Sergeant Suttpen would sell his own mother if he thought there was profit in it, there's no denying that. They had problems with him back in England, apparently. And in Holland. But I'm afraid men like Suttpen and his motley crew are in the ascendant at the moment, given the current moral climate.'

Payne had wanted to bring Suttpen in for questioning, but Norris had shaken his head. 'I'm afraid you don't have any jurisdiction over army personnel and Suttpen's got the backing of Colonel Bassett. I'd be more inclined to pursue this Housing Branch fellow first, Lockwood. He's CCG, so we've some leverage with him.'

Payne had agreed, but reluctantly.

After breakfast, Payne washed, shaved, dressed in his suit and went outside — and saw that all four of the tyres on his utility had been slashed.

Payne walked around the vehicle. With its deflated wheels, the car looked like it was sinking into the ground. There was no way to repair the tyres. The vandal had made sure of that, carving ragged slits six inches long in the rubber walls.

Being without a vehicle would severely hamper his investigation. Payne wondered about the timing of the vandalism.

A soldier came over and stood beside Payne, shaking his head. 'You can't get tyres for love nor money at the moment. And you need all four.'

Payne wondered whether the soldier had had something to do with the vandalism and was taunting him but decided that, on balance, his irritating sympathy was too artless to be anything other than genuine. Payne went back to the police station and phoned Norris to see if he could get him a new vehicle, but there was no answer.

When Payne returned to the utility, Colonel Bassett was standing in front of it, regarding the slashed tyres with an attitude of suppressed fury. The translator, Fraülein Seiler, stood beside him, jotting down notes as Bassett dictated.

'Germans perpetrating acts of sabotage will be summarily shot, regardless of age or sex. Regardless, Miss Seiler, do you hear? *Regardless.* I want that word stressed. The same goes for curfew breakers.'

With his swagger stick and stentorian voice, Colonel Bassett was a ruddy-faced caricature of the retired military type. There were hundreds like Bassett in Germany now, old men that had leapt at the chance to command again as part of the military government of Germany. His staff seemed to regard him as an amiable eccentric, but Payne disliked the man. Beneath his shaggy unkempt eyebrows, Bassett's eyes were hard and dark, the way stubborn, unimaginative men's often were.

'Don't worry, Detective Inspector,' he said when he saw Payne, 'we'll clear this matter up for you. And we'll make the Jerries responsible rue the day.'

'Do you think a German did this?'

'Who the hell else would it have been? We've been plagued with cut telephone lines and smashed windows now for months. Well, not any more, do you hear? They'll stop this, right now, or I'll personally see to it that the civilian population is ridden hard and put away wet. It's the only thing these bloody people seem to understand.'

Payne hitched a ride to the far side of town with some soldiers and had them drop him by the offices of Housing Branch.

A different clerk was on duty. Mr Lockwood wasn't there, though.

'No, I don't know where he is, sir,' the Housing Branch clerk said, irritably. 'He should have been here an hour ago.'

'Is it like him to be late for work?'

'No.'

'I don't suppose the information I requested has arrived yet?'

'That'll be another no.'

Afterwards, Payne left and walked to Lockwood's billet, a semi-derelict townhouse that Lockwood shared with six other CCG men. He knocked at the door of the house and was shown in by a bare-chested man with a pencil moustache.

'Nope, I haven't seen old Lockwood since last night,' he said, when Payne asked.

Lockwood shared his room, which was upstairs, with a young man who was still asleep. Payne shook him awake and the man turned bleary, hungover eyes towards him.

'No, I haven't seen Lockwood,' he said, moistening gummy lips. 'But then I was out all night at a party.'

'Was he here when you got home? Did you hear him leave this morning?'

'Sorry, old man, I was a bit blotto.'

'Do you have any idea where he might have gone?' Payne said, looking towards the immaculately-smoothed sheets on Lockwood's bed. It had either been freshly made that morning or it hadn't been slept in at all.

'Absolutely no idea. But then old Lockwood isn't the chattiest of fellows.'

The man with the pencil moustache was shaving in front of a cracked half of mirror resting on the bedroom's mantelpiece. He wiped lather from the razor, then paused. 'Now that I think about it, someone came to see Lockwood last night. They spoke outside.'

'Who was he?' Payne said.

'You can't expect me to recognise him, old man. I've only been here a week. He was a tall fellow, I think. Heavy set.'

'Was it the quartermaster sergeant, Suttpen?'

The man laughed. 'No, it wasn't old Jacob. I'd have recognised him, don't you worry.'

Payne looked through Lockwood's possessions, but there was nothing of interest. He thanked the men and left.

Outside, Payne stood in the shadow of a broken building. Should he be worried about Lockwood? It was too early to say.

Perhaps Suttpen would know something. Payne had checked the duty roster at the *Rathaus* the night before and he knew

Suttpen was off duty today. He thought about what Norris had said about not bothering Suttpen. Payne decided he didn't care.

He began walking across town.

He had no idea what he'd say to Suttpen, but that didn't really matter. Payne only wanted a chance to take stock of his opponent. In a perfect world, Payne would have let another officer do the talking while he watched from the sidelines. Often you could learn far more from watching a person's reactions than by talking to them.

It wasn't a perfect world, though. He was on his own out here. He would have to do the best he could.

Suttpen and his men were billeted in a beautiful property on the edge of Eichenrode, a place where the urban area began to merge with farms and fields. Outside the house, lines of clothing flapped in the breeze and empty wine bottles, tins and leftover food were littered across the table. As Payne approached, he saw a cat picking through some chicken bones.

A soldier wearing American sunglasses lay on the grass outside the house, sunning himself. When Payne asked where Suttpen was, the soldier pointed towards a pathway that led to a barn.

The barn door opened inwards. Inside, dust motes danced in the shafts of sunlight that came through the gaps between the wall-boards. Goods of every type — lamps, artwork, clothing, silverware, crockery, even a pair of skis and a sledge — were arranged around the walls and floor of the barn. They weren't stacked or dumped, either. The goods had obviously been set out with a view to impressing prospective buyers.

Jacob Suttpen sat at the back of the barn, eating tinned jam with a spoon. He stopped when he saw Payne and his eyes narrowed. He set the tin on the table and rubbed his hands on his battle-blouse. 'Can I help you, sir?' he said in a tone that made it clear helping Payne was the last thing on his mind.

'My name is Detective Inspector Payne. Of Public Safety Branch.'

'Pleased to meet you, Detective Inspector. But I think you must have taken a wrong turn somewhere. This here ain't a *public* place, it's a private residence. And it's totally safe. I make sure of that personally.'

In a single fluid motion, Suttpen swept up a scoped rifle from behind the desk and hefted it in his hand. His smile became broader as he clicked the rifle bolt and put a round in the chamber.

Payne did not move, but he met Suttpen's gaze and held it.

'How would I go about getting new tyres for my utility?' Payne said.

Suttpen drew his breath. 'Why? Has something happened to it?'

Again, the two men looked at each other in silence.

It was him that slashed my tyres, Payne thought. *He wants me to know it was him, too.*

'It's quite an impressive collection you've got,' Payne said.

'Not bad, is it? To the victor the spoils. And I for one intend to spoil myself rotten. The Jerries owe me for six years of my life. To say nothing of being bloody shelled in France in the last lot. Did you serve? In the Great War, I mean.'

'No.'

Suttpen nodded as if some previously-formed opinion had been confirmed.

'Are you a friend of Mr Lockwood?' Payne said.

'Mr Lockwood?'

'Short man, about our age, wears glasses. He works at Housing Branch.'

'Oh, yes. I call him Theo. That's why I didn't twig.'

'How do you know him?'

Suttpen had put the rifle down and now played with a pencil. 'If I were a rude man, Detective Inspector, I'd ask you what bloody business of yours it was. Lucky for you, though, I'm not.' He smiled. 'I know everyone. It's one of the perks of being regimental quartermaster sergeant. Especially in a situation like this.'

'A situation like what?'

The pencil twirled in the air. 'This. Eichenrode. Germany. You might not have noticed, but the creature comforts are a little hard to come by at the moment. That's why people want to get pally with me.'

'And did Mr Lockwood?'

'You could say so. He got me these digs. That's no secret.'

'You have a reputation as a man that can get things. If I wanted something, could you get it for me?'

Suttpen's eyes became wary. 'Depends whether you were asking me as a copper or not. There's rules against entrapment, aren't there?'

'Say I wanted medicines. Vials of vaccine, for example. Could you get me those?'

The momentary confusion on Suttpen's face seemed genuine. 'Probably. But you'd have to tell me first what the hell you wanted with it.'

'What about barbiturate? Can you get that?'

Suttpen laid his hands flat on the table and leant towards Payne. 'Want to know what I think, Detective Inspector? I think you're testing me. You're not asking me about medicines because you want some. You're asking me to see how I react. So let me tell you, nice and clear, that I don't have the foggiest idea what you're going on about. I've bought and sold just about everything you can imagine in my time, but I've never sold vaccines. And if you find who is selling barbiturate, send 'em my way. We can do some business. Now, if it's all the same to you, I'd rather you went now and let me enjoy my day off.'

Payne turned. There was no point in staying. As he reached the door, Suttpen called out to him.

'You're going to be watching me, I know that, Payne. But I'll be watching you, too. This here is mine, do you understand? I earned it.'

Afterwards, Payne walked back to Housing Branch. There was still no sign of Lockwood, so Payne did what any good policeman would have done. He began knocking on doors and stopping people in the street, describing Lockwood to them. He worked methodically along each side of the roads closest to Lockwood's billet, speaking to Army and CCG personnel, DPs and German civilians. Someone always knew something. That was the thing to focus on as the hours of tedium slid past and the endlessly repeated words seemed to be wearing a groove on your tongue.

Persistence paid off. Yes, people did remember the little man with the glasses from Number 26 hurrying along the street the previous evening. People had noticed him because he looked so self-conscious.

Over the course of the afternoon, Payne pieced together Lockwood's movements. Two people had seen Lockwood heading out of town by the north road, hurrying along as if he were late to meet someone, but that was where the trail went dry.

Payne followed the road to the last place anyone had seen Lockwood, then walked a hundred yards out into the countryside. It was nice to breathe air that was free from brick dust, to see the rills the wind blew across the rainwater in the roadside ditches.

Payne paused by an oak tree, looked out across the fields and watched the haze growing within the dells as evening drew in. Then he turned and started to walk back towards the town. As he did so, the cloud cover shifted and the day's last sharp sunlight lit the road.

Payne paused as he walked, wondering what it was that had caught his attention. And then he saw it, a pair of thick-rimmed glasses that lay at the bottom of a ditch, sunlight glinting on the one remaining lens.

12

That morning, Booth took his jeep and drove east out of Eichenrode for fifteen miles, until he saw the divisional signs for Wolffslust prison.

It had taken him thirty minutes of cajoling the previous night to discover where Sergeant Hoyle had obtained the films. Hoyle initially claimed to have forgotten who had brought in the film canisters so Booth had the sergeant begin the laborious process of searching through all the receipt stubs for the information the Field Intelligence unit had received. Curiously, it then took Hoyle only ten minutes to find the correct stub.

'I remember now, sir,' Hoyle had said, brandishing the paperwork. 'It was a corporal from the Devonshires brought us the films, Corporal Peaver. He's part of the forces looking after Wolffslust prison.'

Booth hated Wolffslust. The map listed it as a castle and the first time Booth had gone there, he'd expected a picturesque Schloß. What he found instead was a brick bastion built in a blunt and ugly style that rose from the damp tangle of forest that surrounded it like a toad's head from mud. The wartime watchtowers and wire did nothing to improve its aspect. Much of the prison was below ground and the cell doors opened off stone corridors filled with moss and watery echoes.

Booth read the official report on the occupation of the prison as he drove, balancing the document on the steering wheel. The British advance guard had overrun the prison in late April and found it to be seriously overcrowded — the German authorities had been using Wolffslust to house prisoners from other institutions that had been damaged in air raids. The prison governor and most of the gaolers had fled the day before the British troops arrived, leaving the whole institution in chaos. Many of the prisoners in the overcrowded medical ward had been suffering from malnutrition and some had died. Most of the prisoners belonging to Allied nations had been immediately released, and now the remaining prisoners at Wolffslust were nearly all Germans.

The report was incomplete, though. There was no information on which unit had first found the prison and the report lacked an officer's signature.

Ten minutes later, Booth drew up outside the prison. The British soldiers on duty at the gate were sitting inside the guardhouse drinking tea and smoking. They waved Booth through without looking at his papers. Inside, groups of prisoners lazed in the prison courtyard, playing cards and smoking. One group was cooking a pine marten over a campfire while British soldiers joked with them.

Booth found Corporal Peaver in the mess hall, hands wrapped around a steaming mug of tea. It was clear Sergeant Hoyle had spoken some word of warning to the corporal, as the man began with an apology.

'If I'd known what those films were, sir, I'd have turned 'em straight in to an officer. I didn't realise they were so important.'

'That's quite all right, corporal. I've checked the records. You've done nothing wrong.'

Corporal Peaver was a big, rosy-cheeked man with a Hampshire accent, probably a good fifteen years older than Booth. Booth told him to stand easy, then said, 'What I really wanted to ask is how you found these films. And where. I don't know if you saw the inside of the canisters, but it said something in German about military research. Given the subject matter of the films, it could be important evidence for the lawyers at Nuremburg.'

Corporal Peaver scratched his cheek. 'Where I found them? That's going to be difficult, sir. It was a terrible mess when we got here. The German guards had scarpered and there were prisoners wandering loose all over the place. By the time I got here, they'd ripped most of the admin wing apart and thrown the filing cabinets out of the window. And my unit wasn't the first British one to get here. There'd been other units here before us.'

'How had so many prisoners got free of their cells?'

'Well, some of them were Allied POWS, British and French. Plus, there were a lot of the Germans' forced labourers in here, too, locked up for petty stuff. Apparently, the first British officer on the scene ordered the POWs and the workers released. They in turn went round letting all the others out.'

'Who was this officer?'

'I've no idea, sir. He was long gone by the time I arrived. It was all a bit chaotic back then.'

Booth frowned. 'Do you mean to say this officer released prisoners without first checking what their crime was?'

'I suppose so. Is that a problem, sir?'

'Of course it's a problem, corporal. There might have been serious criminals inside the prison.'

'I hadn't thought of it like that before, sir. But if they were locked up by the Nazis, that sort of makes 'em on our side, doesn't it?'

'Criminals are on nobody's side but their own, corporal. You'd do well to remember that. Logic dictates Nazi Germany must have had its murderers and rapists, the same as any other society.'

‘I thought most of them were in the SS, sir.’

Booth ignored the quip. He was thinking of something else. ‘If the prison was thrown open, why didn’t all the prisoners escape?’

‘To be honest, sir, some of ’em did, but most came back when they saw what things were like outside. I think most of the German lads were sharp enough to realise they were far safer inside a prison than they were out wandering the streets. They’re not a bad bunch, actually. I’ve found they’re pretty well behaved as long as they get three meals a day and we don’t shout at ’em too much.’

Booth lit a cigarette. Something about the situation worried him, though he couldn’t put his finger on it.

‘Let’s get back to the films. Try and think where it was that you found them. It could be important.’

Peaver nodded. ‘Come to think of it, sir, it could well have been down in the cellar, in one of the corridors leading up to the dungeon.’

‘Dungeon?’

‘Sorry, sir, that’s what me and the lads have named it on account of it looking like a dungeon.’

The corporal was right: it did look like a dungeon. The corridor was obviously from the original 17th century Schloß. Bulbous stones protruded from the walls and the floor was patched with puddles; electric lights flickered in brackets on the wall. The corridor ended in an enormous slab of a door studded with iron bands.

Booth dropped his cigarette in a puddle of water and placed his hand on the gnarled wood.

‘What’s on the other side of this?’

‘No idea, sir. It can’t be opened.’

'Good God, man, do you mean to say this door hasn't been opened since May?'

'Begging your pardon, but it's a prison door, sir. It's not meant to be picked. Or opened, for that matter, once it's closed.'

'But there could be prisoners on the other side.'

'With respect, sir, if there were prisoners in there, there won't be none left now,' Peaver said without any hint of sarcasm. 'Plus, I don't think there are any cells down there. Not according to the prison blueprints. I checked that when I realised we didn't have the key.'

'I want this door opened, corporal. If you can't open it yourselves, get a detachment of engineers up here and blow the damned thing off its hinges.'

The engineer detachment promised to be up at Wolffslust by the afternoon. There was no point driving back to Eichenrode, so Booth ate lunch in the mess then spent a few hours trying to impose some semblance of order on the prison.

The first thing he organised was a roll-call of the prisoners. It took forty minutes to establish that there were 314 men currently at the prison but the count had to be redone twice when Booth noticed prisoners who had been outside in the forest sneaking back in. However, even a cursory look at the fragmented documentation that had survived the prison's liberation showed 314 was fewer than half the amount of men the prison had held in April.

Booth told Corporal Peaver to gather up all the prison's remaining paperwork, which actually consisted of a dozen postal bags stuffed with crumpled files, ledgers and ripped, dirty pieces of paper. Booth emptied the first postal bag onto a table.

‘Right,’ he said, looking at the mess in front of him. ‘First of all, I want to know exactly who was in this prison and why. Once we’ve done that, we can start on the most important part.’

‘What’s that, sir?’ Peaver said.

‘Finding out whether the blighters are still here.’

13

Little Otto took the ring of keys from his pocket and rattled the big silver key into the lock. The door creaked as it opened and stale, dusty air wafted out to greet him.

This was Otto's other house, the one he had kept back for emergencies. It did not please him as much as the property on the Brunswick Road — Otto loved to sit in that house's garret, playing with his treasures as the moonlight shone through the hole in the roof — but it would have to do.

Otto put the key ring back in his pocket and rested the packet of quicklime on the kitchen floor. Then he went back outside to where the little man lay on the ground. He checked the bindings that held the man's ankles and wrists together were still tight. Then he took him by the ankles, dragged him inside and sat down to wait for Mr Lockwood to awake.

Otto donned his Mask of Many while Lockwood was still unconscious and made sure that the first thing Lockwood saw as he came round was Otto pushing his masked face towards him and running his fingertips across the loops of twine that bound the lips together. Otto wanted to show the bastard exactly what it was that he valued most in others: silence and compliance.

Lockwood didn't understand. He began whimpering and crying almost immediately, the sound quickly rising to a hysterical crescendo, despite the gag. Otto kicked his head until the man quietened down. He was standing over Lockwood now, staring down at the man's smooth skin that had become streaked with grime and tears.

Should he add him to the mask?

No, Otto had another idea. Lockwood had lost his nerve. He would give the game away. It was only fair that he help to hide Little Otto.

Otto crossed the room. Behind him, Lockwood continued to snivel and weep. Otto took the black pennant from his pocket and rolled it into a blindfold.

Then he reached for the quicklime.

14

Early in the night, Cousin Ursula began screaming. The sound wrenched Ilse from sleep. She lit the paraffin lamp and went to her cousin's bedroom. Ursula's body was totally rigid as she loosed her banshee wails into the darkness. Only her mouth moved, opening so wide it seemed hinged far behind her jaws.

The medicine had served only to make Ursula worse. Ilse had started off applying ointment to some of the cuts and bruises on her cousin's arms and legs, but Ursula had begun to writhe and gasp as if she were lying on hot coals. In the end, poor Ursula had seemed to be suffering so much that Ilse had injected her in the thigh with a syrette of morphine, following the instructions inside the medical kit. That had seemed to quieten her, although Ilse still hadn't been able to part her cousin's legs and examine the damage.

Ilse crossed the room, making soothing noises. Ursula calmed a little when Ilse sat next to her, but she wouldn't stop trembling and her eyes bulged.

Ilse opened the medical kit, took another of the syrettes of morphine and jabbed the needle into Ursula's upper arm. The prick of the needle made Ursula jolt upright, but then she let out a long slow breath and sank back onto the bed, her crumpled love letters clasped between her hands.

Ilse sat stroking Ursula's hair until she fell asleep again, but the sound of the mucous rattle in her chest seemed to have doubled in volume. It was as if something had worked itself loose and was banging around inside her. Ilse held the lamp up and took a good look at Ursula's clammy, jaundiced skin.

Ursula wasn't going to get better, Ilse realised suddenly. She was going to linger there on the cusp of death forever, rattling and shrieking and stinking.

Ilse stood up, trembling herself now. She couldn't take any more. She'd done her best with the medical supplies, but how could you help someone who became hysterical every time you touched her? This whole situation was so unfair. Why did bloody Ursula have to come here of all…

Ilse turned away from the bed, swept by sudden shame. How could she have thought such selfish thoughts? It must be because she lacked food.

She was exhausted, yet she knew there was no way she would get back to sleep again. She went downstairs to the kitchen, poured herself a tot of O'Donnell's whisky and lit a cigarette. She drank the whisky, then poured another, larger this time, and leant against the wall, allowing her thoughts to drift towards happier times, back when they had first moved to Berlin…

She and Rüdiger had hosted such wonderful parties. All the best people had attended. Magda Goebbels had even come one night and stayed two whole hours. For a moment, it seemed to Ilse that she could smell the perfumed scent of those wonderful evenings again, see chandelier light dance on silverware, hear the purr of the conversation. The men had looked so smart in their uniforms. And the flags, red, white and black, fluttering against the walls. Give the Nazis their due, no-one in history had known how to create pageantry quite like they could.

Of course, she'd never taken them too seriously. There had been a brief moment when she'd felt the stirrings of genuine devotion — who hadn't in those heady early days of the war? — but the Nazis were only ever a means to an end for Ilse.

After all, it was all such a lot of garbled nonsense. Anyone that took a moment to look behind the uniforms and histrionic speeches could see that, surely?

Trust an idiot like Rüdiger to take it all so seriously. She could picture him now, sitting in bed, trying to learn the words to his SS oath like some huge idiot child preparing for catechism. And to think that she'd had to exert all her influence at one point to stop him joining the SA. He'd have been in his element there, shoulder to shoulder with all the other bullies and bores. Anyone with any intelligence could see those knuckle-draggers' goose was cooked the moment Hitler took power.

But that was the problem: Rüdiger was not intelligent. That was how they'd ended up in the Warthegau, as the Nazis had named the southern portion of the territory reclaimed from the Poles.

What the hell had Rüdiger known about coal mining? He'd studied Law. But once one of his damned SS chums had filled his head with nonsense, he'd accepted charge of that wretched mine quicker than you could say *Lebensraum* and forced them both to move to some rural hellhole close to Posen. Ilse had made a point of never even visiting the mine the whole time she'd lived there.

She finished her whisky and went upstairs to get a blanket. It was the first time since summer she'd felt the need for a blanket at night. It wouldn't be long now before the cold weather came. God, how was she going to survive the winter?

As she pulled the blanket free from the cupboard, a small wooden box fell to the floor with a thud, spewing photographs across the floorboards. Ilse crouched to pick them up and smiled when she saw they were her mother's photos.

Here was Rüdiger before they married, slim and smart in his Party uniform. And little Johannes in shorts, practising his stiff-armed salute out in the garden.

Ilse held the photograph up to the light.

Dear little Johannes. Ten years her junior, he'd been more like a son than a brother. She thought of how he would snuggle into her bed after bathing, and paused, surprised by the sudden clarity of the memories. She thought of the smell of his damp hair, the scent of his skin. Children always smelt so warm and clean at bedtime.

Johannes had been such an ardent little Nazi. He'd been chomping at the bit to join the *Deutsches Jungvolk* when he turned ten and was let into the Hitler Youth a year early. She smiled when she thought of him on that first day, standing in his pristine uniform in the centre of the kitchen, his hands on his hips.

Of course, there had been trouble. There always was with Johannes. On one evening march, Johannes had beaten a boy from the town with a horsewhip. No-one knew exactly what had happened, but the boy had been left blind in one eye. And two of the youngest members of his Hitler Youth group had returned from a weekend camping trip with pneumonia. They said Johannes had made them stand in the chest-deep waters of a stream for nearly an hour as a punishment.

Johannes was the only one of her relatives Ilse had mentioned on the *Fragebogen* questionnaire. It was Question 101: *Have you any relatives who have held office, rank or post of authority in any of the Nazi organisations listed above?*

What should she have put? Cousin Ursula had three relatives who matched the criteria, but the link between Cousin Ursula and Rüdiger was Ilse. What was the point of pretending to be someone else if she was only going to draw the Tommies' attention to that?

To put nothing, though, had seemed like tempting fate. Better to give them something to look into, to draw their attention. So she'd put Johannes's name down, and listed his full career. *Deutsches Jungvolk* and Hitler Youth, then, later, full membership of the NSDAP and enlistment in the 3rd Division of the Waffen SS, the *Totenkopf*.

There were more photos, but she put them back into the box and closed it, suddenly wearied by the weight of so many memories. A terrible sensation of solitude welled within her. She had no-one now. Rüdiger was dead, killed by partisans in June of '44. And she'd heard nothing from Johannes for two years. Ursula was the only relative she had left.

She went upstairs and sat in the chair beside Ursula's bed, warmed by the whisky. Before she knew it, her head was lolling in time to Ursula's breathing…

It seemed she'd only slept a few minutes, but when she woke silver-white moonlight was filtering through the window. Ilse woke slowly, rubbing her eyes and remembering the sound of a distant boom that had woken her, before she noticed that something was wrong in the room. It took her a moment to understand what it was: the wax and wane of Ursula's breathing could no longer be heard.

She reached for her cousin's arm; she screamed when her fingers found flesh that was cold and stiff.

Her first reaction was to run from the room, desperate to wash her hands. What if Ursula had died from some disease? She spent the next ten minutes scrubbing her hands. She felt dirty all over. Then she went back upstairs, hoping against hope that she was wrong and that Ursula wasn't dead, but, when she stood in the bedroom doorway, she realised there could be no mistaking the horrible twist of Ursula's lips. No live person's face looked like that.

Strangely, she felt nothing. She was too tired, she realised. She went and poured herself another tot of whisky. Instantly, practical considerations crowded in to destroy the release that she had hoped the warmth of the liquor would give her. Ursula was dead. What would she do with the body? She couldn't leave it inside the house: it would rot and smell, and there would be flies. But if she contacted a funeral director — if there was one in the town — the Tommies were bound to come round asking questions. She could lie, say she had no idea who Ursula was, but it would attract suspicion.

No, she would have to bury Ursula herself. There was no alternative.

When she returned to the bedroom her cousin's legs were already stiff, but her arms flapped heavily like stockings packed with sand as Ilse dragged her down the staircase, bumping Ursula's head against the steep steps as she went.

It was cold outside and the birch trees shone silver in the moonlight. She dragged Ursula's body to a patch of ground twenty yards from the house. Then Ilse took a spade from the garden shed and began to dig.

15

When the muffled explosion sounded in the dead of night, Silas Payne awoke instantly.

He lay there, staring into the darkness, wondering whether he'd dreamt the noise rather than heard it. A few minutes later a jeep screeched to a halt in the street outside and someone began knocking at a door across the street. Silas knew that it belonged to the house where an infantry lieutenant was billeted. Running feet sounded on the cobblestones and men's voices began shouting.

Something was wrong.

Payne looked at his watch as he dressed: 03:50.

He reached for one of his civilian suits, but quickly decided his CCG uniform would be more appropriate. Outside, he asked a soldier what was going on.

'We think a mine's gone off in that stretch of field out by the canal.'

'Do you mean it went off alone? Or that someone set it off?'

'No idea.'

When the young lieutenant emerged from the house opposite, Payne asked if he could accompany him.

'I don't know about that, Detective Inspector. This is a military matter.'

'Not if it's a civilian in the minefield. Then it's my business, too.'

That seemed to throw the lieutenant. Or perhaps it was simply too complex a problem for such an early hour. He waved assent that Payne might accompany him.

They climbed into the lieutenant's jeep and drove through the ruined ramparts of the town's gates and out into the countryside. Mist rose from the fields and the moon rode high and full, lining the clouds with silver light.

'What's the situation, sergeant?' the lieutenant said, after they had crossed the Bailey bridge that led over the canal and pulled off the road.

The sergeant nodded towards a nearby fence. 'There was someone out there in the minefield, sir.'

'Do you know who it was?'

'No idea, sir. When we heard the explosion, we came running straight away. Then we fancied we heard someone crying and calling for help. Lucky for us we realised where we were, else one of the lads might have hopped the fence and gone to find the poor sod.'

'And you definitely heard someone cry out?'

'Yes, sir. We think he's still alive.'

'Is that possible if he's stepped on a mine?' Payne said.

The lieutenant nodded. 'Depends what he stepped on. The Jerries used to rig some mines to maim rather than kill.'

He was going to elaborate when the wind shifted slightly and the sound of a low moan was carried on the breeze.

Each man there froze momentarily. Then they concentrated their torches on the darkness, trying to locate the source of the sound. Now they could hear a man's voice, calling out for help. He was speaking in English.

'For God's sake, man, it's away there, over to the right,' the lieutenant said as a private stood on the lowest bar of the fence and shone his torch into the darkness.

'HELP!' the voice screamed, louder now and touched with a genuine sense of terror, as if the man had only just become aware of his predicament. The field seemed to be filled with moving shapes as the clouds above scudded across the face of the moon.

'MY EYES! MY GOD, MY EYES! HELP!' Hysteria distorted the man's voice, but that wasn't what had made the hairs on Payne's neck stand up. Was it his imagination or did he recognise the voice?

'Stay still, you stupid bastard,' a young private said, as sounds of thrashing and other frenzied motions came from the field. One of the privates had a megaphone. 'Stay still. You are in a minefield. Remain where you are and…'

The soldiers were obviously from a fighting unit: when the mine detonated, they all dropped flat to the ground, whereas Payne merely flinched as earth showered around him. The explosion seemed so close it took Payne's breath away; he felt it like a blow in the pit of his stomach and he heard dirt pitter-patter on the brim of his hat. Then something heavy and organic landed with a wet thud on the bonnet of a jeep. One of the soldiers cursed and Payne caught sight of a dark smear that ran across the front of the vehicle before he looked away.

The engineers waited until daylight before going into the minefield to collect the body.

Once the sun began to rise Payne could see clearly where the explosion had taken place, as there was a circle of scorched earth about 20 yards from the fence. Crows hopped and fluttered in this area, pecking at a dark and ragged shape that lay away to the right of the crater caused by the explosion.

While the engineers edged forward towards the body, Payne walked the edge of the minefield, trying to find where the dead man had entered it. Around a hundred yards from the canal, the ground on the other side of the fence had been churned up, as if someone had been kicking and thrashing their legs.

Muddy holes showed where the man had stumbled away from the fence, heading deeper into the minefield.

The engineers had reached the remains and gathered them up and were making their way back with them on a stretcher.

Payne went and stood beside the ambulance. As the engineers carried the stretcher past him, he lifted the tarpaulin that covered it. The lieutenant grabbed his arm and asked him what the hell he was doing, but Payne shook himself free. He had to be sure. He bent closer to the corpse's head.

The face was smeared with mud and the eye sockets were red and blistered, but there could be no doubt. Payne was right: he *had* recognised the voice.

The stretcher harboured what was left of Mr Lockwood.

16

Captain Booth was drinking tea and considering what to have for breakfast when a jeep screeched to a halt outside his billet and Colonel Bassett's adjutant, Captain Fredrickson, got out and ran up the steps.

Booth's nose wrinkled. If Booth merely disliked Colonel Bassett, he actively hated Captain Fredrickson. With his thick black hair, prop-forward's build and abrasively upper-class accent, Freddy was the sort you just knew had been a bully at school. It was oafs like 'Freddy' Fredrickson that would give the occupation a bad name, boorish drunks acting like the overlords of some new European Raj.

Booth's problems with the man had begun back in Holland. That was when Freddy had still been a lieutenant. He'd been serving under Booth in Field Intelligence. They'd been working as part of the division's advance guard, engaged in a sweeping-up operation that involved interrogating men and women suspected of being members of the Dutch fascist party who were therefore also suspected of collaboration with the Germans.

A couple of days after some arrests had been made, Booth had collected the detachment's laundry from a local washerwoman. She was profuse in her apologies: she'd tried everything but she just couldn't get the red speckles out of Lieutenant Fredrickson's shirt cuffs. Was it beetroot, perhaps? Or wine?

Booth discovered what it was that same night, when he walked in on Freddy with his pistol rammed into the mouth of a terrified Dutchman. A second man sat crying on the floor, blood pouring from his mouth.

Booth had taken the matter straight to Division and then on to Corps. Nothing was done. Lieutenant Fredrickson had an impeccable record. It was war. Officers in the field had free rein to use whatever tactics they saw fit.

Instead of being punished, Freddy had been promoted to captain and now served on Colonel Bassett's staff. It was no secret that he had Bassett's ear and had used his influence on a number of occasions to ensure Booth's unit was given irksome duties.

Booth stayed in his office, listening to the low rumble of the duty sergeant's voice in the corridor outside. When he heard Freddy leave, Booth got up and opened the door.

'What was that about, sergeant?' he said.

'It seems there was a bit of a flap early this morning in one of the minefields out by the canal. Someone's been hurt. Colonel Bassett wants you to meet him at the RAMC barracks right away.'

Booth tossed the remains of his tea away, put his mackintosh on and walked to his jeep, chewing his lip.

He'd planned to go back to Wolffslust today. He'd wasted the whole of yesterday afternoon waiting in vain for the engineers' detachment to come and blow open the wretched door. When he had got back to Eichenrode in the evening, he'd had strong words with one of the engineers' NCOs and they'd promised to send someone that morning.

He looked at his watch. With any luck, this business with Colonel Bassett wouldn't take too long.

The RAMC had occupied the remains of the local hospital. When Booth arrived, he saw Detective Inspector Payne walking down the main staircase deep in thought. Booth thought the man's usually calm face looked somewhat perturbed.

'Where's he off to?' Booth asked one of the guards outside the hospital, as Payne pulled the collar of his coat up and walked away into the wind.

'He and Colonel Bassett have had words,' the guard said. 'The colonel bawled him out for bothering Quartermaster Sergeant Suttpen. Then, when the Detective Inspector said he wanted to attend the autopsy, the colonel said it was a military matter and turfed him out.'

'Autopsy? What on earth's been going on?'

'I don't rightly know, sir. But it seems there was some bother in that minefield down by the canal.'

When Booth went downstairs to the tiled corridor that led to the hospital's morgue, he found Colonel Bassett stalking up and down in front of his staff officers, in serious danger of breaking the swagger stick gripped behind his back. He seemed to have been waiting for Booth's arrival. As soon as he saw Booth, Bassett began to speak.

'I'm sure you have all heard what happened this morning in the minefield. If anyone hasn't, I can tell you that one of our men has been killed. But before we look into it, there's something that I want to make abundantly clear.

'When I arrived this morning, that wretched Scotland Yard fellow was here. I've previously held my tongue on this matter, but now I want to spell it out for you all. I don't like policemen. Never have. And I don't want this Payne fellow snooping around in army business any longer, is that perfectly clear? And I don't want a word of today's casualty getting out, understood?'

Bassett regarded each man in turn as Captain Fredrickson whispered something in his ear.

'Thanks to Captain Fredrickson, we know who the dead man was. It seems he worked for Housing Branch, a Mr Lockwood. Now, this just proves why we have to keep an eye on these CCG people. It seems any Tom, Dick or Harry can get a CCG-job as long as he's got a passport from an Allied country and is willing to work, but they're not proper soldiers, remember that.' Bassett turned towards Fredrickson. 'What do we know about this Lockwood fellow? Was he a drinker?'

'Not that we know of, sir,' Freddy said.

'Then what the hell was he doing wandering through a bloody minefield in the middle of the night? And why on earth wouldn't the blighter stay still and wait for someone to rescue him? I want answers, gentlemen. This sort of business makes us look damned stupid in front of Jerry and that is something I won't have. Do I make myself —'

The door to the morgue opened. Shelley, the medical officer, appeared.

'I think you'd better come and have a look at this, gentlemen.'

Mr Lockwood lay under a blanket, although Booth noticed there was a huge dip where the man's waist should have been and his left leg was missing. Shelley angled the lamp towards Lockwood's face then pulled a corner of the blanket back.

Men winced and drew their breath.

'What the devil's wrong with his eyes?' Bassett said.

'That's what I wanted to show you,' Shelley said.

They moved closer. Lockwood's eyes were closed but the sockets around them were red raw and blistered, as if they had been burnt, although there was no sign of charring. The wounds had an unpleasant yellowy colour to them. Shelley motioned towards a metal tray on which a piece of black fabric lay, rolled up and tied into a ring.

'That was found on the ground near the body. It was blown free in the blast, I would imagine.'

'Blown free from where?' Bassett said.

'From his eyes. I think Mr Lockwood went into the minefield blindfolded.'

'You mean someone tied that around his head then set him loose in a minefield?'

Shelley nodded. He lifted the tray and pointed towards two blotches of discoloured cloth on the inner surface of the blindfold. 'And that same someone also poured some type of caustic powder into his eyes. I think that explains why he wouldn't stay still. The pain must have been excruciating.

'I've questioned the engineer detachment and they've found a line of muddy footprints crossing the field. My guess is that Mr Lockwood was set free and stumbled into the centre of the minefield. The first explosion must have injured him without killing him. He then lay stunned for a while. But when he came to again, the pain would have caused him to start moving. I think he crawled across the second mine.'

'Why didn't he just pull the wretched blindfold off?' Bassett said.

'I think his hands were tied behind him,' Shelley said. 'It's difficult to tell, given the extent of his injuries, but there seem to be some scraps of twine embedded in the wounds close to the wrist.'

'Is it my imagination, or is there some sort of design on the blindfold?' Booth said.

Shelley donned rubber gloves and carefully spread the fabric out, to reveal a black pennant. A crude runic design was stitched in its centre, a capital Z, the diagonal crossed with two horizontal lines.

Each man there stared at it. 'Bastards,' Freddy said, then whispered something to the colonel.

Bassett's eyebrows bristled; his eyes narrowed. 'Am I correct in surmising, Captain Booth, that the symbol on that pennant is the one used by those wretched werewolf partisans?'

Booth nodded. 'It's the *Wolfsangel*, sir, The Wolf's Hook. During the advance across Germany, the Nazi regime encouraged civilians to scrawl this on the doors of people collaborating … or, rather, helping us, the Allies. But it's strange that the werewolves would announce their presence so —'

'Am I also correct in recollecting that your assessment of the werewolf threat in this sector was "negligible"?'

'With respect, sir, I don't think this incident proves —'

'What in God's name does it prove then, captain?' Bassett said, his voice rising to a roar. 'I'll tell you what this incident proves. It's a challenge. They've murdered one of our men and they want us to know it was them. Well, by God, if these blighters want to play it rough, I will give it to 'em rough. I want to know how this happened. And I want those responsible caught and punished. If Jerry hasn't realised yet he's lost this war, we will just have to show him, won't we? And if you ain't up to the job, Captain Booth, I'll damned well find someone who is.'

With that, Bassett stalked from the room. Freddy lingered a moment, long enough for his eyes to meet Booth's and a faint smile to flicker across his lips.

'You'd best get cracking, Captain,' he said. 'You've some werewolves to catch.'

PART TWO

1

A little after dawn, Little Otto walked out to the house on the Brunswick Road. He carried with him his big heavy killing knife and a torch. He kept to the paths through the woods as the roads were alive with military activity. That was good, though, it was what Otto had hoped for when he set Lockwood loose among the mines. It would keep them distracted, keep them from looking for Little Otto.

When he arrived at the house, he hid for twenty minutes among the trees, watching the kitchen door, just to be sure. He was aching to return and take possession of his treasures, but he knew he must be cautious.

Finally, when he could take it no longer, he stole across the lawn and entered the house. Inside the kitchen, he closed all the shutters. He didn't want anyone peering in. Then he reached inside his jacket and withdrew the Mask of Many, his skin tingling with anticipation. He sucked in its sweet aromas as he raised the mask to his face and tied it into place. Then he walked across the room and headed upstairs, fingering the key to the garret door and thinking about his Papa…

Back when Little Otto was a boy, his Papa had always called the people they kept in the cellar 'guests'. 'I'm going to see to our latest guest,' he would say to Mutti as he dabbed his mouth and rose heavily from the dinner table. Sometimes, Little Otto would secretly watch through the keyhole as Papa scrubbed his hands with carbolic, tied the leather apron around his wide waist and pulled on the gloves and face mask. When Papa opened the cellar door, Otto could smell the cold air and chemicals that wafted up from below.

The other people who came to the house — the ones that were not taken straight to the metal table in the cellar — had serious faces and uniforms. The women who came wore black and cried into their handkerchiefs.

Little Otto was ten the first time Papa took him down into the cellar.

'This is what I do, Otto,' he'd said, 'what puts food on our table. One day, you will do the same.'

That was the first time he had helped Papa with one of the guests — *their* guests, now — setting the modesty cloth over the body's sticky, stinky parts and bending and flexing the stiffness from the rigid joints.

The guest's skin had been ice cold and blue-white. Little Otto had never seen anything so beautiful. People were hot, noisy, smelly creatures, but the cellar guests were different: death had made them quiet and cold and perfect. He lay awake that night, imagining the spirit of the cellar-guest flitting like a bat beneath the eaves of the house.

Year by year, he learned more of Papa's trade. Papa always worked with a photo of the guest beside the big metal table. First, he used a curved needle and ligature to seal the mouth; then he set the eye caps to keep the lids closed. If the guest was a man, he would shave the stubble. Then the injections began and Little Otto would watch the big white ghost of Papa's reflection slide on and off the curved silver surface of the tank which held the embalming fluid.

One Sunday morning Little Otto feigned stomach ache. Papa wanted to force him to go to church, but Little Otto could always get Mutti on his side. 'Let the boy sleep,' she'd said, stroking his hair, while Little Otto nuzzled his face into her soft bosom and sucked in her hot, swampy smells. He had watched from his bedroom window as they walked away, down the street towards the church. Then he went straight to the cellar.

The new guest was a young peasant girl from the village. Something heavy had fallen on her and cracked her neck. Little Otto pulled the sheet down to admire the perfection of her. Mutti would have looked this way once, he thought, blonde and plump. The girl's hair smelt of soap and flowers. Otto had pressed his face against her cold white flesh, wishing somehow he could dive within her skin and know what it was like to be a different person, to see out through a different pair of eyes.

That was the first time he felt it, that awesome sense of serenity, as if the quiet calm of cathedral cloisters had filled every particle of his being. There was nothing sexual about the feeling, despite what they told him later in life. He never felt so chaste as when he was with one of his guests, the master and the mastered, the god with his disciple.

He feigned illness again the next week and went down to the cellar. The third Sunday was when Papa caught him, the pristine intimacy of the cellar sucked away by the sudden swish of the door opening and Papa's podgy silhouette framed by the hall light.

'My God, boy, what are you doing?'

2

It was midday now and the streets outside the police station were alive with the sounds of military activity: jeeps, lorries, marching boots, shouting voices.

Silas Payne drank tea and watched the soldiers come and go from the window. As with most military activity, the emphasis seemed to be on looking and sounding busy rather than actually getting anything done.

Captain Booth had been right about one thing: this Colonel Bassett fellow was an idiot. Not because he'd embarrassed Payne earlier by insisting he leave Lockwood's autopsy — such petty insults meant nothing to Silas Payne. No, Bassett was an idiot because he mistook knee-jerk impulse for decisive action. If he'd taken five minutes to listen to Payne, he would have seen that all the check points and searches that he was implementing were a waste of time. Mr Lockwood's death had nothing to do with the werewolf insurgency; Payne had been certain of that even before he had caught Shelley, the medical officer, outside the *Rathaus* and asked him for the details of the autopsy.

He sipped his tea as he pondered the matter. The obvious suspect was the quartermaster sergeant, Suttpen, but he had an alibi; Payne had checked. Suttpen had been playing poker the night before with no less than seven men from different units. The game had begun in the early evening and did not end until four in the morning. Suttpen had not left the game at any point.

Back home, Payne would have brought Suttpen in for questioning anyway; given him a good, long session. It was the only way with men like Suttpen: you had to show them you were possessed of limitless reserves of patience as you walked them through the same series of events once, twice, three, four, five times — as many as it took for them to talk themselves into knots. Suttpen might not have set Lockwood free in the minefield, but he knew something about the incident, of that Payne was certain. But Suttpen had the backing of both his CO and Colonel Bassett. Payne would have to wait before he approached the man again.

So, who had killed Lockwood?

Payne sat on his trestle bed with notepad and pencil and began to write down what he knew.

His first contact with Lockwood had prompted the little man to run straight to Suttpen. Payne thought about the conversation he had witnessed between the two men, of the panic on Lockwood's face and Suttpen's contemptuous reaction. The two men were up to something together, that much was clear, although Lockwood seemed to have been regretting his involvement. That same afternoon, an unidentified man had visited Lockwood's billets. Later that evening, Lockwood had walked to the edge of town and disappeared.

Payne thought about the pair of spectacles he'd found. It was clear Lockwood had been abducted, but he hadn't been killed straight away. Instead, the killer had waited approximately thirty hours, then set Lockwood free in a minefield. That meant the killer obviously had access to a place where he had held Lockwood captive. But why choose such a public way of killing him? Why not kill the man and bury him? And why use a werewolf pennant as a blindfold?

There was only one answer, Payne decided: the action had been so blatantly visible that it had to be a ruse to divert attention from something else. What that something might be, though, still eluded Payne. Once again, he had the feeling he was only seeing one small part of a far larger whole.

Payne was still pondering the matter when someone knocked at the door of the police station. He opened the door and found a man in a long, tatty overcoat standing outside. He addressed Payne in German.

'Are you the English policeman? My name is Schaeffer. I have information I need to give you.'

From the man's furtive behaviour Payne deduced that he did not want to impart the information on the stairs of the station, so he invited him in. He stirred the embers of the stove and warmed tea for them both.

Wherever it was that Schaeffer had come from, he had clearly been walking for a long time. The lower edges of his serge coat were spattered with mud and one of his military boots was held together with a twist of ripped fabric. But despite his dishevelled appearance there was a neatness and precision to his manner.

'I shall be brief,' he said. 'There have been murders here recently, have there not? In a house. With surgical implements found.'

Payne's mug stopped halfway to his mouth. 'What do you know about that?'

'It is my belief that certain very dangerous individuals are at large among the civilian population. And it is not what *I* know that should interest you.'

'What do you mean?'

'I was formerly an officer in the Wehrmacht. Until yesterday, I was held prisoner at an internment camp ten miles from here. In this camp there is an ex-Gestapo man. He claims to know who is responsible for these murders.'

'How did he know about the murders if he was interned?'

Schaeffer laughed mirthlessly. 'What else do interned men have to do but gossip with the guards? And men get moved from one facility to another. Somehow or other this Gestapo man has found something out.'

'Tell me about him,' Payne said.

'His name is Toth, Amon Toth. He was a *Kriminalkommisar* in the Gestapo. A few days ago I overheard him talking about this house here in Eichenrode, about the bodies that were found in the cellar. He was laughing, saying that the Tommies did not know what they were up against. He claimed that this murderer had already killed more than a dozen people in Germany during the war and that now the Tommies had set him loose.'

Payne was watching the man carefully now. 'Why do you set such store by what this Gestapo man says? He could have been making it up out of boredom.'

Schaeffer sipped his tea. 'My brother-in-law was a military policeman. When I was last home on leave he told me his unit had been sent to a prison near here, Wolffslust Prison, on two occasions, with orders to execute prisoners. These men were not part of the usual prison population. They were part of a special research programme, run by a doctor. He said they had been transferred from a medical institute in Brunswick after the city was bombed. These men who were brought for the doctor's programme had been serving on the eastern front. They were murderers and rapists.'

'Why are you telling me this?'

'Because it is my duty. *One does evil enough when one does nothing good*,' Schaeffer said. 'Recent German history is surely proof of that. If what this Gestapo man says is true, people could be in danger. I have been to the prison and the security there is very lax.'

But Payne was thinking of something else, of the old woman who had knocked on the door of the police station the day Payne had arrived in Eichenrode. He'd paid her little attention at the time, but now memory of her words sent a chill through his body. 'I've seen him,' she had said. 'The man that raped my daughter. They put him in Wolffslust Prison, but I saw him this morning, walking the streets, free as a bird!'

Payne went straight to Major Norris and said he wanted to question the Gestapo man, Toth.

Norris wasn't keen on the idea, but relented when Payne persisted. 'You won't get into an internment camp alone, though,' Norris said. 'I'll have to ask someone from Field Intel to go with you.'

Payne had instructed Schaeffer to wait for him while he spoke with Norris, but when he went back to the police station, Schaeffer had disappeared.

Small matter. Payne had the feeling that Schaeffer had told him all he knew, in any case.

An hour later Payne was on his way to the internment camp in a jeep driven by a lieutenant named Taylor from Booth's Field Intelligence unit.

Outside Eichenrode, the countryside still bore signs of war. Burned-out vehicles sat beside the road and the grass verges were littered with scraps of clothing, broken pieces of ordnance and discarded army crates, all empty and smashed apart. People moved along the edges of the road, in both directions. Others lived in the woods. As they drove past, Payne could see fires flickering beneath ragged awnings and smoke drifting between the trees.

'What a ruddy mess,' Payne said, looking behind him as a man on the roadside swung a punch at a smaller man.

If Taylor heard him, he did not react.

Payne had been initially happy about going with Lieutenant Taylor — the prospect of a long drive with Captain Booth had not thrilled him — but as they drove in silence and Payne watched the man out of the corner of his eye, Payne realised the man was deeply troubled. Payne knew that nearly everyone called Lieutenant Taylor by his nickname, Tubbs, but whoever had given him the moniker obviously hadn't seen him recently. Taylor now had the sallow skin of a man who had lost a lot of weight quickly. Payne had heard that Taylor had witnessed the clearing of a concentration camp and that he'd not been the same since.

Payne could believe it. Taylor's eyes were bloodshot and he had a nervy, brittle edge to him as if, emotionally, he were staggering forward on his last reserves of energy. It happened to men, sometimes. On the outside they seemed fine but, like the lead of a dropped pencil, they were all broken apart inside.

The internment camp was set up within the grounds of a country manor that had formerly belonged to a German industrialist. The house itself seemed medieval in its size and splendour, but its magnificence was tarnished by a sort of shanty town that had grown up on the lawns beside it. As they drew closer, Payne saw that an area of perhaps the size of a football pitch had been enclosed within barbed wire. Inside, the ground was covered with all manner of makeshift shelters made from blankets, scraps of wood and holes dug in the ground. Watchtowers equipped with machine guns had been erected at each corner of the camp. Groups of British soldiers stood along the perimeter, chatting among themselves and smoking cigarettes.

Payne knew there were camps like this all over Germany now. In the final days of the war the Wehrmacht had begun to surrender in such massive numbers it was impossible to care for them all to the standards demanded by the Geneva Convention. To circumvent this, a new category of prisoner had been invented: DEFs, Disarmed Enemy Forces. Soldiers assigned to this category were not classified as POWs and therefore didn't have to be looked after to the same standards. Payne had heard that there were still hundreds of thousands of Germans locked away in these camps.

'It's quite a contrast, isn't it?' Payne said.

For the first time in an hour, Taylor spoke. 'Oh, I see what you mean,' he said, looking out across the grounds towards the mansion house and the camp beside it. He sneered. 'It won't do German soldiers any harm to see the sort of luxury they were fighting to preserve. I expect most of that mansion was paid for with Nazi war contracts.'

'What'll happen when autumn comes?'

'They'll get cold and wet,' Taylor said in a way that made Payne feel the lieutenant would like the Germans to suffer far worse inconveniences.

As they approached the barbed wire perimeter of the camp, hundreds of eyes turned to meet them, staring from emaciated, dirty faces. The German soldiers wore every conceivable type of filthy and torn uniform and some men still had grubby bandages wrapped around their hands and heads.

Taylor spoke to an officer and explained what they were doing there. A call was put out for the former Gestapo man, Amon Toth. Ten minutes later, Toth arrived at the gates to the camp. He was painfully thin and shabbily dressed in a plain soldier's camouflage uniform. Despite this, he displayed an innate hauteur.

Speaking through the wire, Taylor addressed him in German.

'We've been told you know something about a murder that occurred close to the town of Eichenrode.'

Toth's face became sly. 'Yes, that is true. I fear a beast is loose among you. There could be more deaths. Many more. But I can help to prevent them.'

'And how do you propose to do that?'

For the first time, the German smiled, an ironic curl of the lip, revealing sharp white teeth. His dark eyes sparkled.

'I can tell you who this beast is and how he hunts. And, more importantly, I can tell you how to catch him.'

3

At lunchtime Booth returned to Wolffslust Prison.

He was taking a chance by going back there, as Colonel Bassett had instructed him to prepare a briefing on the dangers of werewolf activity in the area, but Booth wanted to find out what was behind the 'dungeon' door, for the simple reason that if he didn't, no-one else would.

The overcast day gave the hulking brick prison a sinister air. As he pulled up in the courtyard, he saw the promised engineer detachment was already there, unloading equipment from a lorry. Booth went downstairs to the dungeon door and found the sergeant in charge of the engineers bending to examine the lock.

'It's pretty jammed up in there, sir,' he said.

'I know, sergeant,' Booth said. 'That's why I called you.'

The sergeant had a slow West Country accent. He continued as if Booth had not replied. 'Wouldn't be surprised to find someone snapped the key off inside the lock,' he said, poking in the keyhole with a screwdriver. He straightened and banged his fist against the door. 'Mighty fine piece of wood, though.'

'Can you open it?'

'We can dynamite it. But that would ruin the door.'

'Do what you have to do, sergeant.'

Booth left the engineers to it and went back to sorting paperwork. The sound of drilling and banging echoed up through the stone walls of the prison. An hour later one of the sappers came to say they were ready.

'You'll want to take cover over there,' the engineer sergeant said, as he attached electrical cables to a plunger. Booth had the soldiers clear the underground passages and return all the prisoners to their cells. All around the prison courtyard, faces were pressed to the barred windows, watching. Booth took cover and waved to the engineer sergeant, who twisted the plunger and pressed it down.

There was a split second pause, as if the world had caught its breath, then smoke and dust billowed from the corridor, driven forth on a roaring wave of sound. Booth gritted his teeth and put his fingers in his ears. There was a metallic creak, followed by the sound of falling rubble, then the force created by the huge impact shuddered through the roots of the building.

It took two minutes for the dust to clear. When it was safe to descend the stairs once more, Booth saw that the door had been blown clear of its hinges and fallen forwards.

'Right, let's see what we can find through here,' he said, clicking on his torch.

Dust spiralled in the beam of light as Booth crept forward across the shattered door. The air was thick with the smell of explosive. It was pitch dark in the room beyond; Booth searched until he found a light-switch. When he clicked it on, a strip light in the ceiling flickered into life.

Each man there drew his breath.

'What the hell is all this?' someone said.

Booth looked around him. The walls of the large room were of rough ancient stone, worn and stained by centuries of dripping water. In the centre of the chamber was a metal chair with leather restraints for head, wrists and ankles. Beside it was a wheeled metal trolley, also equipped with restraints. A machine with wires, cables and electrometers stood beside the trolley. Metal tools dangled from a rack on the wall.

Booth motioned for the men behind him to stay where they were and moved towards the chair at the chamber's centre. As he got closer, he saw that the metal chair was attached to some form of ratchet and could be tipped backwards with a lever. A square hole was dug in the ground behind the chair. When Booth shone his torch into the darkness of the hole, he saw it was filled nearly to the top with liquid.

He bent to sniff it. It smelt of brackish water.

Booth looked around the room. There were dozens of packing crates and boxes piled against the walls. Booth had the impression that the equipment in the room had been moved from a larger facility and never properly unpacked. Metal filing cabinets in one corner leaked thousands of documents. Beside them were piles of cardboard boxes, also filled with documents. Thousands more sheets of paper were strewn across the floor.

One pile of packing crates had swastikas burnt into the surface of the wood and the words 'Institute of Racial Hygiene' printed below. Some of the crates also bore the strange symbol Booth had seen inside the lid of the film canisters, the sword and ribbon surrounded by runic symbols. *This must be where the films came from*, he thought.

He motioned for the other soldiers to come into the room. Together they began searching the boxes.

Booth took a handful of papers from one of the crates and flicked through them. They were written in neatly-typed German and looked like film scripts. As Booth read them he realised that in reality they were transcripts of conversations held between a doctor named Wiegand and various patients. The patients' names were not given; instead, each one was identified by a number.

He opened another of the cardboard boxes and recoiled when he realised it was filled with human skulls, more than a dozen of them, packed together in the box like bleached eggs.

When he had recovered from his shock, he began to remove the skulls from the box. Each was carefully labelled with a German man's full name. Lines had been scratched into the bone of each skull, forming grids on which various sections had been labelled with words in Latin that Booth could not understand.

Beneath the skulls were a number of neatly folded charts and diagrams. Each chart referred to a different man's skull and was filled with measurements and algebraic calculations of which Booth could make little sense.

As he looked at the names, he paused, wondering why they seemed so familiar. Then he remembered. These were the same surnames that he had read on the insides of the film canisters. He looked at the skulls. No wonder the names had been crossed through.

Booth tried to lift a swastika-marked packing crate down from the top of a pile, but stopped when he realised how much it weighed. He pulled a chair over and stood on it to peer down at the two glass jars that were inside. Both jars measured roughly a foot in width and height and were filled with clear liquid: formaldehyde, by the smell of it. Booth signalled for the engineer sergeant to help him and together they lifted the box down from the shelf.

'Oh Lord, is that what I think it is?' the sergeant said, hurrying to put the jar down on a desk. 'Oh God, it is, isn't it?'

A human brain bobbed within the liquid.

Booth looked at the name on the front of the jar: Tjaden, Albrecht.

He'd seen that same name on one of the skulls. What the hell had been going on down here?

One of the other soldiers had found a box containing hundreds of documents relating to births, marriages and baptisms, together with family trees and genealogical tables. The documents all bore the official stamp of the *Rassenforschungsamt*, the Nazi Race Investigation Office, and all of them related to the names on the skulls.

'They seemed very interested in the racial lines of whoever these people were,' Booth said, as he flicked through the pages. 'There's one here whose family tree goes back to the times of Martin Luther.'

All the documents were originals. The edges of some pages showed signs of having been razored out of books. That explained the wonderful smell of antique paper, but it didn't explain why dozens of parish records had been ruined. Whoever these people were, they must have been important in some way.

'What the hell is this?' someone said, putting a calliper rule down on the desk and withdrawing another tool from a box. It was a curious angle of metal with screws and straps attached to it.

'I think it's a craniometer. For taking measurements of people's heads,' Booth said.

'What for?'

'Anthropometry, I would guess,' Booth said, 'given the nature of these documents. It's a sort of pseudo-science, by which a person's intelligence can supposedly be calculated by taking precise measurements of his or her body.'

On the far side of the room, a door led into a long rectangular chamber. A film screen hung at the far end of the room and there was a film projector to the side of the door.

Wires ran across the walls and were hooked up to speakers in each corner. Apart from that, the room was entirely empty, save for another metal chair with restraints set in the centre of the room. Booth noticed that this one was bolted to the floor.

'I could get this working, if you liked, captain,' the engineer sergeant said, fiddling with wires and switches in the dais beneath the film projector. 'It doesn't look too complicated. If we just plug this thing in —'

The speakers erupted into a burst of static, followed by a deafening blast of sound. So sudden and tremendous was the cacophony that Booth fell backwards with his hands to his ears.

Then he noticed the images on the screen. Naked women stood in a line, some holding children. German soldiers with dogs and whips prowled beside them. The sound was so loud that Booth felt it almost as a tangible thing. Screams. Shouts. Shots. Dogs barking. A wailing wall of noise, a perfect distillation of human suffering, as if a thousand voices were raised in an agony of supplication.

Booth gestured frantically towards the engineer sergeant, who lunged for a lever below the dais. The sound and images died.

'What in God's name was that?' one of the soldiers hissed.

Booth was dusting off his trousers. 'That is precisely what I intend to find out,' he said.

4

For the first time in what seemed an age, Ilse slept late.

For one glorious moment when she awoke and pulled her hair from her eyes, she had no idea where she was. Then the wind stirred and blew through the cracks in the wall and she remembered everything.

Cousin Ursula was dead.

Her last family member was gone.

Ilse walked to the window and looked down at the messy grave she'd dug in a corner of the garden, a long, ragged scar of freshly turned earth. How anyone was supposed to dig a grave six feet deep was beyond her. In the end, all she'd managed to create was a trench perhaps a little over three feet deep in which to lay Cousin Ursula's body — and that had taken her all night. Her palms and fingers were one mass of blisters. She hoped the layer of rocks and rubble she had placed on top of Ursula's body would be enough to deter animals from scratching and scrabbling at the remains.

The enormity of the situation hit her suddenly and she burst into tears. Then sudden fear gripped her and she ran to the other side of the room and looked through the window, towards the rose bush by the path.

No, you couldn't see the other hole, she realised, the hole Ilse had dug when she had first come to the house two months before. The grass had grown back and only the faintest outline of it was visible, a rectangular hole, two feet by twelve inches.

That was good: Cousin Ursula was not the only one of Ilse's secrets buried in the garden.

It was cold when she went downstairs. After days of wishing to be free of Cousin Ursula, Ilse now found the house felt strangely empty. Having two people inside it had given an illusion that the place was still a dwelling; now she was alone again, the house was revealed for what it really was, a battered box of brick and beam without any water or electricity.

Ilse built the fire up and ate some of O'Donnell's bread for breakfast. Then she remembered the wretch would be expecting information about the policeman from her when she went back to work at the transit camp. Well, O'Donnell would have to wait. It wasn't her fault she hadn't seen Booth.

She warmed her toes by the fire and admired the dancing flame as she prepared tea.

When she went back into the pantry she spotted the bundle of letters on the floor. They were Cousin Ursula's, the ones she'd held clutched to her chest all though the long agony of her death. They must have fallen from her hands when Ilse carried the body outside. Ilse went back to the fire with the letters.

Really, she should burn them. They had obviously been important to Ursula; they were private. Yet they were almost the only memento that remained of Ilse's family. She looked at the top letter and the words that were written there: *Liebling Ursula.*

No-one would ever know, she decided, then saw that her fingers were already unpicking the blue ribbon that held the letters together.

Her eyes strayed across the first page. The letter contained precisely what she expected to find, cloying promises of love and undying devotion from some soldier, someone who had served on the eastern front. Ilse frowned when she spotted an allusion to 'playing together as children'. Her frown deepened when she saw the letter was signed 'Johannes D'.

As she skimmed through more of the letters, she realised her suspicion was correct: her brother, Johannes, had written them. There were so many references to childhood incidents and mutual relations, it had to have been him. Ilse frowned even more as she read the sugary protestations of love and promises of marriage that her brother had sent back from Russia.

How could that be? Johannes had always despised Cousin Ursula. He had bullied and taunted her as a child, even though Ursula was eight years older than he. Ilse's expression grew yet more serious as she read on. The later letters were filled with talk of the glory of the Final Victory and how Johannes's unit had imposed 'German culture' on the Slavs.

Good news, my dearest, sweet darling! I have achieved the posting of my dreams. Fortune has smiled upon me and I have been transferred to an elite unit, the SS-Sturmbrigade 'Dirlewanger'. They really are the crème de la crème of our Führer's boys. You should see how their boots and buttons sparkle when they are on parade. We're very popular with the local Slavs. Whenever we visit one of their villages, all the women and men come crowding out into the street and head for the local church to sing our praises. We always give them a warm reception.

Ilse looked at the letter. It was written in pencil on grubby, torn paper. There was certainly nothing about the scrawls that suggested an elite unit. And the whole tone of the letter was wrong: the Johannes she'd known would never have been capable of such saccharine sentimentality.

She looked at the date on the letter. That, too, did not dovetail with her memories of Johannes. It was dated

November 1943. That meant the letter had been written a few months after Johannes's final fateful visit to the Warthegau.

The last time Ilse had seen her brother he had been a changed man. Not only did he have that lean, hard look most of the fighting men from the east had, the cruel spiteful side of his character had come fully to the fore.

Of course, Johannes was the centre of attention at the party Ilse had organised in his honour — how could he not be? But every person who went to congratulate him on the prowess of the German Army walked away from him disturbed. They whispered that he was voicing all sorts of unwise opinions about the Party and the war.

It was inevitable Johannes should fall out with Rüdiger. 'No, *you* don't understand, Herr Hoffman,' Johannes had shouted across the dinner table, after drinking a whole bottle of hock with the entrée. 'We *have* to win this fucking war now, because if the Ivans ever come here and do to us even a fraction of what we've done to them, within a year there won't be any Germans left.'

The dinner party had ended hours earlier than anticipated, by which time Johannes had been lying unconscious before the scullery fire for some time.

Ilse sipped her tea. What had Johannes been doing, exchanging letters with Cousin Ursula? Had he changed? It was possible — sometimes the thought of coming home to a simple plain woman like Ursula was what a soldier needed to keep him going — but somehow it didn't fit her brother's character. If the sentiment wasn't genuine, what had provoked his expression of it? Had Johannes been poking fun at Ursula?

Yes, that was more like it, she realised. Johannes had always possessed an odd sense of humour, the type that enjoyed laughing *at* rather than *with* other people. And who was this

Sturmbrigade Dirlewanger? As far as she knew Johannes had always served with the 3rd Division, the *Totenkopf*.

What did it all mean?

She sipped tea, staring at the fire. And then it suddenly occurred to her in a spike of emotion just how pointless all this wondering and theorising was: they were all dead. All of them. Ursula. Johannes. Rüdiger. She had nothing, now, and no-one.

Ilse looked at her blistered hands, then rose and went to the pantry for the whisky bottle, trying to ignore the tears that had clouded her eyes.

5

Amon Toth sat in the centre of the interrogation room with a booted foot resting on the knee of his left leg. When Payne pulled aside the slat that covered the peephole and peered through, the German raised his hand and wiggled the tips of his fingers towards the door in a dainty wave.

Toth was in his early thirties and good-looking in a chisel-jawed Teutonic way. His hair was platinum blond and exceptionally fine, but his eyes were unusually dark and surrounded by darker lashes. Most SS men Payne had seen were unimpressive without their uniforms, but Toth had presence; there was something of the fallen angel about him, radiant and yet perverse.

Payne pulled the slat closed and said to the duty sergeant, 'What can you tell me about him?'

The sergeant had taken an age to find the right file. 'His name is *Kriminalkommisar* Amon Toth. Not that he told us his real name first time around. According to the file, we picked him up right after the surrender. He tried to pass himself off as a normal soldier when he was first questioned, but one of the inquisitors flagged him as being suspect, so he was sent back to the cage. Then a German soldier told us who he really was: Toth is ex-SS and ex-Gestapo. He was quite high up in Department C.'

'Department C? That was Administration and Party Affairs, wasn't it?' Lieutenant Taylor said.

'Yes. And that's the problem. We know he was linked to the Einsatzgruppen that were going round shooting civilians when the Jerries invaded Poland and Russia, but we can't find any trace of it. Toth's a crafty sod. Most likely he destroyed all of his own records. I know the inquisitors at the interrogation centre in Bad Nenndorf are keen to have a crack at him, but I think they're still gathering the information they need.'

When Taylor and Payne entered the interrogation room, Toth pointed at Payne's civilian clothes. 'Who are you? Why do you not wear a uniform?'

The German smiled when he received no answer. 'I know what you are doing. You are trying to intimidate me with your silence. I, too, have been trained in interrogation techniques.'

Toth spoke good English, but pronounced it with an air of amused contempt, like an adolescent forced to play with children's toys. 'I wish to smoke also,' he said when Taylor lit a cigarette.

'Is that your way of asking?'

'Our conversation will be mutually beneficial, I assure you.'

Taylor handed him a cigarette. Payne could see the lieutenant looked nervous and uncomfortable. That wasn't a good frame of mind in which to start an interrogation, Payne thought.

He was right.

Taylor was a disaster.

Payne had learned that the worst thing you could do when questioning intelligent, voluble men like Toth was to enter into a verbal joust with them, but that was precisely what Taylor did.

'That's *Lieutenant* Taylor, to you,' he said when Toth kept referring to him as Mister.

Toth shook his head. 'I can tell you are not a professional soldier, Mr Taylor. You are like most of your army, a civilian in uniform, a dilettante.'

'Dilettantes that won.'

Toth waved his hand. 'It was the Russians' inexhaustible contempt for human life that broke the Wehrmacht, not your cosseted soldiers. Were it not for the eastern front, your armies would have learned of what the German soldier was truly capable.'

Payne said nothing. The only way to make things worse would have been to interrupt Taylor and undermine the miniscule amount of authority he had managed to establish. Payne awaited his opportunity. Eventually, Lieutenant Taylor said, 'Detective Inspector Payne has some questions to put to you.'

'*Detective Inspector* Payne,' Toth said, pretending to be impressed. 'After the chisel comes the scalpel. Where do you serve? Are you from the famous —'

'I'll ask the questions, Herr Toth.'

Toth smiled at the interruption. 'The voice of authority. At last,' he added, nodding his head contemptuously towards Taylor. 'What is it you need to —?'

Payne made a point of looking at his watch. 'What do you know about the murders in Eichenrode? Get straight to the point, or you're going back outside to the cage.'

Toth made himself comfortable in his seat.

'It has come to my attention that certain crimes were recently committed in a house outside the town of Eichenrode. A man and a woman were found murdered in the cellar, I believe. I am in a position to help you.'

'How?'

'I know who the murderer is.'

'If you know this man so well, tell me what I found at the crime scene in Eichenrode.'

'Oh, I imagine there would have been some scalpels, yes? And some form of sewing implement? And vaccines that perhaps were not all they appeared to be.'

Payne tried hard to hide his reaction, but Toth was good. He watched Payne's face carefully as he spoke and smiled when he saw the evident interest there.

'And what does he do with these scalpels?' Payne said.

'Oh, it's far more fun if you find that out for yourself. And you will do, soon, that I can promise. I imagine your security forces have yet to realise the extreme danger the individual responsible for these crimes poses. If this man has been living free among you since the end of the war there will be more than two victims, I can assure you. You just haven't found the others yet.'

'And who is he?'

'He is what the doctors call a psychopath, a man with no conscience, no morals and no qualms — a monster, if you will, whose only concern is following the dictates of his twisted pathology. He led the Reich's security forces a merry dance for nearly eighteen months before we caught him. And he was extremely active during that period. He managed to kill a total of thirteen men and women.'

Payne was making notes as Toth spoke.

'Tell me how you became involved in this case.'

'My involvement began in Berlin, in July 1943. There had been a particularly heavy air raid and the rescue teams were searching the cellars of damaged buildings for the dead. In the cellar of one building they found the remains of six men and women.

'There was no question of their having been killed in the air raid, as each person's remains had been very carefully butchered and the body parts stored in lime. The matter was first reported to the Kripo criminal police, but when it became apparent three of the dead men were soldiers who had previously gone AWOL, the matter came to the attention of the Gestapo.'

'I suppose you'll tell me these murders were all hushed up and that there's no way of corroborating them?'

'On the contrary, they were widely reported. Especially when more houses with more bodies began to appear across the Reich. They were attributed to English air crews at first. It was a way of stirring up a little extra hate, I suppose. Any of the national newspapers should have coverage of the murders.'

Payne looked at Toth's face. Was he bluffing? No, Toth was too good for that. He must know Payne would check up on what he was saying.

Toth smiled, as if reading Payne's thoughts. 'Although, I must warn you, the newspaper reports do contain one very important factual error.'

'Which is?'

Toth smiled, said nothing.

'You mentioned that this man was caught,' Payne said. 'If that's so, how is it he is free now? Surely he would have been executed.'

Toth smiled and wagged a finger playfully. 'No, Mr Payne. I have no intention of telling you that.'

'And how was it he was able to possess so many houses?'

'Nor that.'

'So, what precisely are you offering us?'

'I can provide a detailed description of your man, both physically and psychologically, perhaps even provide you with photos if I am granted access to the correct files. I can tell you how he hunts, the profile of his victims. I can tell you enough to ensure his swift and easy capture.'

'And what is your price for supplying us with this information?'

'I want safe passage out of Allied Europe. You will take me to some point close to the Spanish border — Perpignan, for example — and supply me with all the necessary documentation. I will then divulge all I know about the nature of your problem.'

When Taylor laughed, Toth sneered at him.

'Do you think it is not already happening? I'll wager if I had been working at Peenemünde on the V-weapon project I would already be in America or England, living like a lord. I know of men with questionable backgrounds — far more questionable than my own — who have successfully bought their way out. There are upwards of 5,000 men in this camp alone. It would be simplicity itself for one man to disappear.'

Taylor had been shifting on his seat while Toth spoke. Now he stood up suddenly and began berating the man in a voice made shrill by emotion.

'You're wanted for war crimes, you bastard. You won't be allowed to wriggle off the hook.'

Toth waved his hand dismissively. 'War crimes? Human history is a litany of massacre. In the last war, the Turks slaughtered the Armenians; the Greeks slaughtered the Turks. What answer would you receive from a Boer, were you to mention concentration camps? Or talk of the civility of British government to an Irishman? Or an Indian? Colonial government is never easy. History will either absolve the Germans or it will accuse all empires of these "war crimes".'

Taylor's face was bright red. Payne saw tears had formed in his eyes.

'Why don't you go and get a glass of water, Lieutenant?' he said.

Taylor left the room, his hands shaking.

'How did you catch him?' Payne said, when the door had closed. 'It will be very difficult to go to my superiors with details of your proposal if I have nothing to offer them.'

Toth blew smoke rings towards the light bulb as he considered this. 'Very well. Check the newspapers and you will readily discover the discrepancy in the official version of the story. And look for details on the military operation codenamed *Greif*. It was that which finally allowed us to capture him. When you have done this, return here with details of when and where I am to be released and we will talk further.'

'Greif? What was that?' Payne said. The word meant gryphon in German.

'I will say no more. But from that you will discover a detail that will be particularly useful if you wish to catch this man. And particularly dangerous, given the current circumstances in Germany.'

When Payne left the interrogation room, he found Taylor outside, leaning against a wall, smoking a cigarette.

'I'm sorry about that,' Taylor said in a flat voice. 'I just … hate them all.'

'Do you think there's any truth to what he says? About Nazis escaping, I mean?'

Taylor waved his hand dismissively. 'One hears rumours, naturally, but I don't believe them. If there were organised routes of escape, why did we manage to capture people like Göring and Himmler? They would have been the first to use these so-called ratlines, don't you think? You don't look convinced, Detective Inspector.'

Payne wasn't. Men were fallible. And greedy. There was always a way.

Taylor put out his cigarette. 'Surely, you don't put any faith in what he said, do you? Didn't you get the impression he was a flim-flam operator of the highest order?'

Payne thought about that as they walked back to Taylor's jeep. He didn't like Toth; that had been his first, overriding impression. There was something oily and unpleasant about the man. Then Payne realised there was one other impression he'd formed while interrogating Toth: he was damned glad their situations had not been reversed.

6

That evening, Captain Booth attended a drinks party hosted by Colonel Bassett's staff.

Military Government social events were the bane of Booth's life: it was bad enough having to serve alongside these idiots, but socialising with them off-duty was torture. Colonel Bassett was the sort of crusty old imperialist Booth would have walked a mile to avoid back in civvy street and the rest of the occupation forces stationed at Eichenrode were just as bad: braggarts, blusterers and blunderers, the lot of them. Most had never seen a shot fired in anger and yet they strutted around before the German civilians like they'd stormed the Normandy beaches single-handed. And this werewolf scare had got them all lathered up. You could see it in their faces: they were excited at the prospect of seeing some 'action', especially now the chances of sustaining a serious injury were minimal.

Booth went to stand beside a window. Outside, the streets were filled with military activity. Bassett had ordered numerous roadblocks and extra guard posts to be established on all the major thoroughfares in the town and the night patrols had been doubled.

Across the room, Booth could see Lieutenant Taylor standing by the drinks table, getting quietly sloshed in the same way Tubbs seemed to do five nights out of every seven these days. Booth sipped his own drink, lost in thought.

In his heart of hearts, Booth knew that what had happened to Tubbs Taylor wasn't really his fault, but he had never really been able to shift his sense of guilt. It had all happened so quickly.

Back in April, a call had come through that a group of SS men had approached 2nd Army's lines to warn them of a typhus outbreak and said that they were offering to surrender. Could someone from Field Intel go up there and help with the arrests? Booth had been all set to go, but Tubbs had said, 'I don't mind popping over there, Jimmy. I've just filled the utility up. What's this place called?'

Booth looked at his notes. 'Bergen-Belsen.'

Tubbs returned two days later, a changed man. He'd never really spoken about what he saw there, but his usual nervy introspection had been replaced by something else, something raw and vulnerable, as if he were a tree stripped of its bark.

That first night after his return Tubbs had wet the bed. He had tried to hide it, rising early and removing the bedding and turning his mattress, but after ten years being educated at boarding schools Booth could read the signs of what had happened.

That was why Booth had ensured that, since his visit to Belsen, Tubbs had been given the lightest of duties: mostly paperwork, carrying out background checks on suspected Nazis, liaising with officers from the Public Safety Branch and vetting the *Fragebogen* questionnaires. Booth and the sergeants handled most of the hands-on stuff now.

That was why it irked him so much that Detective Inspector Payne had taken Tubbs off to interrogate this Gestapo man earlier in the day. Tubbs simply wasn't up to it.

When Booth had asked how the interrogation had gone, Tubbs was noncommittal. That almost certainly meant it had gone badly. Booth had sat in on some of Tubbs's interrogations and he could picture what had happened. Tubbs just couldn't avoid getting genuinely angry. Let the prisoner realise that, and the battle was pretty much lost before you'd even begun.

To make matters worse, Colonel Bassett had bawled Booth out for it.

'I hear that policeman has been out hobnobbing with the bloody Gestapo today, Captain Booth,' Bassett had said as soon as Booth had arrived. 'With the *Gestapo*. And to cap it all, one of your officers went with him to facilitate the process. Did I not make myself clear? I do not want this wretched Peeler interfering with army business.'

Booth had tried to defend himself. 'I'm sorry, sir, but Detective Inspector Payne is investigating crimes that —'

'A bloody Waffen SS officer and his floozy get their just desserts and you call it a crime? Do you know what this Gestapo bastard said to the policeman? He wants to cut himself a deal in exchange for giving us information. That's the real crime. Well, I've pulled the rug from under his feet. I've had him shipped off to the high-level interrogation centre at Bad Nenndorf. They'll know how to look after him there. There'll be no deals cut with any of these bastards, not while I'm in charge.'

A roar of laughter drew Booth's attention back to the party. He lit a cigarette and began mingling again.

Guest of honour at tonight's bash was Professor Svoboda, a small Czech man from the World Medical Association whose surname nobody had been able to pronounce correctly even before the serious drinking began. Accompanied by an escorting officer, Svoboda was touring Germany and Austria to gather evidence on the human experimentation that had taken place in the concentration camps. Svoboda's presence was the reason Booth had agreed to attend the drinks party. He needed to speak to the man.

All of the documents Booth had found at Wolffslust were here in Eichenrode now. Booth had organised a work detail from among the prisoners and had had them load all of the boxes and crates aboard a lorry. The offices of Booth's field intelligence unit were now crammed with them.

Since coming back from the prison, he'd had a cursory look at the documentation and had quickly realised it was so far beyond his field of experience that he would have to seek outside help. All he'd established so far was that there were medical records for more than forty patients, all of whom had German sounding surnames, and that, according to the Nazis' warped racial criteria, their bloodlines were faultlessly Aryan.

Except one.

This man, Patient 14, had a half-Jewish ancestor on his mother's side from three generations back. The word *Mischling* — mixed-blood — had been written at the top of this patient's records in red ink. The word had been underlined and was followed by three exclamation marks. Booth thought there was an almost triumphant flourish in the way the word had been highlighted, as if this was what the investigators had been seeking all along.

That was Booth's sole find of any real interest. Much of the documentation consisted of endless transcripts of conversations that had taken place between the chief doctor, Wiegand, and the patients. The transcripts covered all manner of subjects: childhoods, sexual fantasies, relationships with their parents.

The prisoners at Wolffslust knew very little about what had gone on in the cellars of the prison. Some remembered that in the autumn of '44 soldiers with construction equipment had come to begin work in the cellar. Lorries filled with SS men and civilian workers had arrived with crates of equipment.

Then had come a number of vehicles that had arrived in the dead of night. They contained men in white overalls and 'special' prisoners who were kept apart from the others.

One prisoner remembered helping to drag huge blocks of ice to the door of the cellar. Another mentioned seeing a man in ankle and wrist chains being walked from one of the cells on the lower floor down into the cellar.

Booth poured himself another pink gin and hovered by Svoboda's side, waiting for an opportunity to get the man's attention.

'I say Professor, I was wondering if this symbol meant anything to you?' Booth said, drawing the professor aside and showing him a sheet of paper on which he had copied the sword-and-ribbon symbol found on the film canisters and the crates at Wolffslust.

'It's the symbol of the *Ahnenerbe*,' Svoboda said, his interest immediate. 'It was an intellectual society formed by high-ranking Nazis who were dedicated to "proving" the historical superiority of Aryan culture. Himmler was its principal patron.'

'You know of it, then?'

Svoboda nodded. 'Despite its lofty intellectual trappings, the *Ahnenerbe* was guilty of engaging in all sorts of pseudoscience. In fact, it commissioned a great deal of the medical experimentation on human beings that the WMA is investigating.' The professor's saturnine face became animated and his voice rose. 'Some of what they got up to beggars belief: immersing victims in freezing water, undertaking muscle and bone transplants without anaesthesia, deliberately exposing patients to mustard gas and phosphorus. And don't think I'm exaggerating. I've seen the photographic evidence and I didn't eat for days afterwards. They've got two dozen Nazi doctors in

Camp Ashcan, now. They're going to be tried at Nuremburg right alongside Göring and Speer and all the others.'

'Would you mind if I showed you something?' Booth said.

Twenty minutes later they were at the makeshift cinema in Eichenrode. Svoboda sipped his drink as Booth set up the projector and played the films found at Wolffslust.

Svoboda sneered when Booth played him the film containing the pornographic images, but his interest returned when he saw the footage of the mass killings.

'What do you think it means?' Booth said afterwards.

'Judging by the names on the canisters, it would seem these films served some purpose beyond mere titillation. I would suggest the surnames listed here were those of the patients or test subjects each film was designed to be used with.'

'But why?'

'We'll likely never know. Perhaps they were used to see how patients would react to certain visual stimuli.'

'And what is it that we are seeing? What do the killings and the dead bodies signify, I mean.'

Svoboda's gaze remained fixed on the blanket-screen, as if still contemplating the images. 'The level of the Germans' barbarity — especially in the east — has been an open secret for years. What is not generally known is the extent. The scale of it is quite … staggering. According to depositions taken from high-ranking Nazis and Wehrmacht personnel, there was an organised policy of extermination operative in the east from the very earliest days of the war. At first these killings were undertaken by mixed SS and police units known as *Einsatzgruppen*, men who simply marched their victims into the countryside and shot them beside open graves.

'However, this policy was deemed unnecessarily stressful' — here, Svoboda's voice dripped with scorn — 'for the killers.

Many of them suffered severe psychological traumas due to their experiences and so a new policy was introduced: secret camps were established in Poland and a policy of industrialised slaughter initiated, using gas chambers and crematoria. Some estimates put the number of victims in the millions.

'I think these films document those processes. The first film shows mass executions by rifle. I think the second shows one of the gas chambers being cleared. Those naked women we saw were probably queuing outside a gas chamber. They used to disguise them as showers.'

Neither man said anything for a long while after that, but as they walked outside Booth thought of the dozens of crates of documents he had taken from Eichenrode.

'Are you going to be in this area for long, professor?' he said. 'Because there's something for which I could really use your help.'

7

Next morning Ilse rose early and washed herself using a bucket as best as she could. It was Thursday morning and Captain Booth was coming to see her.

She was downstairs, drinking tea and smoking, when she heard the crunch of his tyres on the gravel outside. She fixed a smile on her face, went outside to greet him … and stopped dead.

Sitting beside the Tommy in the jeep was a young boy with the worst hare lip she'd ever seen. *What the devil is he doing, bringing people like that to the house?* Ilse thought.

Booth must have seen her smile falter, because when he got out of the jeep he put an arm around the boy and said, 'Ursula, this is my friend, Piotr.'

Piotr stuck his bony hand out. Ilse hesitated before grasping the mangy fingers, but forced a smile when she saw Booth frown. Then he said, 'I've brought you some victuals,' and lifted a box of vegetables, fruit and tins from the jeep's rear seat. 'There's fat and potatoes in here. I thought we could fry them. Can I come inside the house?'

Thank God I can say yes, Ilse thought, as she motioned for him to come inside. The suspicion in Booth's eyes had been evident this time. Now she no longer needed to provoke his mistrust.

She led him into the kitchen and made tea, which they drank sitting at the rickety kitchen table. Booth's pensive air continued, though. There was something else on his mind, she realised. He looked tired and nervous, but he wouldn't say what the matter was, so Ilse stopped asking and they drank in silence. Why was it that men always thought they were protecting women when they refused to tell them what the hell was going on?

They smoked cigarettes as Booth began cooking; soon the kitchen was filled with the smell of frying potatoes. God, she nearly fainted when she breathed it in. For a moment, it was as if the hollow in her stomach had become a real thing and she'd felt herself folding in half.

When the food was ready, Booth took the Polack a plateful. The boy set about it with his filthy fingers, seated on the grass. Ilse and Booth sat down together at the table inside.

'Have you heard about the murders that happened a few days ago?' he said, after a long silence.

'Of course. People in the town are talking about them.'

'I don't think you should be alone out here, but I'm going to be very busy for while, so I've asked Piotr to come and look in on you each day. I promise he won't be too much bother. He can chop wood and fix things for you, do some odd jobs. I think you'll find he's very handy to have around. I hope that's not a terrible imposition.'

Ilse did her best to smile. *Imposition?* As far as Ilse was concerned, the Polack was precisely the sort of person she should be locking doors and windows against. Who knew what sort of raddled nonsense went through a head like that?

'Well, if he's to come here, I want him to wash,' she said. 'He smells like a pigsty.'

Booth nodded in agreement. They continued to eat in silence.

'Have you ever heard of the *Sturmbrigade Dirlewanger*?' she said after a while. 'They were part of the Waffen SS, I think. Were they an elite unit?'

Booth scoffed. 'Elite? They were the worst of the worst. Thieves and murderers, for the most part. I think they were originally made up of poachers, the idea being that they would hunt down partisans in the woods. In the end, though, they let all sorts of criminals join.

'The Poles are very keen to get their hands on ex-members, that's how I know about them. According to intelligence reports, the Dirlewangers single-handedly destroyed an entire quarter during that bloody mess in Warsaw last year. The list of crimes attributed to them beggars belief: rape, torture, murder, mutilation. But why do you ask?'

'Oh, nothing, just curiosity. A woman at the camp mentioned something about her son.'

They ate in silence as Ilse considered the information. Thieves and murderers? That couldn't be true, Ilse thought. That was the wretched Polacks spreading lies. And yet Ilse had heard men talking in Berlin about what had happened in Warsaw when the SS had gone to quell the rebellion. There had been little room for mercy so late in the war. Terrible things had happened. Could Johannes have been involved?

They had finished eating now. As they cleared away the plates, Ilse remembered O'Donnell. God, she was supposed to be asking Booth about this wretched policeman. She'd already missed one opportunity to turn the conversation to the subject, so she sat next to Booth and snuggled her head into his neck.

'Actually, darling, talking of the women at the camp, one of them mentioned a curious thing the other day,' Ilse said. 'She claims there is an English policeman here. From Scotland Yard.'

The cigarette paused on the way to Booth's mouth. 'What an extraordinary thing for one of your friends to know,' he said, after a moment's consideration.

'Is it true? Is there a Scotland Yard man here?'

'Quite true, yes. He's not here in an official capacity, though. He's supposed to be training German policemen — his mother was Swiss-German, apparently, so he's a fluent German speaker — but they've all been interned, so he's at a bit of a loose end. He's been looking into this murder business.'

'Is he a good policeman?'

'Do you mean good as in competent? Or good as in a good man?'

'The first one.'

'Yes, he seems very thorough. Hard-working, too. He's a bit of a cold-fish, though. Not an easy man to like.'

'Has he discovered much?'

'He was out interrogating a Gestapo man yesterday. But I haven't had much to do with him, really.'

'What actually happened out at the house on the Brunswick Road? I've heard so many rumours.'

'It's really quite a strange affair. They found a man and a woman strangled to death. The man was Waffen SS, but we've no idea who the woman was — his girlfriend, probably, given the age difference. But it sounds like someone was planning on chopping them up. Apparently there were all sorts of scalpels and surgical instruments there and some —'

An involuntary shiver shook Ilse. Booth looked at her.

'Are you all right, darling?'

'Oh, let's not talk about such horrid things, please,' Ilse said, and meant it.

He placed a hand on her shoulder.

'What's the matter, Ursula? Why do you look so scared all of a sudden?'

'I'm fine. It's just … all that talk of scalpels and strangled bodies. You make me think the *Flickschuster* is loose again.'

She felt the change in him immediately. Booth's body tensed.

'The *Flickschuster*? Who was that?'

'Oh, it's just a story mothers used to scare children,' she said, trying to play the matter down. 'I'm sure what they said about him was exaggerated.'

Booth was gazing at her intently now. 'Do you mean to tell me something like this has occurred before? Look at me, Ursula, this is important.'

Ilse sighed, realising she would have to explain herself now.

'There were murders a few years ago, here in the Reich. They called the killer the *Flickschuster*. But they caught him, a Dutchman. He was executed. I read it in the newspaper. So forget all about it, please. People got so hysterical about the whole thing, he became a stupid story, like the Bogeyman or Jack the Ripper.'

Booth was quiet for a long while. Then he said, 'Jack the Ripper was real,' as he stared at the window, lost in thought.

8

Silas Payne was born in 1901. He was thirteen years old when the Great War began.

The question of his mother's Swiss-German nationality wasn't a problem at first. But, by October 1914, when the British had suffered their first serious reverses and the newspaper stories of German atrocities had done their work, business began to tail off at the grocery shop his parents ran.

His mother tacked signs to the inside of the display windows — This is not a German business — but it did no good. Payne's father came home one night with a bloodied lip and buttons missing from his shirt; the next day, a group of girls spat at Silas as he walked home from school.

Silas was in bed on the night of November 2nd, the night the mob came. There were only a few of them at first, hurling insults up at his parents' bedroom window, but within minutes others began spilling out of the local pubs and a crowd began to form.

Silas had gone into his parents' room as the insults grew in volume and severity.

Hun bitch.

Fuck off back to Germany.

Hang the spy.

Then someone threw a stone and glass smashed downstairs; the crowd's restraint broke with it. They were all over the shop in seconds, dragging the goods from the window. Payne remembered them standing in the street, afterwards, chatting and laughing as they munched apples and sausage and bits of cheese.

Payne's father had been all set to go outside with a walking stick, but his mother had thrown herself on his legs and begged him to stay. They had sat there, the three of them, huddled together on the edge of his parents' bed, listening to the sound of their livelihood being torn apart.

And then the whistle had sounded, a single three-beat blast that had silenced the crowd immediately.

When Payne peered from the upstairs window he saw the local police sergeant standing between the crowd and the shop window, taking his tunic off and flexing his big fists open and closed.

'You all know me,' he said in a low, calm voice, 'and I know most of you. So believe me when I say that the next one of you blighters to take something from this shop is going to have to go through me to get to it. Is that perfectly clear?'

The crowd wavered and men began whispering. The quiet seemed to last forever but when no-one made a move, the police sergeant cracked his knuckles and smiled, the master now of the situation. 'It's a mighty cold night, lads, so either we get straight to it or we all go home. What's it to be?'

That had broken the spell. Some laughed at the sergeant's temerity, others pulled their caps down to hide their faces and slunk towards the shadows. As quickly as the crowd had formed, it was gone.

'Don't you worry, Mrs Payne,' the sergeant had said afterwards, as Payne and his parents began salvaging what they could from the wreckage, 'I'll see those animals don't trouble you again.'

He'd been true to his word, too, prowling up and down their street each hour, on the hour, for the next two weeks, whistling tunelessly and swinging his truncheon. And, as Silas had watched the man, feeling the calming aura of strength and safety he exuded, he had realised one person *could* make a difference — it was all a question of persistence and determination. From then on, Silas Payne had known precisely what it was he wanted to do with his life…

Payne blinked eyes that were gummy with sleep. He sat up on the creaky trestle bed in the police station and pressed a hand to his chest. His heart was hammering, the way it always did when he dreamt of that night back in 1914. Even now, more than thirty years later, Payne remembered the hysterical terror and confusion of the experience with total clarity; during the whole of his career in the police force, nothing had ever come close to it. He rose, made coffee and got straight to work. He knew from experience that the best antidote was to occupy his mind.

As soon as it was light, Payne went to the *Rathaus*. He kept going over what the Gestapo man, Toth, had told him. Was there any truth to his claims? There was only one way to find out, Payne decided.

The cellars of the *Rathaus* were extensive. A veritable warren of corridors connected dozens of vaulted stone chambers, some of which must have been over five hundred years old. There was a chaotic lack of orderliness in most of these chambers: Eichenrode had been bombed by mistake back in '44 and most of the books and paperwork salvaged from the town's library had been stored haphazardly in the cellars.

Payne picked his way through piles of cardboard boxes towards a desk that stood at the back of the main chamber.

'Am I right in thinking there are some boxes of German newspapers down here?' Payne said to the soldier on duty, steadying himself by placing a hand on the wall as he stepped over a box.

'How do you say newspaper in German, sir?' the man asked.

'*Zeitung.*' Payne wrote the word down for the man.

'Ah, yes, I recognise that word. Down that corridor, turn right, chamber on the right. You'll find all the *zai-tongs* you could want in there, sir. But I don't think they've been sorted.'

He was right. There were boxes and boxes of newspapers but they were all jumbled together. Once Payne had located all the relevant boxes, he took them to a desk in a side chamber and began the laborious process of sorting the newspapers by title and date. First, he divided them into their relevant editions. The boxes contained copies of three newspapers: *Der Stürmer*, *Völkischer Beobachter* and *Das Reich.*

An hour later, Payne leant back in his chair and sighed. He'd become totally side-tracked, he realised, massaging his temples. His head was swimming and not just from the effects of staring at newsprint under the dim light. He had never realised quite how cynically perverse the minds that had controlled Germany had been.

Within the pages of these newspapers, every single event of the last ten years of European history had been turned about-face, upside down and inside out: British aggression had started the war, Stalingrad was a great feat of German arms, the Russians were Asiatic barbarians who had launched a war of extermination against the virtuous and peace-loving German people and the Jews and Bolsheviks were responsible for everything…

Payne could pinpoint the moment when the war had begun to turn against the Germans: the smug tone common to all the publications was replaced by an ever more histrionic incitation to 'resist', 'punish traitors' and 'hold on until the Final Victory'.

The closer the publication date to the end of the war, the more the newspapers shrank in size. They provided a graphic depiction of the melting of the Reich's power and of the delusional nature of those final months. The *Völkischer Beobachter* had still promised Final Victory even when it had diminished to a single sheet of paper.

Payne took a moment to regain his concentration. Then he set to work.

He examined the copies of *Der Stürmer* first.

So, this was Julius Streicher's infamous Jew-baiters' bible. Owing to its worldwide infamy Payne had always imagined *Der Stürmer* as a great tome of a publication, but it was really little more than a pamphlet. It was quite gratifying to see Streicher's tripe limited to so few pages. The pre-war issues had sixteen pages. By the '40s, though, it had been reduced to a mere four pages.

What it lacked in size, it made up for in offensiveness. Payne paused to examine the cover of one issue on which a fat-lipped man in Hassidic garb and ringlets was feeding an Aryan child into a sausage machine with pound and dollar signs on the barrel.

An issue of *Der Stürmer* dated September 1942 was the first to report anything that might corroborate Amon Toth's claims. The headline read 'New Jew Horror' and described the discovery of a Brunswick house at which 'Jew blood rituals' had been practised, killing 'more than four good Aryans'.

It described in graphic detail how the victims were slowly bled and tortured by Jews still hiding in the Reich. The article claimed the 'Jew killers' went on to mutilate their victims' corpses, although in what way was not specified.

That was hardly surprising, Payne decided. The article — if that was the correct word for it — was short on any real details as to what had happened. It ended with hysterical warnings to 'watch for the Jew among us' and never to hesitate in denouncing 'race-traitors' who might be hiding 'murdering Jewboys'.

Payne threw the copy of *Der Stürmer* back into the box with the others, glad to be done with it. Still, the article had served one purpose: it had given Payne a date he could use as a reference point when searching the other newspapers.

Payne then turned to the copies of the *Völkischer Beobachter* and Goebbels's own personal newspaper, *Das Reich*.

Both covered the series of murders. This time they were attributed to a new terror weapon being employed by — depending on which newspaper you read — English spies parachuted into the Reich for the purpose or enemy aircrews that had bailed out over Germany. According to the articles, these 'murder squads' lured Germans into secluded places and killed them before mutilating the bodies. Goebbels had even written a brief editorial on the subject in *Das Reich*:

But London is mistaken if it believes it can by terror break German morale. We have said it a hundred times before and will say it a hundred times again: today's German people has nothing in common with the German people of 1918. Our morale breakdown then was a one-time exception, not the rule.

Proof of their desperation has seen them turn to the cruellest of methods. Even when shot from the skies by the steel ring of defences that surrounds the capital, the English aircrews fall among us and behave like animals, murdering and mutilating. This latest outrage shows to what lengths they are prepared to go: a young soldier, home on leave, murdered alongside his fiancée, their bodies mutilated in the most horrific ways imaginable.

By early 1943, though, both newspapers had begun speaking of a single killer, a man they took to calling the *Flickschuster*. Payne paused. How could he best render that name in English?

Translated literally, it meant a person that cobbled or patched something together, like a shoemaker, but Payne sensed the word was used more figuratively in relation to the killer: the Patchwork Man might be a more accurate translation.

The reports in the newspapers mentioned the discovery of a cellar full of dismembered body parts after an air raid on Brunswick. Some of the body parts had been buried under the floor of the cellar; others had been shoved into a furnace and burnt. The newspapers said the remains of six people had been found in the cellar, although bone and tooth fragments found in the stove indicated there might have been more.

Payne read on, cross-referencing each news story.

Another 'House of Horror' was discovered in Berlin in July 1943. This was the crime Toth had mentioned investigating. Again, the bodies were discovered in the cellar of the house. This time, though, witnesses spoke of a tall, well-built man who had been seen leaving the house on a number of occasions.

According to the newspapers, a Dutch worker named Wilhelmus van Rijn was arrested in May, 1944 and charged with the murders. The captions that accompanied the grainy photos of van Rijn surrounded by Gestapo agents highlighted his bulbous eyes and 'Jewish features'. A large amount of coverage was given to the show trial and subsequent execution.

Payne stopped. Execution?

He checked his notes. Toth said they had caught the murderer but had mentioned nothing about the man being executed. What did it mean? Clearly, Toth knew something the newspapers had not reported.

The Dutchman was probably innocent, Payne decided. If not, why would Toth have deliberately steered Payne towards looking in newspapers, knowing the stories published there would undermine his claims? Is that what he had meant when he said the newspaper reports contained an 'important error'?

Payne massaged the back of his neck. He was tired. And hungry, he realised. It was nearly eleven and he hadn't had any breakfast.

He rose from the desk. Then he stopped and frowned.

A familiar voice was echoing off the walls of the cellar. It took Payne a moment to place it: Captain Booth. He leant against the door frame and listened to the captain's voice.

'…looking for German newspapers. Anything really, the more populist the better. Why? I'm looking for details on a series of murders that happened here in Germany during the war, sergeant.'

Payne frowned. How the hell had Booth discovered the same line of enquiry? It was too much of a coincidence. He would have to speak to the man. He rose and stepped out into the corridor.

'Hello again, Captain Booth,' he said, hands in his pockets. 'Do you know, I think I might be able to save you a lot of time and effort.'

9

Later that afternoon, the two men sat opposite each other in Booth's office, the relevant German newspapers piled on the table between them.

They had spoken for half an hour in the cellar of the *Rathaus*. Payne had shown Booth everything he'd found in the newspapers about the *Flickschuster* series of murders. Then he had told Booth about the claims made by the Gestapo man, Toth.

It was very strange. Booth had spoken to Tubbs at length about the interrogation, but the lieutenant had mentioned nothing about a series of murders that had already taken place in Germany. Then again, though, Tubbs was all over the place emotionally.

'Your theories are all very well and good, Detective Inspector,' Booth said, 'but I think there's one serious problem: according to the Jerry newspapers, they caught the killer. Guillotined him in June last year.'

Payne shook his head. 'They got the wrong man. At least, that's what I think Toth was intimating. He claimed more killings occurred after the Dutchman's execution. Killings that weren't reported.'

'But Toth is looking to save his neck. I've seen his files. Even though the evidence is incomplete, it seems likely he'll be indicted for war crimes. He'd say anything to get out of that.'

Payne nodded. 'That's very true and we'll have to bear it in mind. But it doesn't mean we can discount everything he's told us. Didn't you once mention to me that you had a list of German policemen?'

'That's correct. Why do you ask?'

Payne indicated the newspapers. 'According to these reports, there was a man from the Kripo criminal police in this area that headed up the investigation into the house they found in Brunswick, a policeman by the name of Metzger. It would be useful to find him. Perhaps he could tell us more.'

Booth nodded and promised to dig out the relevant files. Payne continued to look at his notes.

'Do you know anything about this Operation Greif? Toth mentioned that, too; said it was relevant.'

'Yes, I remember it very well. It was the German codename for a false flag operation the Jerries ran last year — *their* soldiers in *our* uniforms up to mischief behind the lines.'

Booth rose, rummaged through a filing cabinet and withdrew a file.

'Here it is. According to this, Operation Greif was a false flag operation organised by an SS man, Otto Skorzeny, the same man that organised Mussolini's rescue in Italy. In October 1944, Skorzeny got the green light to gather together a special unit of SS personnel that could speak English. The troops were trained in Grafenwöhr, in Bavaria, then moved to Münstereifel in Westphalia for the beginning of operations. During the December '44 Ardennes offensive, Skorzeny's men donned American uniforms and wrought havoc behind the Allied lines. Many of the men involved are now being sought in connection with war crimes.'

Payne frowned. 'What possible connection could it have to what I am investigating?'

'Perhaps Toth used it as window dressing. You know, a little bit of truth to sweeten the odour of an otherwise entirely rotten barrel of fish. I can look into it, though, if you like.'

Payne nodded almost imperceptibly and murmured 'thanks' as he pored over his notes. Booth sat back in his chair and watched Payne work.

What he'd previously mistaken in the policeman for haughtiness was actually concentration, Booth realised. That was why Payne gave the impression of being such a cold fish. Little that was outside the immediate focus of his attention seemed to really register. Booth wondered if it was an inevitable consequence of a life spent trying to catch others out.

Booth had the desk sergeant run over to the mess and bring them a round of sandwiches and a flask of tea. As Booth tucked in, he told Payne of what he had found in the basement of Wolffslust prison.

'Do you think it could be related to what you are investigating?' Booth said when he'd finished.

'It's possible. And even if it's not related, the possibility that hundreds of serious criminals were released is something that needs to be looked into. We need to ascertain who this British officer at Wolfsslust was,' Payne said, 'the one who went in with the advance guard and oversaw the sacking of the prison. Perhaps he might know something.'

'I've looked into that already,' Booth said. 'I'm afraid there don't seem to be any records as to precisely which unit overran the prison. It was all very chaotic back then. But I've got Lieutenant Taylor investigating. Tubbs is a bit of a wiz when it comes to unravelling army red tape. If anyone can discover who this officer chap was, it will be Tubbs. And I wouldn't like to be in that officer's shoes if we do find him. Christ, if Toth is right and this idiot has released a mass murderer, it's going to make the British look bloody stupid,' Booth said.

'Have you had time to examine the medical documents you found at the prison?' Payne said.

'No. Since the business with Mr Lockwood in the minefield, Colonel Bassett has had me working overtime investigating this alleged werewolf cell. I've got a Czech professor looking at the documentation, though. Hopefully, he'll get back to me soon. But I have done some digging elsewhere.

'From a Nazi perspective, every one of the men in this medical programme seemed to possess faultless bloodlines, so I phoned their names through to Corps HQ. That's where they store the *RuSha* files, the ones we captured from the SS Race and Settlement Main Office. I'll phone now and see if the archivist up there has had time to cross-reference the names with the lists they've got.'

'Hello Killy,' Booth said when he'd been connected. 'Had any luck?'

Corporal Kilminster was the chief archivist at Corps HQ. 'Hello, sir,' he said. 'I'm not sure whether it constitutes luck or not, but out of the forty-odd names you gave me, thirty-one appear in our files.'

'So the others weren't SS?'

'Not necessarily. It could be that the others are in the files somewhere and I just haven't found them yet.'

'What have you got on the men you have found then?'

'All of them were SS officers with equivalent ranks of lieutenant and above. But that's beside the point. The interesting thing is where these men served. Out of the thirty-one I've found records for, seventeen served as concentration camp guards and the others all served in *Einsatzgruppen* in Poland and Russia.'

'So, all of these men are potential war criminals?'

'They would be if they weren't all dead.'

'Dead?'

'Yes, sir. Every one of them was killed in action, sir.'

'Are you sure? Because I got their names from the records of a medical programme they were all part of.'

Booth wrote the dates of death down. He and Payne then cross-referenced the names with the data Booth had taken from the medical files. Five minutes later, Booth was back on the phone to Killy.

'Are you absolutely certain about those dates you gave me?'

'Of course.' Killy sounded slightly peeved at the inference they might not be. 'Why?'

Booth didn't answer that. He was too busy tapping a pencil against his teeth and wondering why, according to Killy's official files, every single man on the list had supposedly died a week before they entered Doctor Wiegand's medical programme.

10

That same day, Ilse had to work at the transit camp.

As she pulled on her woollen stockings a sudden thought occurred to her. What with one thing and another, she'd forgotten what was, potentially, her biggest problem: the hag woman that knew her real name.

She thought about her problem as she walked to the camp. It was obvious the woman intended to blackmail her. If not, she would already have gone to the Tommies and denounced her.

The best thing to do was avoid her, Ilse decided. If they didn't see each other, the woman wouldn't be able to make her demands. Ilse hurried her pace and arrived at the camp twenty minutes early, before the other German women had got there. She volunteered to work in the laundry room again.

I'll have to get a transfer to work somewhere else, Ilse thought as she tipped piles of dirty clothing into the vats of boiling water. Yes, that was the best idea. She would have to speak to Booth about that. Not that Booth had paid her much attention the day before. After Ilse had mentioned the *Flickschuster* murders, Booth had become so pensive she could hardly get a word out of him.

At midday Ilse volunteered to walk across the camp with a wheelbarrow and fetch a fresh crate of detergent from the stores. She wanted an excuse to see O'Donnell and tell him what she had learned about the murders. She steered the rickety wheelbarrow along the camp's main road, but when she was out of sight of the laundry she turned to the right and headed towards the admin building.

As usual, it was chaos outside that building. Hundreds of people had formed into straggling, swaying queues, all of which converged on a single doorway. Ragged children danced between the legs of the adults and the air was filled with a dozen unintelligible languages.

When Ilse asked the guard on the door where O'Donnell was he pointed across the way to a gap between two buildings.

O'Donnell was talking with the soldier, Suttpen.

The two men seemed to be arguing. As Ilse watched, Suttpen raised his fist at the Irishman, who shook his head and began explaining something. Suttpen looked at his watch. Then he nodded, turned and stalked away.

When O'Donnell walked back towards the admin building, his face was furious. Ilse turned away. Nothing would induce her to speak to him now. She hurried back across the camp towards the storehouse.

The rest of the day passed in the usual fug of monotony. Ilse thought about what she had witnessed. What were those two up to? Because it was clear they were up to something. She knew that the soldier, Suttpen, was even worse than O'Donnell. Rumour had it he exchanged food with German women for sexual favours. What connection could he have to O'Donnell, though? The men gambled together, she knew that, but what she'd witnessed had seemed something far more serious than a simple argument over money. As well as being angry, both men had looked worried about something.

At five o'clock the Red Cross woman signalled that Ilse could go. She took her coat from the peg, trying to flex some feeling back into her raw, swollen fingers. She returned to the admin building and asked for O'Donnell, but he wasn't there.

Her route home took her near to a field where some of the camp inmates slept in tents. She was close to the camp gates when a sudden series of screams erupted amid the rows of tents.

Ilse's first reaction was to flinch; then she realised the screams were of happiness.

An old Jew wearing a ridiculously small fur coat stood with his hands clasped towards heaven in an attitude of profound gratitude, tears flooding his cheeks as a young woman knelt in the dirt, hugging his legs and kissing his knees.

Ilse had never seen two people happier to see each other. All around people stared and the air was suddenly heavy with raw emotion. Some smiled. Others cried. The Jews were hugging and kissing now, touching fingers to each other's faces as if to ensure the flesh each felt was real. The young woman trembled all over and kept making small steps on the spot, as if the ground burnt her feet.

Ilse hurried past, surprised to find her own eyes moist with half-formed tears. Then she felt a hand grab her arm. She spun round, expecting to see O'Donnell.

It wasn't him, though. It was the hag.

'If you run away this time, I'll tell the Tommies who you are,' the old woman hissed.

'I don't know what you're talking about,' Ilse said, but her voice quavered as she spoke.

'Your name is Ilse Drechsler. You were married to Herr Hoffman's son, Rüdiger.'

'Let me go.'

The woman's grip increased.

'Not so high and mighty now, are you? Where's your car and driver? Where's your precious Party, Ilse?'

The soldiers at the gate had begun looking towards them. Ilse pulled the woman out of their sight.

'What do you want from me? Money? Food? I have neither.'

The hag sneered. 'I'm not going to blackmail you, don't worry.'

'Then what do you want?'

'I want you to come with me, to my home. I want to show you something.'

'Don't be so ridiculous.'

'Ridiculous?' The woman's voice rose as she spoke. 'You dare to call me ridiculous, Frau Hoffman?'

She enunciated the last two words with exaggerated clarity. Ilse hissed for her to be quiet. The hag smiled triumphantly.

'If you want me to be quiet, come with me. If not, I will go straight to the Tommies and tell them who you really are.'

Ilse had no choice but to comply. They left the camp and walked in silence along country lanes, back towards the edge of the town, then turned into a street where the buildings were little more than brick boxes filled with rubble and broken wood. Dazed, dusty women sat in the street, half-heartedly trying to scrub clothes in makeshift tubs, while tattered children played.

The hag took Ilse to a set of steps that led down from street level to a cellar door.

'In here,' she said.

The dark room smelt of cabbage and damp brick. There was little in the room apart from a few sticks of furniture and what seemed to be half of a sideboard, its splintered edge pushed up against the wall. A child, wrapped in blankets, lay on a makeshift bed in a corner of the room. The child moaned and whimpered softly as the hag approached. She made soothing noises, then turned and motioned for Ilse to approach.

'This is what you must see,' the woman said and flung back the covers.

Ilse stifled a cry as she saw the wretched, twitching thing beneath the blankets was not a child, but a young man. His legs ended in puckered stumps a foot below his hips and his face was missing an eye and most of the teeth. The remaining orb rolled and darted beneath the scarred lid like that of a frightened horse. Saliva dripped from the jabbering lips and gums.

'There,' the woman said. 'That is all I have left of three sons. No, look at him, you heartless bitch,' she said, when Ilse tried to turn. 'My eldest was killed in Africa. My second died in Italy. And this … this is how my youngest came back from the fighting in Normandy. I had everything I wanted in life. Then you Nazis came and turned the world upside down and now I have nothing. Less than nothing. What argument did I ever have with the English or the Americans? Or the Russians? Or even the damned Jews?'

Ilse wanted to flee, but she found herself paralysed by the woman's cold fury.

'What do you want from me?' Ilse said. Her voice trembled as she spoke: she was genuinely afraid of hearing the reply.

The woman looked at Ilse and as she did so the blaze of hatred in her eyes, which had been suppressed before, flared up; her lip curled. 'You were a Nazi, Frau Hoffman. For years you strutted around in front of the ordinary people, making out you Nazis were something special when in reality you were selfish, arrogant shits, the whole lot of you. So, I want you to say sorry. I want you to look at my son, I want you to hold his hand and I want you to apologise.' She came so close now that Ilse could smell her breath, which was rank with acorn coffee. 'You people, you Nazis, you filled their heads with drums and dreams of glory. But this is where you led them. That is why I want you to kneel beside his bed and ask his forgiveness. This is your fault and you must admit it. Then I will decide whether to tell the Tommies who you really are.'

Ilse could not move. It seemed to her that a hundred possible courses of action were flashing through her mind as she stared down at the crippled soldier, but she could not decide which one to take. When the hag put a hand on her shoulder and pushed her down, Ilse's knees buckled. She knelt beside the bed.

The man's scarred hand was hot and dry when she held it. She opened her lips but no words emerged. The woman prodded her.

'I'm sorry,' Ilse whispered.

'Again.'

'I'm sorry.'

The woman knelt beside her.

'Kiss his brow and tell … don't you dare try to run, you bitch!'

But Ilse was up now and stumbling towards the door.

'Come back,' the woman hissed. Behind her, the lump on the bed began to rock and cry, flapping his stumps impotently against the wooden board in an effort to rise.

'I'm sorry. I'M SORRY!' Ilse cried, then turned and ran for the door. She fell and grazed her knee on the stairs outside, but she got up again quickly and did not stop running. Children stopped and watched her as she fled along the street, weeping hysterically, but their dead eyes showed no emotion. They had seen far worse things.

11

Captain Booth's interest in the *Flickschuster* case had confirmed Payne's suspicions. This business with the dead bodies and Lockwood had nothing to do with Nazi partisans. There were no werewolves. Something else was going on, Payne was certain of it. That was why at midday he walked out to the murder house on the Brunswick Road, carrying a canvas sack filled with tools.

It was always good to return to a crime scene. Payne found it helped focus his mind on the facts that had been learned in the intervening period. And he nearly always spotted something new, some tiny detail he had previously overlooked … and it was the tiny details that usually made the difference between success and failure in a criminal investigation.

There was a lot of military traffic on the roads today, so Payne walked along the grass verge, the sack thrown over his shoulder. Before he reached the murder house, he walked to a property that was on the hillside opposite, the only one that overlooked the crime scene. Really he should have done this when he first began investigating the matter, but he'd been distracted.

There had been a fence outside the house once: lines of torn earth showed where the fence posts had been ripped out. The house's shutters were all gone and the lower floor windows were boarded up from the inside.

Payne knocked at the ruined front door. When no-one answered, he peered through the chinks in the window boards. An elderly woman's face appeared at a second-storey window.

'*Wie kann ich Ihnen helfen?*' she said.

'Could you come down, please?' Payne said in German. 'I need to ask you something.'

'Are you a soldier?' she said. 'When will you people go back to your homes and leave us in peace?'

Payne thought about showing her his CCG identity card, but thought better of it: telling her he was a policeman might not calm her, given the reputation that the first wave of Allied soldiers to reach Germany had acquired. 'Come down and speak to me; then I will leave you in peace.'

It took the woman a while to remove whatever it was that was holding the front door closed. When she did so, it fell inwards. The old woman was wrapped in a ratty dressing gown. She was trembling, Payne noticed, although the day was not cold.

'How long have you lived here?' Payne said.

'All my life.'

'Who owns that house over there?' he said, pointing towards the murder house.

'Herr Tauber.'

'Where is he?'

She shrugged. 'Someone in the village said he was killed fighting with the *Volkssturm*. I've not seen him since November.'

'Did you ever see anyone come to the house? In the last few months, I mean.'

The old woman thought about this. 'There were some English soldiers, but that was back in May. They only stayed a few weeks. Then people came in a lorry sometimes.'

'A lorry?'

'Yes, a big one, painted green.'

'Who were they?'

'Travellers.'

'Why do you say that?'

'They had suitcases with them. And they were always gone the next day. I think they only ever spent single nights there.'

'How many people did you see?'

'I don't know. Four, maybe five couples. And lights. I saw lights in the house at night sometimes.'

'When?'

'I'm seventy-three. I can't remember things like that. Every few weeks or so.'

'When was the last time?'

'Last night.'

Payne froze.

'Last night? Are you sure?'

The woman nodded.

'Which windows did you see the light in?'

'That one, at the top,' she said and pointed her stick towards the garret window.

When Payne got to the murder house, he went straight to the well in the garden and prised the top off it with a crowbar. This was something else he should have done when he first began investigating.

It took a bit of brute strength to break the wood free from the padlocks, but he managed it in the end. Payne tossed the wooden cover to one side and put his hand to his nose. The chemical smell he had detected on his first visit was stronger now; there was no doubt it was coming from the bottom of the well.

Covering his mouth with a handkerchief, he shone his torch down into the dark cylinder of the well shaft. The red bricks seemed peppered with white powder, as if someone had thrown sacks of flour down into the darkness. The chemical smell rising from the well was unpleasantly strong and caught in his throat.

Payne rested his hands on the edge of the well-head and dropped a stone into the darkness. The faint thud that sounded a few seconds later told him the well was deep and dry. Payne was unsure whether it was his imagination, but his nostrils seemed for a moment to detect the faint whiff of decay amid the chemical stench. He replaced the crowbar in the sack and headed towards the house. The kitchen door was closed but not locked. It creaked as he pushed it open.

It was pitch black inside the kitchen; the blacked-out windows were all closed.

Had the soldiers left it like that? Payne closed his eyes, trying to picture the kitchen as he'd left it. No, the windows were definitely open then: he remembered shafts of dusky evening sunlight that had crossed the kitchen and shone on the enamel surface of the sink.

Payne used his torch to guide him to the nearest window and fumbled the latch open. Gloom disappeared as summer sunlight flooded the room. He crossed to the other pair of windows and opened those, too. The hatch to the cellar was closed. He opened it and went halfway down the stairs.

It was just as he'd left it.

He returned to the kitchen and headed for the stairs that led to the upper stories, but stopped when he had only reached halfway across the room. The muddy footprints Sergeant Beagley's men had left on the kitchen floor had dried to dust and were still perfectly visible — except in one place near the door, where the dust had been scuffed. It looked as if someone had dragged something across it.

Payne cursed himself for not being more careful. He couldn't be sure whether he'd done it himself while crossing the kitchen to open the window.

'Hello?' he called up the stairs. 'Is anyone there?'

No answer.

He said the same in German and French.

The only response was a faint creak.

Payne crept upstairs a single step at a time, one hand on the wall to steady himself, neck craned upward. His heart was racing. This was not something he'd considered properly. He had always made a habit of returning to murder scenes, but never alone. There was something about places where violent death had occurred, he realised now: some echo or scent to which the animal in human instinct responded.

He paused at the top of the stairs. Sunlight flooded through the shattered windows. He checked each room, but there was no sign of anyone having been there. In the smallest bedroom, he paused and stared at the ceiling. Motes of dust were falling from a crack in the plaster. As he watched them, the beam above him creaked very slightly.

He tiptoed up the stairs to the garret, to find that the solid door at the top was closed. Payne turned the handle and leant his weight against it. The door would not budge. He ran his hand across the rough surface of the door. There was no way he could force it, even if he could get a run at it. He tried the handle again, rattling the door in frustration, then walked back downstairs. The house was utterly quiet now, although it seemed to Payne's jangled nerves the silence was more that of a breath being held.

When a window shutter banged in the wind he nearly jumped out of his skin. Then he was running helter-skelter downstairs, out through the kitchen and on into the daylight in the garden.

He stood in a shaft of sunlight, one hand pressed to his chest, and let the warmth calm him. It had been years since he'd had such a bad case of the heebie-jeebies.

Then he went out and stood on the side of the road. He knew that an army vehicle would be along soon.

Twenty minutes later, two soldiers in a jeep that Payne had managed to flag down returned with a long wooden ladder balanced along the length of their vehicle.

Payne had originally hoped to get some engineers to open the garret door but they were all too busy working on the minefields outside the town, so he had been forced to resort to Plan B. If they couldn't get into the garret via the door, they would have to use the hole in the roof.

The two soldiers shouldered the ladder and followed Payne across the grass towards the back of the house. The sun shone bright and strong; its light glinted on the thousands of tiny fragments of shattered window that lay among the grass.

'That's where I want to get to,' Payne said, indicating the ragged hole in the building's crow-stepped roof.

The elder of the two soldiers was called Bill Ainsley. He scratched his cheek and shook his head like a builder assessing a tricky piece of work. 'Are you sure it's safe up there? Look at those roof beams, they're all cracked. It could be a death-trap.'

'I've been up to the garret on the inside,' Payne said. 'It seems structurally sound.'

The ladder was just long enough to reach the edge of the collapsed roof.

'There you go, sir,' the younger soldier said, when the ladder was in place. 'Do you want me to foot it for you?'

Payne looked up at the ladder. This was one practicality he hadn't considered. It was a long way up. Christ, how high was it? Eight yards? If he fell from that height he'd break his neck.

The young private beside him smiled when he saw the doubt on Payne's face.

'Do you want me to go up there, sir? I used to be a window cleaner, so heights don't bother me.'

'If you wouldn't mind, son. Just see if there's a way to open the door from the inside.'

The young soldier climbed the ladder. He paused at the very top and examined the splintered brickwork around the edge of the hole.

'Seems solid enough,' he said as he pulled himself up onto a roof beam, swung his legs over into the hole and dropped down. A few seconds later, his blond head appeared amid the cracked roof tiles.

'It's a bit of a mess up here,' he said, 'but it seems solid enough.'

'What can you see?' Payne said.

'Well, there's a ruddy great hole just behind where I am standing. But the other half of the room seems fine. There's a load of clothes up here. And suitcases.'

'Suitcases? How many?'

The head disappeared for a moment.

'I can see seven. But there might be more.'

'Can you see if the door opens from the inside? It might be bolted.'

'Will do, sir.'

'And you watch your footing up there, Charlie,' Ainsley said. 'You've come a long bloody way if it's only to go and break your neck now.'

Charlie grinned. 'Don't worry, Bill, it's fine up here. I think the mortar went through and —'

The young soldier's head snapped downward so suddenly, both Ainsley and Payne cried out. It was as if the floor beneath him had collapsed but there was no sound. Then a hand flailed in the opening and Payne heard a muffled scream before the sound was cut short. A faint gurgle followed, then silence.

Ainsley continued to shout the soldier's name as Payne began to climb the ladder, taking the rungs two at a time. The ladder wobbled and jerked beneath him as he neared the top; roof tiles slid away and smashed on the ground below. Payne ignored them as he took hold of the jagged masonry on either side of the hole in the roof and lowered himself down into the garret.

'Charlie?' Payne said. He saw a pair of boots poking from the rubble. There was no answer.

The garret was little more than a triangular crawl space formed by the peak of the roof but there was enough space to walk upright at its centre.

Charlie lay on the floor, totally still. A huge puddle of blood had pooled beneath his head and throat. Payne knelt beside him, felt for a pulse. There was none. Then Payne lifted the boy's chin, and drew his breath when he saw the horizontal rent in his throat that had severed both carotid artery and windpipe.

How the hell had that happened? Had he slipped and impaled himself on something? Payne stood … and the figure pounced, rising up from behind a pile of rubble with a terrible cry.

Payne caught a momentary glimpse of motion through the fallen beams, then cried out as he realised the face rushing at him was formed of patches of leathery skin, the lips sewn shut with thick loops of twine; animal eyes blazed from the ragged eyeholes and then the man-thing was upon him, pushing him backwards as it hissed and wailed, a shrill German voice that screamed *'I'll keep you awake while I cut you!'*

Payne put his hands up to protect himself, but the thing swung the rock it was clutching and struck Payne on the side of the head. He stumbled backwards, fell, and landed on his buttocks with a thud. His teeth rang with the impact of the rock and he tasted blood; his head swam and his vision blurred.

The thing came at him now with a huge knife, slashing at the air, but Payne managed to kick out and catch it a painful blow on the shin. He heard a piercing scream of pain and then the creature was gone. Payne heard a key rattle and a door open and close. Footsteps sounded on the wooden stairs.

Payne's head swam as he stumbled to the breach in the roof and shouted down.

'Bill, get your rifle and go round to the front. He's getting away.'

Payne tried to lift himself up through the hole in the roof, but his hands slipped on the jagged edge of the breach and he cried out as he cut a gash in the fleshy part of his palm. He heard three shots ring out and another of those terrible, high-pitched screams.

Then his head swam, his knees buckled and everything became dark…

12

Booth spent the morning helping Professor Svoboda sort through the medical documents he had found at Wolffslust. At midday, he went to get some lunch. On the way back he stopped in on Tubbs Taylor.

'Have you made any headway in ascertaining which unit overran Wolffslust prison, yet?' Booth said. 'Or who this benighted officer was that set everyone free?'

'I'm still collating, actually, Jimmy.'

'Well, I don't want to press you, Tubbs, but I'm going to need something soon. Do you want me to give you a hand?'

'No. I work better alone.'

It was the second time in as many days Booth had asked Tubbs about his progress and for the second time he went away with the impression that Tubbs was dragging his feet. Booth returned to his office and lit a cigarette as he considered the problem. He'd no evidence, of course, so there wasn't really anything he could do about it. The last thing he wanted to do was to confront Tubbs about it. Still, it was a damned nuisance. If there was one thing Tubbs Taylor was good at in life, it was sorting through paperwork, and yet, after two days of ferreting, Tubbs still had nothing for him.

When Booth returned to Professor Svoboda the man's face was clouded with worry.

'I've had a chance to peruse some of these documents now, captain,' he said. 'They are absolutely fascinating. And highly incriminating of the medical staff involved.

'As we feared, this medical project was indeed commissioned by the *Ahnenerbe*, under the auspices of a psychiatrist, one

Doctor Hans Wiegand. The project began sometime in 1940 at the Institute of Racial Hygiene in Brunswick. However, as a result of the damage caused by the October 14th air attack on the city last year the project was then moved to the cellar of Wolffslust prison.'

Booth looked at the documents Svoboda handed him. 'What was this Wiegand up to then?'

'It seems the original thrust of his research was to determine where the psychological breaking points were in a sample of men, with a view to finding out how much strain combat troops could stand. I suppose the fundamental purpose was to discover how much horror a man could take before he ceased to function psychologically.

'However, as the war progressed, the thrust of the research changed. It seems that from 1942 this Doctor Wiegand began to concentrate solely on SS men who had broken down as a result of their duties. That is why you found so many men who had belonged to the Einsatzgruppen or were concentration camp guards. It was these experiences that had caused them to break. And the SS hierarchy wanted to know whether this 'weakness' was due to hereditary or genetic factors. Could it be assessed and measured? Could it be isolated? Could it be stopped? That is why the genealogy of the patients was studied in such obsessive detail. After all, in their view, the Einsatzgruppen were only killing animals, *Lebensunwertes Leben.* Do you know what that means? Life unworthy of life. That is the classification that was applied to those deemed racially unsound by the Nazi regime.'

'So, the *Ahnenerbe* wanted to know why their racial thoroughbreds had become so skittish?'

'Precisely.' Svoboda handed Booth another sheaf of paper. 'As you can see, the patients' breakdowns took a variety of forms. Some showed signs of hysteria — crying, nightmares, bed-wetting, insomnia — while others were deemed to have enjoyed the killing duties too much. They became, in the words of the report, '*demi-human predators*' given to extremes of violence deemed unsuitable even by their SS overlords. We must not forget how prudish Herr Himmler was. By his own warped standards he considered himself a civilised man. His SS butchers were expected to spend their days killing but then return to their families in the evening as if nothing had happened.'

'So what happened to these men?'

'It seems Wiegand's "patients" were subjected to the most extreme forms of psychiatric stimuli: electric shocks, immersion in iced water, the film images that first alerted you that something was going on. Some were given lobotomies, others were sterilised via radium injections in the testicles. Their responses were then studied.'

'But how could this Doctor Wiegand get away with it if these men all belonged to the SS?'

'You mentioned you had discovered a discrepancy in the dates of the men's deaths. These men, once brought into the project, were not to survive it. That is why the officially recorded dates of their deaths precede the dates on the medical records by a few days or weeks. They faked the actual death dates.'

'Could they do that?'

'You may have noticed that many of these documents were stamped by the *SS und Polizeigericht zur besonderen Verwendung.* The Extraordinary SS and Police Court was a secret tribunal convened to deal only with highly sensitive issues which were desired to be kept secret even from the SS itself. Basically, it could do whatever it wanted.'

Svoboda handed Booth the last of the files.

'According to the records, the patients were liquidated once they were no longer useful to the programme. However, it seems Wiegand had between two and four subjects being tested at any one time and that his work continued right up until the end of April 1945.'

'Which means one or more of these men could have been at Wolffslust when the British overran the prison?'

Svoboda nodded.

Booth blew air as he sorted through the paperwork, his eyes lingering on the words *demi-human predators*.

He needed to warn Ursula.

Svoboda began to speak again when both men became aware of shouting and a commotion outside. A jeep shot past Booth's window, beeping its horn. He opened the window and called to a soldier.

'What the devil is going on, Private?'

The soldier's expression betrayed a mixture of excitement and anger.

'Werewolves, sir. They've killed another one of our lads. Slit his throat by all accounts.'

PART THREE

1

Little Otto snuck in by the coal chute. Then he went upstairs to wait for Suttpen.

He had lost it all: the house, the clothes and jewellery, the suitcases, the travel documents: ten weeks of work gone, just like that. He touched his fingertips to the scratch on his face, to the place where the Mask of Many had been ripped away. That was the bitterest loss. The mask had required months of patient work, slicing and drying and stitching.

It had all happened so quickly. He'd killed the first blasphemer that had entered his sanctuary, high up in the rafters of the house. But when the second came Little Otto had known the game was up and fled down the stairs, out through the kitchen door and across the lawn.

How he had wailed when the edge of the mask caught on a branch and he felt it tear from his face. He'd been running so fast that he was several steps past it before he could stop and turn back. Then bullets had begun to snick the ground beside his feet and the air had filled with the whipcrack report of rifle fire, forcing him to flee, wailing and screaming as he did so…

Little Otto had first killed as a young man, but it had been a noisy, messy affair that had given him no pleasure. He knew it was wrong but when the urge came, it gave him no rest until it was satisfied, so he preyed upon drunks and tramps and whores, the human refuse of Germany's industrial cities. He had longed to spend time with them afterwards, to press his face to theirs and feel the heat slowly fade from them, but it was too risky. It was impossible to obtain the privacy he needed in order to enjoy the experience fully. The police were always sniffing around.

That was after the first war, when Germany had become a republic. When the Nazis arrived on the scene, he was initially dismissive of them. How could he not be? In the early days, they were nothing but brown-shirted thugs, brawling and breaking bones with their hobnail boots. But when Otto had first seen men from the SS on parade, resplendent in their ebony and silver plumage, he knew he had found his place within the new order.

When war came they had trained him as a medical orderly and sent him to the eastern front, but not to take part in the war. Little Otto was part of one of the special commands charged with cleansing the conquered territories of Jews. It had been a crude and ugly business, the spirit of Nazism made manifest. Like the other men, Little Otto had dulled himself with alcohol and got on with it as best he could, but the Jews always seemed to sense what awaited them and they filled the air with their crying and religious whimpers as they were made to dig the pits.

The experience had inflamed the unquiet voices in Little Otto's head and when the urge to kill returned, it was a hundred times stronger. He could no more stop it now than he could stop himself from breathing…

Otto tensed when he heard the rumble of a vehicle approaching.

He could start a new mask by killing Suttpen, he thought, but then decided against it. Suttpen was big and strong. Otto would have to slice him quickly and he never liked working with bodies that were messy with blood.

No, killing Suttpen was a necessity, nothing more: the bastard could ruin everything. Suttpen had been out at the camp that morning, arguing with the Irishman. And he'd confronted Otto, hissing in his cheap pimp's voice that he knew what Otto had been up to and that he wanted his cut.

No, Otto would not wear anything made from Suttpen. Besides, Seiler had more travellers for him. He would start his new mask with them. Then he would deal with the doctor and move on.

Headlights flashed across the window. A vehicle stopped outside. Otto wrapped his big fingers around the handle of his killing knife. So Suttpen wanted his cut, did he?

Otto would give the bastard that all right.

2

It rained that night. Ilse hardly noticed. She was exhausted. The experience with the woman and her crippled son had drained her last reserves. She built the fire up when she came home, wrapped herself in blankets and drank tea and whisky, but she continued to tremble all over. It was one thing for the Tommies to despise her, but how could a German woman hate her so?

She drank far more whisky than she should have. Eventually, she slipped into unconsciousness and was released from her troubled thoughts.

At daybreak, she woke suddenly with her head swimming and her mouth filled with saliva. She rushed to the kitchen door, stumbled outside and vomited. That calmed her nausea, although her mouth was foul with the taste of whisky and tobacco. She leant against the wall.

People were moving on the road that passed the end of Ilse's garden, some going eastwards, some towards the west. The grass sparkled as the sunlight picked out droplets of water. The wind smelt clean and fresh.

She laughed as a thought occurred to her: she would probably be better off if she set up a tent and slept in the garden. The air inside the farmhouse was thick with the cloying smell of mould and damp rubble. She turned and headed back towards the house.

That was when she saw that the muddy ground outside the kitchen door was covered with fresh footprints, the kind a man wearing boots would make.

She caught her breath in fear as she saw now that the trail of footprints led from the woodland straight up to the kitchen door and then back again. A half-remembered dream came to her of someone knocking at the door during the night. She shivered as she realised it wasn't a dream.

Could it have been Booth? No, he had been on duty. Who was it, then?

It was probably only some refugee seeking shelter from the rain, she told herself. People saw the building and assumed no-one lived there. After all, it was a ruin. She examined the boot prints. It looked as if only one man had come. Still, that was bad enough. He might come back.

Ilse went inside and sharpened the largest of the kitchen knives. Then she checked that the locks on all the windows and doors were sound.

She was actually glad when the Polack arrived. He came earlier than usual, dragging a huge bundle of firewood behind him. He accepted Ilse's greeting, then set to work stripping the branches of twigs, carefully collecting them in a wicker basket that Ilse gave him.

Later that morning, she found the Polack dragging a huge water butt round to the front of the house. She asked him what he was doing, but his response was incomprehensible. At the front of the property the house had collapsed in such a way that the rubble formed a steep slope that ran up to the undamaged portion of the roof. The Polack rolled the empty butt up this slope. Ilse noticed he had a length of rope coiled around his shoulder and a hammer and nails tucked into his belt. Once more she asked him what he was doing, but this time the Polack did not seem to hear her, so intent was he on trying to balance the water butt upon a ledge of relatively flat rubble.

She left him to it and went inside to make herself tea. The rest of the morning was filled with the sound of hammering and sawing and the crunch of the Polack's boots on the rubble slope.

At midday, Ilse heard a new sound, the clanking of metal. She went outside and saw that the Polack had managed to secure the water butt close to the edge of the flattened ledge with lengths of shattered roof beam. He had also taken pieces of metal pipe from the house's ruined plumbing and strapped them together. One end of the pipeline was attached to the water butt; the other ended in a shower nozzle.

The Polack had stripped to the waist and was carrying buckets of water from the stream at the bottom of the garden. When he saw Ilse staring at his contraption he became agitated and, even though Ilse could not understand a word he was saying, she got the distinct impression he was telling her she had spoiled a surprise.

For another hour, Piotr trudged back and forth, carrying brimming buckets from the stream, one in each hand. Finally, his mangled face appeared at the window and he beckoned for Ilse to come with him.

She went outside. Piotr was hopping from foot to foot in excitement. She saw that the final section of the pipe had a lever attached to it, close to the shower nozzle. He motioned for her to open the lever.

When she did, there was a faint gurgle — and then water began to spurt from the shower head.

It was a ramshackle contraption — water leaked from a dozen fissures along the length of pipe and the spray that emerged from the shower-head was little more than a trickle — but it worked. Ilse could not help smiling as she held her hand beneath the water, angling the shower-head back and forth.

Piotr made motions for her to undress.

'You're mad if you think I'm going to undress in front of you,' she said, but her irritation faded when Piotr greeted her refusal with such a look of such wide-eyed bemusement she realised there had been nothing salacious about his suggestion. Even so, Ilse waited for the boy to leave before she began searching for the lump of scented soap she had brought with her from Berlin.

She started to undress next to the shower, but felt horribly exposed, so she waited until the sun had set and darkness had come before she went back to it and stripped naked. The ground was warm beneath her bare feet and the moonlight shone silver on her pale skin as she opened the lever and stepped beneath the stream of water.

The water was freezing cold and emerged in a dribble — but that feeble jet of water seemed to Ilse a luxury the like of which she had not felt for an age. She allowed the water to play across her whole body, then shut off the tap and soaped herself, covering her skin in a wonderful lather of scented suds. She stood for a while enjoying the smell, then washed the soap off and wrapped herself in a bathrobe.

Clean, at last. How long had it been since she could say that? She'd forgotten what it felt like. She felt lighter somehow. *Now* Booth could say she was beautiful. She was a woman again.

The evening air was pleasantly warm, so Ilse smoked a cigarette outside, still wrapped only in a towel, watching clouds scud across the silver face of the moon. Then she dressed and walked barefoot back across the grass to the house.

And stopped.

The kitchen door was open.

Wide open.

She was sure she'd shut it before she went to shower. Her heart raced as she went closer and saw fresh boot prints in the earth by the kitchen step.

'Who is it? Who's there?' she said, cursing her own stupidity.

'Come in and you'll find out, won't you,' a man said in German. Ilse felt her knees weaken as fear gripped her. She'd left the knife inside.

She heard a chair scrape and footsteps sounded on the kitchen floor. A man's figure stepped into the doorway, a burly man in ill-fitting peasant clothing, silhouetted against the flickering light of the fire.

Ilse took two steps back and bent to pick up a rock. The man laughed. The sound stopped Ilse dead.

She recognised that sound.

'Hello, my little *Gräfin*,' Johannes Drechsler said. 'Don't you have a kiss for your own dear brother?'

3

'Ah, good, I see you're awake.'

The voice came to Payne through clammy cobwebs of consciousness. His head was full of fuzzy dreams. He blinked and smacked gummy lips, wondering where he was and why he was lying in a bed.

'You've had quite a shock, Detective Inspector,' Captain Booth said.

Payne jerked as memory returned. A terrible sensation of panic filled him, but he could not remember what had caused it. Payne swung his legs over the edge of the bed, gasping. His head ached.

'What happened to me?' he said, touching the lump on the side of this head.

'We were rather hoping you'd tell us, Detective Inspector. We've spoken to the soldier who was with you when the attack occurred, but his report was rather garbled. Do you remember anything about your assailant?'

Assailant? Yes, Payne remembered something now, but the memory seemed fragmented and unreal, like some half-recalled nightmare. Payne struggled to concentrate on the facts, to winnow out the false information fear and surprise had caused him to register.

'There was a man in the garret of the house,' he said slowly, speaking for his own benefit as well as Booth's. 'He must have been there when I arrived at the house and was therefore trapped by my presence. I sent a soldier up into the garret. Whoever was there attacked him, slit his throat. When I followed the young soldier up, the same man attacked me. He hit me with a stone. I must have passed out.'

'What did this man look like?'

That was the bit Payne was trying to focus on. The only images he had were grotesque and distorted. 'He wore a mask, I think. A mask made of leather.' Payne stretched. 'How long have I been unconscious?'

'They brought you in yesterday evening. It's the afternoon of the next day now. Here, let me get that for you,' Booth said, when Payne reached a tremulous hand towards the water pitcher beside the bed. 'You've missed all the excitement in the interim.'

'Excitement?'

'Colonel Bassett is convinced you were attacked by werewolves. He's turned the whole district upside down. Random searches, roadblocks, patrols. And the curfew's been brought forward by two hours. Some of the men are joking it's the most work they've had to do since D-Day.'

Payne sipped water as he listened. His head hurt. 'You don't agree about it being werewolves, though, do you, Captain Booth?'

'No. No, I don't,' Booth said, after chewing his lip. 'I'm convinced now that there is a maniac on the loose, a man from Wolffslust prison. That's why I wanted to come here and speak to you. Why are you investigating Quartermaster Sergeant Suttpen?'

Payne shrugged. 'I've said all along that I suspect he is involved somehow. Whether he has anything to do with the killings is another matter, but I should have brought him in for questioning a long time ago. If Colonel Bassett won't let me speak to him, perhaps you could have the MPs pick him up?'

Booth scratched his cheek. 'There's the rub, Detective Inspector. Quartermaster Sergeant Suttpen has gone AWOL.'

'AWOL? When?'

'No-one knows precisely. I spoke to the MPs and mentioned your suspicions. That was yesterday evening. They went out to speak to Suttpen this morning, but no-one can find him.'

'They waited a whole night before trying to bring him in?'

'To be fair to the MPs, they didn't have a great deal of choice, what with Colonel Bassett blustering and bullying about his wretched werewolves.'

'What happened at the house?' Payne said. 'After I was attacked, I mean.'

Booth's face became serious. 'As you mentioned, young Smith was presumably killed by your assailant. The other soldier, Private Ainsley, managed to loose a few shots as the man ran from the house. Then he ran out to the road and flagged an Army lorry down. After that, practically the whole ruddy garrison was put on alert. It's been bedlam these last twenty hours or so. Most of us have been up all night.'

'What did you do with the suitcases and clothes? And did you notice the well?'

It was only now that Payne realised how strained Booth looked. The captain's face was sallow and grey.

'That's another reason I wanted to speak to you. There's going to be a conference later on to discuss what we've found at the house. It's really quite an … extraordinary situation. You were right to look in the well. I suppose it was you that prised the top off?'

'Yes.'

'By the time I arrived, they'd got you and the dead man out of the garret and taken you off to hospital. Everyone was rushing around, promising vengeance on the Jerries and not really taking a blind bit of notice of anything else. But then I spotted that the well had been opened.

'Well, I took one sniff and knew something was amiss. Dry wells are not supposed to smell like that. Anyway, once the white powder inside the well was identified as quicklime, I sent for a team of engineers. They established that the well was around ten metres deep and dry. Then they sent a man down.'

'What did he find?'

Booth went to speak but words failed him. He ran his fingers through his hair.

'I think it's simpler if you come downstairs to the mortuary and see for yourself.'

When the RAMC medical officer, Shelley, emerged from the mortuary thirty minutes later he was pale and his hands shook. Silas Payne followed him out. He removed his face mask and rubbed away the smear of Vaseline beneath his nose.

Captain Booth had waited for them outside.

'Tell me something, Detective Inspector,' he said, extinguishing his cigarette, 'have you ever seen anything like this before?'

Payne's eyes flickered towards the door to the mortuary. The metal tables with their blanket-covered mounds were visible through the door's rounded window. He shook his head.

'That's what I thought,' Booth said. 'I saw the aftermath of plenty a battle during the war and I've not seen anything that gruesome since Falaise.'

Payne turned to Shelley.

'What are your conclusions?'

Shelley rubbed his long chin. 'You'll understand that as an army doctor I've not really had much experience with autopsies,' he said. 'But we did do a little theory work at Med.

school. I've arranged the body parts that were found at the bottom of the well as best I can. Each cadaver has been dissected, post mortem. The dissection follows a similar pattern in each case, with saw cuts made below the knee, at the top of the thigh and below the chin. There are seven bodies in total, four men and three women. Each is complete bar one omission. There are no heads. Not a single one.'

'What does that mean?' Payne said.

'I don't know.'

'How long have they been dead?'

'It's not possible to say with any degree of precision, owing to the effects of the quicklime. That stuff sucks all the moisture out of flesh, causes it to mummify. I would guess two of them died fairly recently, probably within the last three weeks. The other five died before that, although I can't really be specific. We had a hell of a time cleaning the lime from the body parts: water makes the ruddy stuff caustic.'

Payne had his notebook and pencil out. 'How did they die?' he said.

'Again, I can't say with total certainty. But given that the first two victims — the Waffen SS man and his girlfriend that you found in the cellar of the house — had been strangled, I made a detailed examination of the neck stumps and found indications that the seven victims in the well also died from strangulation.'

'So, our killer drugs his victims, then strangles them. Then he cuts them into little pieces and throws them into the well,' Booth said. 'What possible purpose does it serve?'

Payne shrugged. 'Who can say? Look at the Jack the Ripper crimes. What explanation is there for what he did to those women? And yet, in the killer's mind, the savagery served some purpose. But that's presuming the crimes are related.'

'Surely they must be,' Booth said.

'I agree. But it's dangerous to make assumptions until we have concrete proof.' He turned to Shelley. 'Do any of the bodies have the SS blood group tattoo?'

Shelley shook his head.

'But that doesn't necessarily mean they weren't SS,' Booth said. 'Only fighting troops tended to have the tattoo. Also, the Germans seemed to have used the tattoo less and less as the war went on.' Booth looked at his watch. 'It's nearly time for the conference. We need to tell people what we've found. Do you think it is the same man, Detective Inspector? Is it the *Flickschuster*?'

'It's either the same man or someone who knows of his crimes.'

Shelley lit a cigarette. 'There's something else I'd like to show you before we go to the conference,' he said.

Booth and Shelley followed him upstairs to his office.

Payne shuddered when he saw the leather mask that lay face upwards on a sheet of brown paper in the centre of Shelley's desk. It was the one his assailant had worn.

The mask depicted a human face in a rough sort of a way. The surface of the mask was creased and crumpled as if made of different layers, like papier-mâché. Crude stitching formed a seam along the line of the lips. Payne found himself unable to examine the thing for long: there was something unwholesome about the mask, something that made him shy away from too detailed an examination.

Booth leant down to examine the mask more closely.

'Is that leather?'

Shelley extinguished his cigarette and took a sip of water. 'No. It's human skin.'

Booth jerked upright. 'Surely you're joking?'

Shelley shook his head. 'What you are looking at there is called in dissection a facial mask. An incision is made across the hairline, down along the jaw and across under the chin; the skin is then peeled away downwards from the scalp.'

'But why would anyone create such a thing?' Booth said. 'Have you ever heard of anything like this, Inspector?'

Payne nodded. 'There was a series of murders just before the war. Three prostitutes were beaten to death in the space of a week. They were really savage attacks and in each case some of the victim's fingernails had been pulled out post-mortem. Then we noticed the girls' hair had been snipped, too. And that was how we caught him, in the end. He had the nails and the hair in an envelope underneath his pillow.'

'But why?'

'It was a type of trophy, a keepsake. These people kill as part of some strange ritual only they understand.'

The three men stood in silence, regarding the mask.

'If it's human skin, why is it so thick?' Payne said after a while.

'Yes, that puzzled me at first, too.' Shelley leant on the table edge and began indicating parts of the mask with the tip of his pencil. 'If you look, there are parts where the mask appears not to coincide. And the eye holes are an odd shape. It took me a while to realise why: there is more than one facial mask here. It's quite possible there are four or five of them, placed one within the other and glued together.'

'Are you saying our man is a doctor?'

'No. But I would say that whoever did this had rudimentary medical knowledge. That's another reason the edges are so ragged.'

Payne thought about the surgical tools he had found beside Konrad Jaeger's body. 'Presumably the killer was about to operate on the two original victims but was interrupted?' Payne said.

'That must be the case,' Shelley said, 'I'm certain of it.'

'I'll tell you something else we can be certain of,' Payne said, looking at his notes. 'Given the ritualistic nature of the crimes, I think our man already has a real taste for killing. He won't ever stop. Not unless we catch him.'

4

The conference was held that evening in the main room of the *Rathaus*. All the heads of the military government in Eichenrode were there. The mood inside the room was sombre.

The members of Colonel Bassett's staff had gathered at one end of the large conference table, whispering among themselves. When Booth entered the room, Freddy looked up and for a moment his eyes burned with hostility. Then Freddy began speaking again with Bassett, who was clenching his big fists and nodding as he listened.

Seven suitcases of all shapes and sizes had been placed on the table, together with a mass of male and female clothing. The mask lay next to them on a sheet of brown paper.

'We all know why we're here, so I won't bore you with preliminaries,' Bassett said. 'Another one of my men was killed yesterday. Had his throat slit with a knife. Now, it's perfectly clear to me that this was the work of werewolves. And it's my fault. I want you all to know that. I've been far too lenient.

'Our problems in this area began with cut wires and vandalism and I did nothing. After that, we had pit traps and still I did nothing. Then a CCG man was blindfolded and set loose in a minefield. Only then did I react, but it was already too late. The rot had set in.

'We've been too soft on the Jerries. But I want every man in this room to know that it's going to stop now. I didn't lead my men halfway across Europe only for them to have their throats slit by masked maniacs months after the bloody war ended.

We're going to catch this killer in short order. Do I make myself clear?'

Every pair of eyes in the room was fixed on the table. Bassett hadn't led his 'men' anywhere: he'd been appointed by the military government a week after peace was declared.

'Another thing: I don't want a word of this to get out to the Jerries. Not the soldier's death. Not the suitcases. Not the bodies in the well. We can't have them gloating about this.

'Now, I've spoken to the soldier that survived, this Ainsley fellow, and managed to get precious little sense out of him,' Bassett continued. 'I've allowed you to attend this meeting, Detective Inspector, in the hope that you can shed some light on the incident.'

Payne had been staring at the table while Bassett spoke. He began to explain what had happened at the murder house in clear, concise words, but Colonel Bassett interrupted him.

'You say you saw *someone* in the garret of the house. Please be more specific.'

'It was a man. He was wearing a mask. That one there, on the table.'

Each person at the table looked at the leather mask. Bassett was the only one able to fix it with his gaze for any length of time. He turned to Shelley.

'You've given this the once over, Captain Shelley. What are your thoughts?'

Shelley explained what the mask was. A few men at the table winced as he spoke. Colonel Bassett looked at the mask again, and his moustache began to tremble. His cheeks flushed red.

'Disgusting,' he murmured, then repeated the word twice more.

'I've consulted with Captain Booth and Detective Inspector Payne,' Shelley said. 'We do not concur with the opinion that this was the work of werewolves. We feel we are dealing with a deeply disturbed individual, a psychopath.'

Colonel Bassett gave a rumble of displeasure. 'Individual? What the devil are you two talking about, man? There were seven bodies chopped to pieces and stuffed down a well and you think it was one person? This is clearly the work of an organisation.'

Silas Payne shifted in his seat. 'I think it would be foolish to jump to any conclusions until we know the identities of the victims in the well.'

Captain Fredrickson was sitting next to Bassett. He smoothed his dark hair down, looking very smug.

'I think I can shed some light on that, Detective Inspector,' he said. Freddy stood up, opened a file and threw a handful of Red Cross travel permits on to the table. 'We found these among the victims' belongings.'

'So these people were DPs?' Payne said, examining the documents.

'That's the way it looks. Three Poles, two Czechs, a Frenchman and a Dutch woman. Precisely the sort of people werewolves would prey upon.'

'But it makes no sense,' Payne said. 'The other two victims were Germans. These people could have been, too, travelling on false papers.'

'Or they might have been capos in concentration camps,' Freddy said. 'Or informers. Or spies. Or just unlucky. Thousands of people were killed in the weeks after the war ended. I understand you're used to peacetime policing, Detective Inspector Payne, but I'm afraid this werewolf attack is a little beyond your experience. And, if you'll forgive me, your capabilities. What we have here is clearly the sort of terror tactics the werewolf insurgency was trained to engage in. They exist to promote confusion and dissension and generally do everything they can to ensure the occupation is as problematic as possible. They want to intimidate us. I spoke with a Russian officer when I was in Berlin and you wouldn't believe the things the Jerries got up to out there.'

Colonel Bassett was nodding his head.

'With all due respect, Colonel,' Booth said, 'Detective Inspector Payne has informed me of the results of his investigation and I, too, have grave doubts as to whether this business represents action by the Werewolf insurgency.'

'Informed you, has he?' Bassett said. 'Well, that just proves this matter would have been better handled by the military from the get-go.'

Payne took a deep breath. 'Perhaps I could continue to pursue my own investigations in parallel with the military response. I believe the army currently has a number of German police personnel in custody. Men from the Kripo criminal police and other security forces. Perhaps —'

'Men from the Kripo *and other security forces*,' Colonel Bassett interrupted. 'You know what the Detective Inspector means by that, don't you, gentlemen? The bloody Gestapo is what he means.'

Bassett rose and rested his meaty knuckles upon the table.

'We all know you've gone cap in hand to the Huns once, Payne. I won't let it happen again, do you understand? As far as I'm concerned, your involvement with this matter is over. Now, I'd like you to leave, if you don't mind. We've army business to discuss.'

The conference rumbled on for another twenty minutes while Bassett and Freddy outlined the military response to the situation. An interrogation centre was to be set up in the centre of town and every German male within a five mile radius to be brought in for questioning.

After the conference, Booth went to find Payne.

'I'm afraid this was always going to happen,' he said. 'There's just no talking to Bassett once he's got an idea into his head.'

'Can we speak to Toth again?'

Booth shook his head. 'Not if he's at Bad Nenndorf. The security there is very tight. Added to that, Colonel Bassett has muddied the waters for us. I'm afraid it's absolutely impossible.'

'What about the policeman, Metzger, the one we read about in the newspaper reports? Can we find him? He ran the original *Flickschuster* investigation.'

'Yes, that's a possibility. If he's in one of the civilian internment camps, the security won't be anywhere near as tight.'

'I'll head out to the Red Cross camp tomorrow and see if I can discover anything about these travel permits. But we need to find out where Captain Fredrickson found them in the first place.'

'There's something else we need to know about Fredrickson, Detective Inspector,' Booth said. 'We need to understand why the hell he is bending the Colonel's ear. It's him that's pushing this werewolf idea, I'm sure of it.'

5

Ilse and Johannes sat opposite each other at the kitchen table, sister and brother together again. For ten minutes, Ilse was genuinely glad to see him. Then she began to notice how different Johannes was now from how she remembered him.

First, there were the scars: a starburst of livid tissue that crossed his jaw-line and another, thick and red, on the back of his hand. They were only the most noticeable blemishes, though; the whole of his being seemed nicked and notched now, like an old ham bone. And his demeanour was different. He had been sly and cheeky as a boy, but what had once been merely a mischievous air had an undercurrent of genuine malevolence to it, now.

The conversation came in spits and spurts. They spoke about their experiences at the end of the war. Johannes said he had deserted at the end of April and had been living in the woods ever since. He did not mention where he had been serving or with which unit.

'You look older, sister,' he said. 'And you're thinner. There's grey in your hair. Just here.' He reached across the table and brushed dirty fingernails through the hair at Ilse's temples. She resisted a momentary impulse to flinch. Something about her little brother scared her now, she realised.

Johannes finished his tea. 'Haven't you got anything stronger, my *Gräfin*,' he said as he finished his tea.

Ilse shook her head. She was damned if she would share her whisky with him. It irritated her that he kept calling her *Gräfin*, duchess: it had been their father's pet name for Ilse.

Johannes looked at her, eyes hooded. 'Are you sure you don't have any liquor, *Gräfin*?'

'Oh, certainly, what would you like? Shall I open the bar? And stop calling me that. I'm not your *Gräfin*.'

'What would you prefer I call you, then? Ilse Hoffman?'

He laughed at the way the sound of her real name made her flinch. 'Yes, I'm sure the English solider you're fucking would love to know all about Rüdiger. Who did you tell him you were?'

Ilse ignored the question. 'What do you know about that?'

'You don't think I would just saunter up to the house and knock, do you? I've been watching you for days, waiting for the right moment. And don't worry, I won't harm your Englishman. I've enough problems as it is. You've done well to get one so quickly, though. You were always a little sharp for most men's tastes. What was it father used to say about you — "All thorns and no rose"?'

'He never said such a thing.'

Johannes shrugged. 'Believe what you like.'

More silence. Then Ilse said, 'Do you know anything about Cousin Ursula?' as she watched Johannes's reaction carefully.

'I know quite a bit about her, actually. She used to write to me when I was in Russia. And I used to write back. That was one part of the week the boys really looked forward to, listening to Cousin Ursula's love letters. They used to help me compose the responses. I think the dumb bitch thought I was going to marry her.' He laughed, a harsh bark of a sound.

'That was wicked of you, Johannes, to taunt poor Ursula like that. She came here. To this house, I mean. Men at the frontier had raped and beaten her. She died of her injuries a few days ago.'

If the information meant anything to Johannes, he did not show it. He picked food from between his teeth with a fingernail.

'Where will you stay tonight, Johannes?'

Again the crooked smile. 'Do you mean to say I can't stay here?'

'Of course not. There's no room.'

'But this is my house, too, now. And I intend to sleep here.'

Ilse said nothing. Johannes watched her then said, 'Don't worry. I've no intention of staying here for long. Or in Germany for that matter.'

'Where will you go?'

'Spain. Then on to South America. The Tommies are hanging SS men like me.'

'Well, you would do well not to hang around too close to Eichenrode. Someone might recognise you. And the Tommies are searching houses. They think there are partisans here continuing to fight. People have been murdered.'

Johannes nodded, as if the information pleased him. 'I can get going tomorrow. If you're prepared to help me, that is.'

'Help you? What can I do?'

'There are people here that can get me the documents I need: ID papers and travel permits.'

'And you want me to speak to these people? I have no influence with —'

'I want you to pay. I need some of your money.'

Ilse laughed. 'And what makes you think I have any money?' Her laughter grew as she waved towards the cracks in the wall, the piles of rubble, the fractured roof beam. 'Oh, that really is wonderful, Johannes. Money? Yes, you're right, how much would you like? Did you not hear? I really am a *Gräfin* now and this is my castle.'

Johannes peeled the skin from another potato and watched her in silence until her laughter faltered. For a moment, fear gripped Ilse. Did he know about the box buried in the garden? No, he was bluffing. He must be.

'You can't really believe I have any money, Johannes,' she said when the silence became uncomfortable. 'It was all I could do to get out of the Warthegau with the clothes I wore. You've no idea what it was like for civilians when the Russians broke through. It was chaos. I had to run for my life, literally.'

Johannes held the strips of potato skin in the palm of his scarred hand, crushed them into a single mass and swallowed them. 'But you didn't run straight here, though, did you? You said yourself you went to Berlin.'

Ilse felt her face blush. 'What of it?'

'Remember when I visited you in the Warthegau? Rüdiger told me about his deposit box at the bank. His escape plan, he called it. Of course, back then he was thinking about what would happen if he ever fell out of favour with the Party, wasn't he? But I bet that was the first thing you went to collect when you got to Berlin. In fact, I'm willing to bet that was the whole reason you went there in the first place.'

'I don't know what you're talking about, Johannes.'

'Yes, you do. Don't think I can't spot when you're lying, sister. And don't try to hide your face by looking out of the window. You know we could always read each other.'

He laughed when she refused to turn.

'What do you need with travel permits, anyway?' she said, more to fill the silence than anything. 'You can go cross country. Travel at night. You're a soldier. Live off the land.'

Johannes laughed. 'It's amazing how quickly those words come to the lips of those who've never tried it. Live off the land? Live off what, precisely, when every turnip from here to the Pyrenees is probably already dug up. There are millions of people on the road, now. You must have seen them. They are like ants, everywhere at once, on the roads, in the woods, crossing fields, on the riverbanks. There is no land left to live off.'

After that pronouncement, Johannes took firewood — more than Ilse would have used for a whole week — and built the fire up to a roaring blaze. Then he took a tattered blanket from his gunny sack, spread it out before the hearth and lay down and slept. Just like that. He had no pillow, but within seconds his breathing slowed and he was deeply asleep.

The flames cast flickering light onto the gaunt angles of her brother's face. Ilse watched him sleep, then went to stand on the porch. The moon was nearly full and bathed the countryside with silver-white light. To the east, lights shone amid the dark bulk of the town, serving only to highlight its cracked and irregular skyline.

Winter was around the corner, the harsh, unforgiving winter of northern Germany. Lord, how would she survive then? She had Booth, but what would happen if he was recalled to England? Would Booth look after her? Marry her? Take her with him?

That was about the best she could hope for, but what would that be like? If the English here hated Germans, what would they be like in the towns and cities that had been bombed?

No, there was no future with Booth. He was a pleasant young man. In other circumstances, she could have loved him. But not here, not now. She would not be dependent on a man's goodwill for her own happiness.

She stood and smoked a cigarette, weighing the pros and cons of the situation.

Johannes was right. She *had* gone to Berlin to get Rüdiger's box from the bank vault.

She'd been lucky to get all this way without having the box stolen. When the soldiers took her car at gunpoint she'd thought she would lose the box, but they'd never thought to check her luggage. Ilse had seen in their eyes that all they were thinking of was saving their miserable hides and so she had unloaded her suitcases from the boot, then handed them the keys. It had given her a secret thrill to think of the riches that were right under their noses. All told, she had eight thousand dollars and some jewellery.

But Johannes knew. She could be sure of that; they *could* read each other. He knew she had the money here, hidden, just as she knew Johannes would stay until he got his own way. And there was that something more to her brother, now, a part that was deep, dark and different, the part that said, *This time I am asking. Next time, I will simply take.*

She looked out at the darkness for a moment longer, then turned and headed inside.

She sat on the stool beside the fire and shook Johannes. He emerged from sleep with such a sudden jolt that Ilse jumped back, stifling a scream: for a moment, there was no recognition in his eyes, only a leer of bestial aggression.

'It's me, Johannes. Ilse. Your sister.'

Johannes's hand fell from the hilt of his hunter's knife, but his eyes remained narrowed.

'Don't ever wake me like that again. What do you want?'

'You can have your money, Johannes. But I have one condition.'

Johannes yawned. Then he smiled. 'I would expect nothing less, my *Gräfin*. Name your price.'

'I want to go with you.'

6

Payne couldn't sleep. Each time he closed his eyes he saw the young soldier's face emerging from the hole in the roof, waving cheerfully and then disappearing from view. By now, the boy's commanding officer would have written the letter home. Payne could imagine the mother, hair-scarf tied above her head, scrubbing at a washboard, nattering across the fence in the back garden about what she would do when her little Charlie came home.

He'd had men die before — three of the officers at Payne's station had been killed during the war — but this was different. Deaths in peacetime held meaning again. In some ways that was a thing good, he supposed. For six years, death had been a mere statistic. Now, when someone died, once again whole communities would grieve, whole countries. A murder would become front page news once more.

Payne sat in his pyjamas, feeding wood into the potbellied stove, a blanket wrapped around his shoulders, listening to the patter of rain outside. It was times like this, in the deep, lonely reaches of the night, that he was best able to think.

Colonel Bassett's emergency council had confirmed Payne's worst fears. Bluster and bullying was all very well in the barrack house, but it was fatal to a police investigation. With his checkpoints and house searches and random interrogations, Bassett was about as subtle as a drunken elephant.

There was no arguing with the man, though. He'd had two full companies of men mobilised. They were sweeping the woods and countryside around the murder house, knocking on doors, waking Germans, watching roads and generally making a nuisance of themselves everywhere within a five-mile radius of Eichenrode. Tomorrow, they would be rounding up German civilians in order to question them.

But that was beside the point. There was a killer on the loose, a man who killed to satisfy his own strange needs.

Payne considered what he knew of the killer's *modus operandi.*

He kept trophies: that was the key. Not just the mask, but the suitcases and clothes, too. But why had the victims been carrying full suitcases in the first place? That was crucial to understanding what had taken place in the murder house.

Payne thought about the Red Cross travel permits. The old woman in the house across the way had mentioned a lorry arriving and seeing people with suitcases. The victims must have been expecting to travel somewhere, somewhere beyond Europe most likely: that would explain why the killer was able to give them vaccination shots. The travel documents were the key, Payne realised. He needed to discover if Konrad Jaeger, a known war criminal, had also been travelling with Red Cross permits. And he needed to look into Suttpen's disappearance as well, to determine whether the man had bolted or been silenced.

Eventually Payne dozed in his chair. The sun woke him, creeping above the horizon, casting the bright, golden light that often follows a night of rain. A little after eight, a soldier knocked at the door with a message from Major Norris: Payne's new tyres had arrived, sent straight from Army HQ.

Miracles would never cease.

Payne borrowed a jack from the army unit billeted across the way and changed the tyres. Then he drove out to the Red Cross transit camp.

From a distance it looked a little like a military camp; up close, though, you started to notice the people were not soldiers.

Some sat listlessly by the roadside; others wandered in the shade beneath the trees. There were men, young and old, and women of all ages. Children played on the dust esplanade at the centre of the camp, kicking stones. Everyone was dressed in a curious motley of garments. Some wore suits and shirts and long coats, while others still wore the striped pyjamas that they had been issued in the concentration camp. White DDT powder leaked from trouser legs and shirt sleeves as they walked. A Belgian nurse attended him when he arrived at the camp gates and offered to show him around. Payne said nothing about the travel documents found at the murder house. He wanted to find out how the camp was run before revealing his hand.

'We've got all sorts here, Detective Inspector,' the nurse said. 'Armenians, Poles, Latvians, Lithuanians, Estonians, Yugoslavs, Greeks, Ukrainians, Czechoslovaks. The first thing we do when they arrive is to register them. Then we classify them according to their pre-war nationality and sort out whether they are able to return to their own countries. We also check them for signs of disease and malnourishment. Then we try to find information on missing relatives. It's all very complex and chaotic at the moment. I don't think humanity has ever had to try and sort out a mess on this sort of scale before.'

'What do you do after you register them?'

'We shower them, dust them down with DDT and try to get them some decent clothing.'

'What about travel permits? Who can get those?'

'That depends on each case. Many of these people were brought to Germany against their will and don't have any documentation. Others have only the identity papers given to them by the Nazis, which obviously no-one wants to use anymore.'

'But when are these travel permits issued?'

'We try to encourage people to stay put, simply to keep them off the roads. But obviously, people are looking for relatives, so when they've tried one camp, they head on to the next. And people of certain nationalities try to stay together. Certain camps get a reputation for having large populations of one ethnic group and then more of the same people arrive at them. They need some form of ID to get them past the checkpoints and across the new internal borders in Germany.'

They were in the centre of the camp now. Here were neat rows of marquee tents distributing food and outdoor showers. Nurses and volunteers stood behind trestle tables upon which sat steaming vats of porridge.

Payne paused as something caught his eye. Behind the tables, there was a pile of hessian sacks. Some bore the Red Cross symbol. Others had British Army markings. He walked closer and examined one of the sacks. It bore the markings of the Army depot in Eichenrode.

'Do you know a man called Suttpen?' Payne said. 'Jacob Suttpen? He's quartermaster sergeant here.'

'Yes, of course,' the nurse said. 'We get some of our supplies from him.'

Payne nodded. He'd found his link between Suttpen and the camp. He needed to find the quartermaster sergeant. He was certain the man was at the centre of this whole business.

'Could you show me where the travel permits are issued?'

'Of course. You can speak to Mr O'Donnell as well. He runs the camp.'

The admin office of the International Committee of the Red Cross was like Bedlam: there was no other way to describe it. Hundreds of people crowded the building and every one of them seemed to Payne to speak a different language. The whole spectrum of human emotion was visible within a few feet of the door: anger, despair, joy, apathy.

A man with a lilting southern Irish accent was in charge. He introduced himself as Mr O'Donnell, but any trace of affability disappeared when Payne said he was a British policeman.

'What is it you want exactly, Mr Payne?' he said, interrupting Payne's attempt to explain precisely that. *He made a point of calling me Mister, as well*, Payne thought. The man had been drinking, Payne was certain. As a teetotaller, the smell of spirits on another's breath always hit him like a slap in the face.

'I'd like to know how a person goes about obtaining a Red Cross travel permit.'

O'Donnell's lips pursed. 'It's a complicated process. But as you can see we are rigorous in checking each applicant before the documents are actually issued.'

Yes, Payne could see that. The chaotic line outside fed into perhaps half-a-dozen smaller lines inside the building. At the end of each one Red Cross personnel sat behind desks with translators whose function seemed to be to question the refugees and check that each person was actually a native speaker of the language they claimed as his or her own.

Payne had arranged for a list of the seven names found on the travel documents at the murder house to be sent to the camp. He asked O'Donnell about it.

The Irishman shook his head. 'We've no record of issuing travel permits to any of those people.'

'Are you sure?'

'Didn't you just hear me? I had one of my nurses look through the records, then I double-checked it myself personally. Those people were not issued travel permits at this camp.'

The Belgian nurse was still with them. At mention of the travel documents, she had looked away suddenly.

'And yet the permits exist,' Payne said, dividing his attention between O'Donnell and the nurse now. 'And they've got the official stamp. I've seen them myself.'

'What you have or haven't seen, Detective Inspector, is beside the point. There is no record of these people having passed through this camp.'

O'Donnell made it clear that he considered their business concluded and began walking away, but Payne was far from finished. He caught O'Donnell up in a couple of strides and kept pace beside him.

'Is it possible there could have been some mistake? Perhaps the documents were issued in another camp but stamped here? Or could you have lost the relevant records?'

'I have neither the time nor the inclination to explain the intricacies of Red Cross procedure to you, Mister Payne. There are millions of people currently without any form of valid documentation.'

'How would someone obtain them illicitly?'

O'Donnell stopped. His bloodshot eyes blazed. 'What the devil are you insinuating?'

'Is there a register?'

'Yes, there's a register, but I'm damned if I'll let you look at it.' O'Donnell's face flushed a yet deeper shade of carmine. 'I know all about the British police, Mr Payne. You and your fucking G-men and Black and Tans. They smashed some of my brother's teeth out. So if you think I'll tell you anything, you're wrong. As far as I'm concerned, you're not much better than the Nazis.'

With that, O'Donnell turned and stormed away, waving a hand in the air and shouting curses in Gaelic.

The nurse held Payne's eyes for a moment until O'Donnell turned and shouted for her to follow him.

She hurried away.

7

That day had turned into a nightmare for Captain James Booth.

During the morning, Colonel Bassett's patrols began to round up German civilians and bring them to a temporary interrogation facility that that wretch Freddy had set up. As there were only three fluent German speakers on the whole of the staff of the British Military Government in Eichenrode, most of the interrogators had to use German translators which, as far as Booth was concerned, defeated the whole object of the exercise. It was bad enough having to do it in the first place, without knowing the whole thing was a complete waste of time.

The more Booth thought about it, the stranger it seemed that Freddy would be such an enthusiastic adherent to this werewolf idea. A galumphing bully Freddy might be, but he wasn't stupid; yet by promoting the idea so forcefully Freddy had actually created an enormous amount of work for himself, something that he would normally have assiduously avoided.

Booth conducted more than a dozen interrogations during that morning. At lunchtime, he took a break and motioned for Tubbs to follow him out of the interrogation building.

'Have you had any luck finding that officer's name, yet, Tubbs? The one at Wolffslust?'

For a brief moment, Tubbs looked guilty. Then he shook his head.

Booth stepped closer and dropped his voice. 'What's going on, Tubbs? I just don't understand it. I can't help feeling you're dragging your feet on this one.'

Tubbs had a way of twisting his wedding ring when he became nervous or upset. He was doing it now.

'Come on, Tubbs, out with it. I know something's up. You should have found that information for me days ago.'

Tubbs sighed. Then he said, 'The truth is I've known all along who the officer was at Wolffslust. And actually, it was *officers*. There were two of us.'

It took Booth a moment to realise the implications of what Tubbs was saying. 'Do you mean to say you were there?'

Tubbs nodded. 'Freddy and I went into Eichenrode with the advance guard. I think Freddy wanted to make sure he got decent billets. When we reached the town some combat troops radioed in about the prison, so we went there to take charge of the situation.'

'You mean to say you had a hand in causing all that chaos?'

Tubbs shrugged. 'Most of the prisoners were already free when we arrived there. Anyway, the looting and vandalism were already going on.'

'Why didn't Freddy stop it?'

'I think the situation went to Freddy's head a little, especially when we found some of the Allied prisoners in the medical ward. They were terribly thin. Freddy went wild after that and ordered all the prisoners to be released. He even organised a little ceremony. He had the men of each nationality march through the prison gates singing their national anthem, led by a flag bearer: first the Russians, then the Dutch, the Belgians, the Poles and the French.'

Booth was thinking aloud now. It all suddenly made sense. 'And presumably that is why Freddy is so hell bent on convincing Colonel Bassett that we have a werewolf problem here? Because it's just possible that Freddy has released a bloody maniac?'

Tubbs shook his head. 'No, that isn't it. I don't think Freddy believes in your killer theory at all.'

'Then what on earth is the problem?'

The wedding ring was turned full circle. Tubbs's gaze returned to the floorboards. He seemed to be fighting some internal battle. When he sighed, it was a sigh of capitulation. He looked up.

'Freddy doesn't want attention focused on Wolffslust, because he shot two of the German guards.'

'What?'

'When we got to the prison, there were still two German guards locked in a room. Freddy stood by as the prisoners pelted the men with stones. Then he marched the guards round to the back of the prison and shot them both in the head. They're buried in the woods, somewhere close to the walls. That's why he fudged the report. He realised there might be consequences.'

'Why on earth didn't you say something before, Tubbs?'

Taylor looked towards the window. His eyes were wet with tears now.

'Do you know what Freddy and I found when we came into Eichenrode? The bodies of three young German boys, hanging from the trees on the main street, tongues poking out, blue in the face. They couldn't have been more than ten or eleven years old. They'd tried to contact the Allies and tell them the best way to enter the town to prevent any more killing, so the town commandant had them executed. The war was hours from ending and yet he still killed three children.

'I made a note of the bastard's name: Glasisch. He walked into captivity a few days later. I had to interrogate him. Do you know what he said to me? *Endlich ist mein Krieg vorbei.* At last, my war is over. He even tried to shake my hand.'

Tubbs stared at his right hand, turning it from side to side as if it were now forever sullied. Tubbs gave a great gulp and his voice became ragged. The tic in his eye trembled a few times, the way Booth had noticed it did when Tubbs was really upset.

'Why didn't you tell someone about Freddy?'

'Do you think I was going to dob Freddy in just because he shot a couple of Jerries? Do you know what I saw at Belsen when I first got there? The Germans deserve to be punished, Jimmy.'

Tubbs was going to say more, but stopped mid-word. He looked upwards and the light reflected the tears in his eyes. Then he began weeping. It happened so suddenly it took Booth a moment to react. He stood and put a hand on Tubbs's shoulder and the man seemed to unravel before his eyes.

'You're all done in, aren't you, old man? It's OK.' Booth fetched whisky and poured Tubbs a stiff measure. Tubbs drank it down before he got up and dried his eyes.

'I'm sorry,' he said. 'I shouldn't have told you that. About Freddy I mean. I'm going back to the interrogations, Jimmy. Do what you have to about Wolffslust. I just don't care anymore.'

'Tell me one thing, Tubbs. Where did Freddy find those travel permits? The ones at the murder house.'

'They were stitched inside the linings of the suitcases.'

Booth went back to his office. He wouldn't waste any more time on the interrogations. He knew what he would say to Freddy if the bastard tried to make any trouble.

He sighed as he considered what he should do about Tubbs's admission. If he went by the book he should report the matter straight away. But what if Tubbs withdrew his statement? He would be accusing a fellow officer of murder. That wasn't something you could do lightly. He would have to think it through.

A lorry rumbled past outside, bringing more German civilians in for questioning. Booth suddenly felt very tired. He was sick of the Army and everything that went with it. All he wanted now was to find a home for Piotr and then settle down in a quiet part of the English countryside with Ursula. Somerset, perhaps, or Gloucestershire.

At midday he went to the police station and told Detective Inspector Payne about the Red Cross permits.

'We need to find Jaeger's suitcases,' he said, when he'd listened to Booth's explanation.

'How would we do that?'

'Beagley, the sergeant who reported the finding of the first two bodies. We need to find him.'

'Can you be sure he has the suitcases?'

'Someone does, I'm certain of it. Jaeger and his woman had plenty of clothes with them and I'll wager they weren't carrying them in their arms.'

They found Sergeant Beagley standing by the door of a wooden barrack hut, supervising an entire company of men as they packed belongings and equipment into duffel bags and stripped bedding from bunks. Beagley rolled his eyes when he saw Payne.

'You've a damned nerve to come out here, copper. I've said everything I have to say to you.'

'That's enough in that tone of voice, sergeant,' Booth said, stepping into the barrack hut behind Payne. 'You're to answer Detective Inspector Payne's questions as if you were speaking to an officer. That's an order, sergeant. And stand to attention when you address us.'

Beagley gave Booth a grudging salute.

'Begging your pardon, sir, but my CO spoke with Colonel Bassett and he said I was to go to him if the Inspector came round bothering me.'

Payne stood his ground. Some policemen enjoyed the argy-bargy of police work, but Payne prided himself on getting what he wanted without ever raising voice or hand. 'I hear your unit is being taken back to England, sergeant.'

'Yes. So?'

Payne moved until he was standing shoulder to shoulder with the sergeant. Then he turned his head and said in a low voice, 'Because earlier in the week you lied to me, sergeant, and I mean to know why. You can either tell me now or you can do it when you're back in England. It's your choice, but I'll tell you one thing: as soon as you step off that gangplank in Dover, you *will* be on my turf. I'll have officers waiting for you at the port and they'll take you in for questioning as soon as you leave the ship. This is a major investigation now. What's it to be?'

Payne felt the man bristle. Then Beagley sighed in the deep, weary way people do when preparing to unburden themselves of a secret.

'What do you want to know?' he said.

'Why did you break into the house?'

'We went inside to see if there was anything we could nab. In case you hadn't noticed, the whole of Germany has become one vast Tom Tiddler's ground. Everyone else is going home with their pockets stuffed and yet me and my boys, we've always missed out — mainly because we were too busy fighting.'

'And I presume you found something?'

'Suitcases. There were two suitcases on the floor of the kitchen. They were nice ones, brown leather with big chunky locks. And filled with clothes.'

'So your men removed evidence from a crime scene?'

'They didn't know it was a crime scene. It was just another bombed-out house, like dozens they'd seen before. Most of these lads came into the forces as teenagers and they've had five solid years of war. If they've learned to grab what they can when they can, you can hardly blame them.'

'What did you do with the suitcases?'

'We cracked 'em open and started divvying up the clothing that was inside. Some of it was real nice stuff. Then someone went down into the cellar and … well, you know what we found down there.'

'Where are the suitcases now?' Payne said.

It took only a couple of minutes to locate the suitcases; Beagley had been planning to take them back to England with him.

Payne stood the larger of the two suitcases on a table, opened it and examined the silk lining. He saw that at the top right hand corner about four inches of the seam had been carefully unpicked and then re-stitched.

Payne used his penknife to cut the lining open, then turned the suitcase on one end and shook it. A Red Cross travel pass dropped out onto the floor.

'Bingo,' Booth said.

They checked the other suitcase. That, too, contained a travel permit, hidden within the lining of the suitcase.

Payne held the permits up to the light to examine better the passport-sized photos in each.

They were undoubtedly of Konrad Jaeger and the woman whose body had been found in the cellar of the house. Jaeger's travel pass identified him as Tomas Novak; his nationality was listed as Czechoslovakian. The woman was also described as Czech.

Payne handed the documents to Booth. 'We have our proof. We know now for certain that a man wanted for war crimes has somehow obtained a Red Cross travel pass that could have got him out of the country. I'll bet he had to pay handsomely to get it, too. We also know that Suttpen has links with the Red Cross camp. I think we really need to find out who requisitioned the murder house. I'm willing to bet that Lockwood and Suttpen had something to do with it.'

They drove to the offices of Housing Branch. The clerk was none too pleased to see Payne, but when he saw Booth's uniform his attitude changed. Booth told the man to find the boxes containing the relevant requisition chits. Booth and Payne sat down and began sorting through them.

'Here it is,' Booth said an hour later, handing Payne a file.

According to the file, the murder house was first requisitioned on May 5th 1945 by a combat unit of 30 Corps that had been moving in to occupy the area. That unit had left the house on May 14th. It had then been requisitioned for 'Army Stores' by Regimental Quartermaster Sergeant J. Suttpen on May 19th. The receipt stub was signed by Mr T. Lockwood.

That was the link between the two men, as Payne had suspected all along. He showed the file to the clerk and said, 'I need to see the details of all the houses requisitioned as army stores and signed for by Mr Lockwood.'

The clerk grumbled, but he did as Payne asked. When Payne offered to come back for the paperwork later, the clerk said, 'No, I want you to see how much bloody work it is trying to find this nonsense.'

It took him another hour to find the relevant documents.

There were four properties in total. Each one had been requisitioned as an 'army store' and each had been signed for by Suttpen and Lockwood.

Payne thought about what that meant: Suttpen had probably been paying Lockwood to requisition specific properties, he decided. Yes, that made sense. It explained why Lockwood had looked so panicky when Payne first mentioned the matter to him: Lockwood's name had been on the requisition receipts but he had no idea what was behind them. Did Suttpen? That was the burning question.

'I think this Lockwood chap was accepting bribes to keep certain properties aside,' Payne said. Booth nodded and looked away sharply, his face flushed.

'Do you know something that you think you should tell me, Captain Booth?'

Booth sighed. 'I don't really want to go into details, Inspector. But I can tell you that, yes, you are entirely correct in your supposition.'

Payne indicated the list of addresses. In that case, I think we should drive out to each of these properties and take a look at them.'

The requisitioned properties were all in secluded locations, well beyond the outskirts of the town. First on the list was the house by the Brunswick Road. The next two houses had been locked up. Payne pressed his hands to the windows at each of them, trying to see in.

'For storerooms, they look mighty empty inside,' he said.

Booth nodded. 'It's as I said before, Detective Inspector. The very idea of having army stores in such a secluded location — and unguarded — is ludicrous. I suppose Mr Lockwood had to put something down though, didn't he?'

The fourth property was the furthest from the town, an isolated two storey farmhouse hidden behind a copse of silver birch. A wooden placard was nailed to a tree at the end of the driveway. It said, 'DANGER, TYPHUS', in English, German, French and Polish. Similar messages had been daubed across the exterior walls of the house, and the windows and doors in the lower storey had been boarded shut.

'We must have made a mistake,' Booth said, indicating the signs. 'No-one's been here for weeks.'

Payne said nothing. He began checking the boards on the windows one by one, to see if any were loose, but they were all firmly nailed shut.

Booth was looking at the warnings daubed on the walls. 'That message about typhus could be genuine, you know.'

'I'm willing to take the risk and enter if it means we'll get some idea of where Suttpen has gone. He's the key to all of this,' Payne said, walking round to the back of the house. The windows and doors were boarded up here, too. Payne stood with his hands in his pockets, looking up at the second storey windows. They were free of boards but they were all fastened shut; the glass in all of the windows was intact.

Booth lit a cigarette. He was thinking aloud. 'As we know that Suttpen was able to get houses requisitioned on the sly, I suppose it's possible he might also have had entrées into other bureaucratic channels.'

'What do you mean?'

'I'm thinking about the travel documents we found in the suitcases. Supposing they are false, they would had to have come from somewhere, wouldn't they? Do you think Suttpen might have had something to do with it?'

'It's possible,' Payne said, as he completed his circuit of the house. 'It'll certainly be one of the first questions I ask him. I know he was supplying the Red Cross with army foodstuffs, which means he had a few favours to call in. And there's definitely a market for false travel documents. Mr Suttpen doesn't seem a man that would pass up on a good business opportunity.'

'But how does that tie in with these people being killed? Who would go to the trouble of obtaining these travel documents if they just wanted to kill the people for whom they were intended?'

Payne shrugged. 'I admit that part of the equation doesn't add up.'

They had reached the far side of the house now. The door here was boarded up. Then Payne saw other doors close to the ground.

He pulled the doors open, revealing a short metal chute leading down into darkness. The chute was black with coal dust but scuff marks were clearly visible on its surface. Payne knelt to examine it. It was wide and high enough for a man to slide down and a rope had been tied to the top of the chute. He thought about the first time he'd seen Suttpen and the black marks on the seat of his trousers. This must have been how he'd got in and out.

With only a brief moment's hesitation, Payne climbed inside the chute and slid down it.

He found himself inside a small, square chamber. Payne crossed the room, climbed the stairs on the far side of it and tried the handle on the door. It was not locked.

The door opened into the kitchen. Payne pushed it open a crack and looked inside. Gloomy daylight filtered through the boards on the windows. Payne sniffed the air. It was rank with the smell of death. He covered his mouth with his handkerchief.

'Lord, what's that smell?' Booth said when he also came down the chute but then relapsed into silence: he already knew the answer.

As they climbed the steps to the upper storey the low buzz of flies became audible, the smell stronger.

They found Suttpen on the floor of the front bedroom, lying at the centre of a huge pool of dried blood, his throat cut wide open. Payne shone his torch on Suttpen's face. The skin was marbled blue with decay.

'How long has he been dead?' Booth said.

'It's difficult to say. I'd guess at least a day.'

'Why was he killed?'

'That's the real question, isn't it? We know Lockwood procured these requisitioned properties and we know Suttpen was involved. Why did they want these houses in the first place? And for whom did they want them?'

Booth began searching the other rooms while Payne examined Suttpen's pockets. They were completely empty.

'Have you found something?' Payne called, when he heard Booth swearing in the other room.

'You'd better see this, Detective Inspector. Whatever the murderer's motive was,' he added, when Payne entered the bedroom, 'I think we can rule out robbery.'

Booth gestured towards a hole in the floor on the far side of the room where two of the boards had been prised up. Payne shone his torch at the hole. The light reflected on jewelled surfaces and brightly shining metals.

'Lord, look at this,' Booth said, kneeling beside the hole and holding up an ornate silver plate. 'This must have come from a church.'

They levered up a third floorboard and found rolls of canvas. The tattered edges suggested that they were paintings that had been torn from their frames. Booth unrolled one of the canvases and revealed a portrait of a nobleman in doublet and breastplate. 'This must be hundreds of years old. Where the hell did Suttpen get all of this stuff?'

'You told me Suttpen had been looting right across Germany.'

'Yes, but we've never came across anything like this before. Look at this stuff. This must have come from a cathedral or a museum,' Booth said, fishing out an ornate candle snuffer.

'It doesn't look German, either, does it?' Payne said, examining a square religious icon. Cyrillic lettering was imprinted in the silver lametta that covered its edges. There were more icons among the booty and an ornate Bible written in a language that he thought was probably Polish.

They took Suttpen's loot and loaded it into the boot of Payne's utility. Booth said he knew of a unit that was specifically charged with tracking down cultural items looted by the Nazis and returning them to their rightful owners. They would take care of any objects handed over to them.

They left Suttpen's body where it was. When they returned to the town Payne and Booth drove to the RAMC barracks and arranged for it to be collected by an ambulance.

'I don't think Suttpen did loot all that stuff,' Booth said as they drove back towards his billet. 'I think that stuff was looted by the Germans when they reached the east.'

Payne nodded. 'If Suttpen was involved in helping get war criminals out of Germany, the loot could have been part of his payment.'

'But why were these people killed?'

Payne shrugged. 'At least we have a good idea *how* they were killed. They had suitcases and travel documents. They clearly expected to go somewhere. However, at some point in the proceedings they were given a vaccination which contained a barbiturate. Then they were strangled.'

'Well, I've heard about these organisations that are supposedly helping Germans to escape the country. Ratlines, some of the chaps are calling them.'

'Except that if we're correct about this, it's not a ratline that's operating here,' Payne said. 'It's a rat trap.'

8

The first thing Johannes told Ilse to do was meet a man named Eugen. Johannes said he'd already contacted the man through a go-between, a young boy from the town, but that Ilse would have to take over negotiations for the travel permits now.

After she had agreed to do as he asked Ilse made Johannes leave the house and promise not to come back until evening. Piotr would be there soon and she couldn't risk his seeing Johannes. And she needed time to dig up the box.

When she told Johannes to leave he gave her that sardonic smile of his and picked up his gunney sack and sauntered out of the house and away across the fields towards the copse of trees that stood beside the stream.

When he had disappeared from view, she took the shovel and dug the metal box up. She carried it through to the kitchen table and removed from it the money and the jewellery. She took half the money and hid it inside one of the cracks in the wall. The other half she stuffed inside her knickers. Then she headed towards the town.

There were more checkpoints on the roads than usual. The Tommy soldiers were more suspicious than she'd experienced before: enough to make Ilse wonder what on earth was going on. She made sure she took her accustomed route into town, the way that she walked when she was going to the transit camp. The soldiers on the checkpoints knew her and once they'd looked at her papers they simply waved her through. As she walked along the road she saw lorries rumbling past filled with German prisoners.

Johannes said he had arranged to meet Eugen in the centre of the town at 10 o'clock. Ilse arrived fifteen minutes earlier and waited in the agreed place, hovering in the queue by the standpipe.

She recognised the man long before he sidled over to her. He was a small ferrety-looking fellow who was loitering in the shadows of a ruined building and observing the queue with sharp eyes. When their eyes met, the man nodded and walked around the perimeter of the square, twice. Finally, he walked towards the queue, passed close to Ilse and whispered, 'This way.'

Ilse followed him out of the square, through the ruins of a building and on to a café, one of the few in the town that was still open for business. Eugen led her to a booth at the back of the cafe.

She recognised him, Ilse realised when they sat down and she had the chance to look at him properly. His name wasn't Eugen. He was one of the doctors from the town that was collaborating with the Tommies. What was his real name? Seiler, that was it, Doctor Seiler.

Seiler sat with the fingers of his small hands folded into each other. As he spoke, his thumbs beat together. His attitude was all mock civility and regret but his eyes glittered greedily.

'How many are you?' he said.

'Two. Myself and a man.'

'And where do you want to go?'

'To Spain.'

Seiler hissed. 'That means travelling through France. You will not find many friends along that road. It is far safer to head south, through Bavaria and on into Austria and Italy. There are people along that route sympathetic to Germans. But the route you choose…' He hissed again and shook his head.

'Are you saying it is impossible?'

'No, of course not. Anything is possible. For the right price. Regrettably, though, there has been a change of circumstance since last I communicated with your friend,' he said. 'Just as the transport of certain goods requires greater precautions — and a corresponding increase in cost — the same is true of our little network. I'm afraid things have become very complicated in the last few days. The British are watching the roads. And for that we must ask more.'

'How much more?'

'The price will now be two thousand American dollars. Per person. Plus another thousand for sundry expenses.'

Ilse swallowed. Five thousand? That was more than half she had.

'And what does that price include?'

'Everything. Documentation. Road transport to within a few miles of the German border. Vaccinations.'

'Vaccinations?'

'If you plan to travel abroad it is advisable. Certain diseases long since controlled in Europe are still rampant in South America. Plus, given the current state of the world, infection is a constant danger. Look what happened after the Great War: the Spanish influenza ravaged the continent.'

'Five thousand dollars seems an exorbitant price.'

'Please understand that I am a mere go-between. It is an associate of mine that actually runs the network, so there is no point in trying to haggle with me. And if his price seems expensive, you are welcome to shop around.'

Seiler stood to leave. Ilse put a hand on his arm.

'Don't be hasty, sir,' she said, 'I was merely checking.'

Seiler smiled and sat back down.

'A wise decision, Fraülein.'

'When do we pay?'

'I want three thousand now. The other two thousand you will pay when my associate collects you.'

Ilse went into the toilet and counted the money out, then returned to their table and slid the money to Seiler under her hand. Seiler counted the money beneath the tabletop, folded the bills and popped them into his top pocket.

He said he could have the travel documents ready for the next evening but that he would need photographs. Johannes already had four passport-sized photos, but Ilse had used all hers when she'd had Ursula's documents changed. Seiler said he could get her some for one hundred dollars and told her to meet him that evening at a property on the outskirts of the town.

Ilse went home and sat beside the fire, watching the clock. At six, she left to meet Seiler again. She had thought about reburying the box, but decided simply to carry what remained of her stash with her. It was the only way she could be sure it was safe.

As she walked across the fields behind her house, she fancied she saw someone moving among the trees opposite. She called out Johannes's name, but there was no answer. It was so gloomy beneath the trees that she got nothing more than a glimpse, but nevertheless she drew her scarf tight around her head and hurried across the fields.

Seiler was waiting for her outside the house he had named, tapping his watch. He took her into an outhouse. A white sheet had been hung from the wall. A stool was placed before it and a box camera stood on a tripod. Seiler took the photos using an old camera and a magnesium flash, then hurried her back outside. The flash made dots swim before Ilse's eyes.

'What happens now?' she said.

Seiler handed her a piece of paper and a key. 'You must go to this address tomorrow evening. There is a door at the back of the house that leads into a cellar. Wait there. My associate will come to meet you, bringing your travel documents. He will also vaccinate you. Then he will drive you to your destination. You should pack a single suitcase each.'

It was dark when she began to walk home. The Tommies were patrolling the main roads with jeeps and lorries, so she took the back roads home, smoking a cigarette as she walked.

It was over. She was going. There was no alternative. She had already parted with more than half her money.

A twig cracked somewhere in the darkness. Ilse quickened her step, looking behind her as she walked through the gloom.

She didn't see the men until it was too late. They emerged from the trees and surrounded her before she'd even realised they were there, four of them, all raggedly dressed.

'Who are you? What do you want?' Ilse said in English, although she already knew the answer as the men grinned and fanned out around her. There was no mistaking the hungry malice in their eyes. They wanted her bag. Then they would beat her. After that, who knew what they might do?

Ilse moved backwards a few steps as the men advanced, seeking the moment to strike. She picked up a thick stick from the ground and waved it at one of them, but the man to her right side stepped forward and punched her hard on the side of the head. The blow sent her tumbling to the ground and made her ears ring.

All four of the men leapt forward, shouting in a foreign language. Ilse kicked out as one tried to pull the bag away from her and another began to paw at her legs. She felt a hand go up her skirt. One of the men laughed. Ilse could smell his foul breath.

She was now lying on the ground and still trying to keep hold of her bag when she saw a shadow sweep in from the right, coming silently and swiftly towards the men from behind.

Two of them fell in an instant as a blade rose, glinting in the moonlight. Then the shadow struck at the third man and there was a horrid cracking noise as the man fell back, screaming and gurgling. The fourth man tried to run as the sinister new presence turned and threw something. The man fell to the ground.

The clouds moved and Ilse saw that it was her brother pulling his hunter's knife from the man's back. The third man lay writhing on the ground, clutching at his face, sobbing and gurgling. Johannes Drechsler strode up to him, raised his boot and twice stamped the heel of it on the man's throat. There was a horrible silence.

'Get up,' he said, staring at Ilse, his expression unnaturally composed.

'Thank God you were following me,' said Ilse, panting.

'I wasn't following you. I was following our money. Now help me get this shit off the road,' Johannes said, grabbing the ankles of a corpse and dragging it towards the bushes.

Ilse and Johannes returned to the house. It was now completely dark. Ilse was trembling. Despite all those years of war and all those millions of deaths, she'd never before actually seen anyone killed.

Johannes took bread from the pantry and ate in silence. Afterwards, he lit a cigarette.

'What?' he sneered across the table when Ilse's gaze fell upon a red stain on the outside of the cigarette packet.

'Did you take that from one of the dead men?'

'They're fuck all use to him, now, aren't they?' Johannes said. Then he laughed mirthlessly. 'Why do you look so shocked, sister? What was it you thought I was doing all those years in the east? Learning to play the balalaika?'

'I know where you were sent to serve at the end of the war. You were in a penal battalion, weren't you? The Dirlewangers.'

Johannes mimed silent applause.

'They say your unit murdered civilians. Is it true?'

Johannes laughed. 'Murder? On the eastern front? You might as well ask a man tossed into the sea why he becomes wet. Murder, you say?' His laughter increased in volume.

'What was it you people thought your precious little Fuhrer wanted his troops to do in Russia?'

'What happened to you, Johannes?'

It was the wrong thing to say. His expression, already surly, became angry.

'What happened? You and your fucking husband happened. You filled my mind with all that Nazi shit. Do you remember? We were to be the first among nations, the chosen people. And little Adolf was to lead us there. I believed you. Do you hear me? I believed every fucking word about destiny and honour and the new order. I believed it all, right up until the war started to go wrong.'

His lip curled. 'Do you know how many good men I saw chewed up on the Russian front? And while our men froze to death for lack of winter clothes, the newspapers spoke of strategic retreats and well-fed pigs like your dear Rüdiger in his pristine party uniform urged us on to make the supreme sacrifice for the Fatherland. But what happened when the shelling came close? We, the *Frontkämpfer* in our shabby uniforms, bore the brunt of it, while the party men were running for their miserable lives. And then, when I dared to criticise the way the war was being fought and brought it to the attention of your dear husband, I was sent to a penal battalion.'

'What do you mean?'

Johannes's smile was back. 'It was Rüdiger who had me thrown out of the *Totenkopf* division. One of his SS chums was friends with my commanding officer. After that visit to the Warthegau, Rüdiger had him watching me. They got me on some trumped-up charge and threw me out. I had two choices: a concentration camp or the *Dirlewangers*. Do you know, in a funny sort of a way, I felt far more at home with them. At least they dispensed with all the moralistic bullshit, all the pageantry. You and Rüdiger would have loved some of my boys.'

'I don't know what you mean.'

'Don't you?' That hint of darkness within her brother flashed across Johannes's face and the effect was like deepening cloud on a showery day: the chill of it filled the kitchen. 'Without Nazis like *you*, Ilse, there would never have been Nazis like *me*. Remember that.'

'That's a lie.'

Johannes was working himself up to a crescendo now. 'Do you want to see what it was like? What the east was really like?'

He fumbled in his pocket, withdrew a crumpled photo, folded in half. Five soldiers were surrounding an old man, forcing him to kneel while they pinioned his hands behind his back. One of the soldiers had grasped a clump of the man's hair, pulling it upwards. Two of the others, grinning for the camera, held either end of a woodsman's saw, the teeth of the blade resting on the old man's neck.

'What you can't see is what the rest of the lads were doing to his wife,' Johannes said in a low voice. 'They made a real mess of her.'

Ilse stared at the photo. She began to tremble again. She pushed the photo away.

'Enough of this, Johannes. Please, I can't stand anymore.'

Johannes looked at her for a moment and began to laugh, pounding the table with the flat of his hand.

'Do you know what's so funny now, my *Gräfin*,' he said suddenly, and the humour fell from his face, quick as a slammed door. He stubbed a finger at the photo. 'That's *exactly* what that old bastard was saying when I took that photo.'

That night Johannes found the bottle of whisky. It happened before Ilse realised what was going on. One moment, Johannes was fumbling around in the pantry in search of more food; the next he was swigging from the neck of the bottle. The dark light in his eyes grew as he drank.

When he had finished the whisky, he rummaged in his gunny sack and withdrew a bottle of Korn, which he began swigging like a bottle of beer. Ilse tried to chide him for drinking like a brigand, but when he turned towards her his raw eyes were wet with tears and he did not seem to recognise her. She locked the door when she went to bed. She could hear Johannes fumbling and crashing around downstairs long into the night.

Next morning she found him lying fully clothed in the pantry, surrounded by broken glass. She sighed heavily, hands on hips. The floor was sprayed with vomit.

She sat in the kitchen, staring at the embers of the fire. Then she took out the piece of paper Seiler had given her containing the address. She recognised the name of the street: it was on the other side of the town, one of the country roads lined with farms and summer houses. She picked up the bottle of Korn and realised there was still some left. She went to pour herself a glass but put the bottle down when she noticed the bloodied fingerprints on the label.

God, how could she travel anywhere with her brother? It was like being locked in a cage with a wild animal. But she'd spent so much money, three thousand dollars. She was trapped with him, now. Her mind raced, weighing pros and cons as she played with the piece of paper. She would have to go with him as far as Spain. It was too dangerous to stay in Germany. She'd already been recognised once. It could happen again and perhaps the next time the person would want more than a simple apology. But it would be impossible for her to go to South America with Johannes. She wanted to get away from her brother as quickly as she could.

Groans sounded from the pantry as Johannes emerged, hair unkempt, eyes bloodshot. He walked straight to the table, picked up the bottle of Korn and sucked at it greedily. 'What's that?' he said, nodding towards the paper Ilse held.

She handed it to him as she said, 'Go outside and wash. You smell like a brewery. There's soap on the mantelpiece.'

Johannes said nothing. He chewed a piece of stale bread, his expression contemplative as he stared at the address. Then he slid the paper under the bottom of the bottle, took the soap and walked outside.

Ilse went upstairs to pack. From her bedroom window she could see Johannes on the far side of the yard. He pulled off his ragged tunic, revealing his broad chest and pale, grubby skin, but left his trousers and boots on. Thick tendrils of scar tissue ran across one breast; his shoulder bore the signs of old burn-marks.

Ilse watched as he soaped and lathered his upper body beneath the makeshift shower. As he lifted his arms and tilted his head back to let the water fall onto his face, she saw that he was smiling in the same way that he had sometimes smiled as a boy. From this distance it was almost possible to believe he was still the young man she had once known.

That photo of the men with the saw — it must have been a fake. He was kidding her. He'd always been such a liar when he was a boy. Yes, that was it. It was probably just one of his stupid jokes. Surely he couldn't really have done —

Ilse froze when she saw Johannes spin round and lower his arms slowly. The change in his attitude was so precipitate that it made Ilse catch her breath. Johannes resembled a hound catching scent of prey.

Ilse shivered as she followed his line of sight and saw Piotr standing nearby clutching a bundle of firewood, ready for his day's work, his mangled mouth trying to smile as he caught Johannes' eye.

She banged on the window but Johannes was already loping towards the trees, waving for the boy to come closer while the fingers of his other hand sought the handle of his hunting knife, tucked into the back of his trousers.

9

Detective Inspector Payne woke before dawn and put on his CCG uniform.

Booth had sent him a note the previous evening saying he had found where the policeman, Metzger, the man who had investigated the early *Flickschuster* murders, was being held. It read: *Former Eichenrode police chief held at Civilian Internment Camp 42. Inmates not regarded as serious security risk, so do not foresee any problems about you speaking to him (touch wood). Make sure you don't go in civvies, though. Colonel Bassett has made it clear he doesn't want you speaking to Germans, but I think you'll be OK as long as you flash your CCG papers and get in and out quickly.*

Civilian Internment Camp 42 was twenty miles outside the town. It consisted of four block houses made of brick and wood, surrounded by barbed wire. It was here that the men and women from the Eichenrode district who were suspected of being minor Nazis — bureaucrats, Hitler Youth leaders, Gestapo informants — were interned. The fence posts and barbed wire that surrounded the camp were the only items that looked new. Paint was peeling from the wooden walls; the windows of the blockhouses were cracked and dirty.

The soldier on the gate looked at Payne's ID and wandered away without saying anything. When he returned a few minutes later, accompanied by a rotund army officer, Payne thought the game was up. However, the man introduced himself as the camp commandant. He listened as Payne explained what he wanted, nodding occasionally.

'That shouldn't be a problem, Inspector,' he said, after examining the chit Booth had filled out for him. 'Step this way, I'll show you where Herr Metzger is.'

German men in civilian clothing stood in groups outside the block houses. As Payne and the commandant approached, they stopped talking and turned thin, nervous faces towards them.

'I hate the way they look at me,' the commandant said. 'They remind me of stray dogs. I never know whether to make them salute me or not.'

They stepped into the chill, gloomy interior of one of the blockhouses. Men stirred on banks of wooden bunks, then looked away. Some smoked; others merely stared at the roof. There were no bunks at the far end of the blockhouse, where the prisoners slept on straw palliasses.

'We don't actually have any facilities for interrogation here, Detective Inspector,' the commandant said. 'For all the heavy stuff, the prisoners get taken over to the larger facility.'

'It doesn't matter. I only want to speak to him.'

'He's down there at the end. I'll leave you to get on with it. Let me know if you need anything.'

The police chief, Metzger, was in his early fifties. He was sitting on the floor in his shirtsleeves, hair unkempt, pot-belly pressing against the front of his shirt. Payne greeted the man in German. Metzger's eyes flickered slightly, as if showing interest.

'What do you want of me?' he said.

Payne handed him the photos of the two bodies he had found in the cellar. Then he handed the man black and white shots of the body parts taken from the well. He let Metzger examine them. Then he said, 'Do you remember a killer called the *Flickschuster*?'

Metzger's eyes became guarded. He was clearly registering something, but didn't want to show his hand.

'I might do.'

'I need your help.'

Metzger gave a short, bitter laugh.

'You must think me a fool, Herr Detective Inspector. First, you take my gun and my badge. Then, you take my belt and boots and give me straw to sleep on and just two bowls of soup each day. You do everything you can to take my dignity from me. And yet you come here to ask my help? I suppose you're going to make me an offer, tell me you can get me released? Or get me reinstated in my job?'

Payne shook his head. 'No. I don't think you'll ever work at that again.'

Metzger was taken aback for a moment. Payne's honesty had unsettled him. 'Then why should I help you?'

'Because you were a policeman once and you helped hunt this man. People are dying. And if you ever took any pride in your uniform, you'll tell me what I need to know, so that I can catch this monster before he kills again.'

Metzger thought about this. Then he stood up.

'Let us take the air together, Detective Inspector. Tell me what you know.'

Payne told him everything. Metzger listened in quiet concentration. When Payne had finished, Metzger said, 'You are right to suspect that the Dutchman they executed had nothing to do with it.

'As you have seen from the newspapers, the first set of *Flickschuster* crimes was discovered in the autumn of 1942, in Brunswick. We found bodies in the cellar and more buried in the garden, and a bath tub filled with quicklime. I don't think they ever found out how many victims there were. Then other houses containing bodies were found. There was one in Regensburg. And another in Berlin.

'The more victims were discovered, the more the political pressure increased. I knew the arrest of the Dutchman was mistaken. The authorities had a way of rushing things through when they were trying to please their political masters.

'Anyway, there was a "trial", the Dutchman was found guilty and they guillotined him. Then they found the house in Würtemburg. For the first time, there was no official announcement of the crimes. We heard about them, though, through a Gestapo man who worked from our office. He just couldn't resist boasting whenever he knew something the rest of us didn't, especially when he had a few beers inside him.

'After that, there were more murders at Grafenwöhr, in Bavaria. That was in October '44. And others were uncovered at Münstereifel in Westphalia last December.'

'Why do you think they kept the subsequent killings secret? Was it to avoid embarrassment over the false arrest?'

Metzger drew closer and dropped his voice. 'Part of it might have been that. But I think it was mainly for a different reason. I think the authorities had realised by then that the killer was an SS man.'

'An SS man?'

'Think about it. How was it the killer was able to get access to so many houses? Well, a Kripo man I knew named Gohrum found out the answer. In each case, they were houses the SS authorities had confiscated from Jews. They were supposed to be given to the families of SS men or turned into offices, but someone had fudged the books and so they lay empty. And when the killer began using them, nobody dared ask who he was.

'But the real proof was when those bastards from the SS special court began sniffing around. That was when we knew it had to be something serious because it took a lot to get them to leave Berlin.'

'SS court?'

'It was a special tribunal that looked into crimes committed by SS personnel. Basically they could write their own rules. Dangerous bastards.'

Payne told Metzger about the Red Cross travel documents. 'Did you see anything like this during the *Flickschuster* case?'

Metzger smiled. 'That was the most interesting part. The killer was cunning. Do you know how the Gestapo became involved in this crime? They were investigating something else, what seemed like a totally separate incident at the time, a clandestine organisation that could supposedly help get enemies of the regime out of Europe: deserters, Jews, communists. They had managed to infiltrate this group with a Gestapo man posing as a Jew. But then the Gestapo man disappeared. Do you know where they found his body?'

'At one of the killer's houses?'

'Exactly. He had an unusual birthmark on his chest, so they knew it was him. Plus they found his clothes and wedding ring and ID papers in the attic. And that was when the authorities realised what was really happening. The killer was like a spider and the false escape network was his web. These people went to the killer expecting to escape Germany. Instead they were murdered. And, of course, when they disappeared, no-one was looking for them as they were *supposed* to disappear. It was a fiendishly inventive plot.'

Metzger had been going to say more when the camp commandant appeared, looking perturbed.

'I say, Detective Inspector, I've just been on the phone to HQ and they don't know anything about this interrogation of yours. I'm afraid I'll have to ask you to leave.'

There was no point in arguing. Payne walked back to his car, thinking about the suitcases in the attic, the travel documents. Christ, it had all happened before.

He stopped by his car and looked at his notes. Those names, Grafenwöhr and Münstereifel, he'd heard them before, too.

He searched through his notebook. When he came to one particular page, he ran back towards the camp and knocked on the door to the guardhouse.

'Can I borrow that?' Payne said, pointing at the telephone. 'It's important.'

10

Captain Booth woke an hour before dawn and made himself a thermos of hot, strong tea. Then he went to the building where the boxes of documents he had found in the cellar of Wolfflust prison were stored. He pulled a desk and chair close to the stove, sat down and poured himself a cup of tea. Then he opened the first box, withdrew the pile of papers from within it and set to work. Somewhere among the files, documents and transcripts of conversations was the killer's identity, Booth was sure of it.

He worked for three hours before he realised the task he had set himself was near impossible. Nearly fifty SS men had gone through Doctor Wiegand's programme between 1941 and the end of the war, and each patient's case had produced hundreds of pieces of paper.

He looked at the piles of cardboard boxes. He needed to find some way of narrowing the parameters of the search. He and Payne had discussed the possibilities the day before. Because of the dates of the *Flickschuster* crimes, they could be fairly certain that their man had not entered Wiegand's programme until mid-1944 at the very earliest. That still didn't help very much, as some of the patient records were fragmentary and others lacked dates.

Booth spent the morning trying to put some order to the mass of notes. At lunchtime, Payne phoned and told Booth what the German police chief had said.

'The killer used the lure of a false escape network to reel his victims in. I think he's doing the same here. And it definitely wasn't the Dutchman,' Payne said. 'There were more

Flickschuster crimes committed after the Dutchman was caught and executed.'

'When and where were these other crimes committed?'

Payne opened his notebook. 'In Würtemburg. And then in Grafenwöhr in Bavaria. That was in October '44. And Münstereifel in Westphalia, in December. Do you recognise those names, Captain?'

Booth tapped his pencil against his teeth. He did recognise the names but he couldn't remember from where.

'It was Operation Greif,' Payne said. 'The men of the SS unit trained in Grafenwöhr during the autumn of 1944. Then they began operations out of Münstereifel in December. That's what Toth meant when he said Greif was of special significance. Our man was part of Operation Greif. That was how they found him. The fact he had murdered in those places meant they could pin him down to specific areas at specific times. He'd created a trail they could follow: the murders coincided with his movements as part of Operation Greif. And that means our man might not have entered the programme until January 1945.'

Booth was nodding. 'If you're right, it means something else. It means our man can speak English. He may even be fluent.'

'Yes. That was what Toth meant about him being especially dangerous. He can blend in. But that might be to our advantage. If he is fluent, he must have some link to an English speaking country. Keep looking through the files. I am going to follow up on the travel documents. I need to speak to one of the nurses from the Red Cross camp. I think she knows something about O'Donnell.'

Booth set to work again, searching through the paperwork. Hours passed. Outside, it began to rain. Army lorries rolled past, their tyres spattering mud against the windows of the building. At three, hunger got the better of him, so he stopped for an hour and went in search of lunch.

He had to force himself to go back to the paperwork. His eyes were hurting from sifting through type-written documents all day.

He sat down, opened up a new box and lit a cigarette … and there it was, the information he had spent all day hoping he would find.

Patient 43. His parents were Germans but he had been born in South Africa, where he had learned English and Afrikaans. *Christ, this is him*, Booth thought as he read through the details and saw the date Patient 43 had entered the programme: January 22nd, 1945.

Booth put all the other paperwork aside and concentrated on the details of Patient 43.

Twenty minutes later, Booth had telephoned the archivist at Corps HQ. 'Killy? I need you to pull the *RuSha* files on a man named *Scharführer* Otto Flense. Joined the SS early 1936. Served as a medical orderly with the Order Police in Poland and Russia, attached to the 14th Army as part Einsatzgruppen I. Can you check if you have his personnel files? Would you mind dropping whatever it is you're working on and doing it right now? I'll take the flak.'

Booth put the phone down. His hands were shaking as he reread Doctor Wiegand's notes on Patient 43, this man named Otto Flense.

A variety of visual stimuli were shown to the patient. He experienced severe reactions to film reels A, B, D, E and F. He proved indifferent to reels C and G.

Patient 43's pathology is founded upon the tangle of contradictions that form the very centre of his being. He considers himself a witty, sophisticated and intelligent man, but his conversation is actually dull and repetitive. There is no more substance to his personality than there is to the wooden hoardings on a film set. The epicentre of his being is a monstrous and overwhelming selfishness, if that word can be applied to a patient whose psyche understands only the concept of self; beyond that, there is only vacuum. He is torn between an infantile self-absorption and a deep-seated loathing of his own mediocrity. Just as the coprophile is drawn to his or her own feculence, patient 43 seems obsessed by the evil within himself.

He values others only in as much as he can dominate and use them. Many aspects of the patient's case are typical: the restrictive, religious father, the doting, permissive mother; the adolescent patterns of petty crime and cruelty to animals. Indeed, his first description of the sensation of 'empowerment' associated with his crimes comes from his killing of cats and dogs as an adolescent, although, interestingly, his experiments with burning and hanging the animals were discontinued as 'they squawked too much'.

The unusual post-mortem treatment of his victim is, I feel, fully explained by his father's working as a mortician. Patient 43 grew up in an environment where death was a commonplace and, crucially, divorced from any sense of tragedy or pain. The patient described first helping his father with the dressing of corpses at the age of ten but was not allowed to speak with the relatives of the deceased until well into adolescence.

Interestingly, it is this familiarity with death which seems to be the fulcrum upon which his pathology rests, as the trauma of his experiences on the east front, particularly the liquidations en masse of Jews as part of Einsatzgruppen I, are paramount in understanding the deviant reasoning behind his crimes. The unrestrained displays of suffering he witnessed there seem to have clashed violently with his preconceptions of death; indeed, to have shattered them utterly.

In conversations with me, he has described the eastern front killings as 'crude and brutish' and seems to regard them as having offended his aesthetic sensibilities. He talks of making his victims 'perfect' through his ritual and reserves the highest praise for the 'silent and painless' way in which he dispatches his victims. However, again we see the contradictions at the root of this case, as Patient 43 admits to having killed a number of times long before he was sent to the eastern front and has also proved to be a savage and opportunistic predator, quite capable of acts of extreme violence should he feel his secret to be threatened. He is a —

Booth jumped when the phone rang. His hand trembled as he reached for the receiver.

'You're in luck,' Killy said. 'I've got him here. Otto Flense, born 1906. Ugly-looking brute.'

'Killy, take the whole file, put it in a briefcase and get the first dispatch rider you can find to bring it to me right now. I can't stress how important this is.'

The file arrived an hour later, the soldier on his motorcycle skidding to a halt outside Booth's billet.

Booth opened the file and removed the single photo inside, a head and shoulders photo of Flense in SS uniform, staring into the camera.

Killy was right: Flense was an ugly bugger. His nose was big and bulbous, his eyes small, crafty and cruel. His fair hair was shaved into a severe line just below the crown of his head. Booth had hoped that he might recognise the man, but he was disappointed. Flense looked like a hundred other SS men.

And yet…

There *was* something. Booth angled the photo towards the light. Was it his imagination or was there something familiar about the man's face, the arrogant set of his jaw-line? Had he seen the man before?

He was still examining the photo when a knock sounded at the door and Sergeant Hoyle's face appeared, pale with worry.

'What is it, sergeant?'

'There's a bit of a problem at the interrogation centre, sir.'

'Problem? What sort of a problem?'

'With Captain Fredrickson, sir. I think you'd better get over there right away.'

Booth jogged from his jeep to the building where the makeshift interrogation centre had been set up and followed Hoyle towards the steps that led to the cellar. As they descended them, Booth noticed a smear of blood on one of the steps.

There was more inside the door, a trail of red droplets that led along the corridor and towards a room at the back of the cellar. Booth heard shouts coming from the room. He hastened towards the door and flung it open.

Freddy was standing with his back to the door, bellowing at a youth who was sitting on a chair.

'What the devil's going on, Captain Fredrickson?'

Freddy turned. His face was red and sweat covered his forehead. 'Oh, it's you, Booth.'

'Yes, it is me. Now answer my damned question. What are you doing?'

'This little shit,' Freddy said, twisting the boy's head round to face Booth, 'is the root of our werewolf problem. A patrol picked him up last night. He was trying to cut some telephone lines. Got him bang to rights. He had wire cutters, pliers and a knife on him.' Freddy gestured towards the tools and weapon which lay on a table beside him.

'What's his name?' Booth said.

'Putzi.'

'Do we have anything on him?'

'He was a student at the Napola Academy close to here. And that's enough for me.'

Booth wasn't listening. He was looking at the boy's bruised and bloodied face. 'Have you struck him, Captain Fredrickson?'

Freddy snorted. 'I might have tapped the little bastard a couple of times, just to keep him on his toes. But there's no permanent damage, I've made sure of that. I want him to be awake when they shoot him.'

Booth motioned to Hoyle to leave the room. Then he said, 'Christ, Freddy, how much longer are you going to continue with this charade?'

Freddy flexed his fists. 'Charade? What the devil are talking about?'

'This. The boy. The interrogations. I know why you're doing it. I know what happened at Wolffslust. About the German guards.'

'What about the German guards?'

'You killed two of them.'

Freddy's eyes narrowed. 'You've been chatting with that weasel, Tubbs, haven't you? That's absolute rot about the guards. You want to get your facts straight before you make accusations like that, Captain. As it is, you're for the high jump anyway when Colonel Bassett finds out what this chap has told me,' Freddy said, gesturing towards the boy slumped on the chair.

'And what's that?'

'This one is just the tip of the iceberg. He's got a Waffen SS accomplice hiding out in the woods, something you would have been aware of if you hadn't been chasing your tail with nonsense about murderers. That's why I'm trying to sweat some answers out of the little swine.'

'How could you possibly know he has a Waffen SS accomplice?'

'Two days ago a local woman, a friend of young Putzi's mother, came here to denounce a known Nazi, someone she recognised from before the war. Apparently, she saw young Putzi acting suspiciously in town and decided to follow him, whereupon said woman saw Putzi speaking to this SS fellow.'

'And how did she know he was SS?'

'Because she got a damned good look at the bugger and she recognised him as a local man. That's his *RuSha* file over there. Ex-Waffen SS. And wanted for about every war crime you can possibly imagine. But do you know the really interesting bit? This SS bastard is planning on getting himself some false travel documents.'

'How?'

'That's what I'm trying to get out of our friend here. He spoke to someone in the town about it. Apparently this SS fellow is going to have to pay 2,000 dollars for his documents. But little Putzi won't tell us who the contact is.'

'How can you be so certain this woman recognised the man?'

'Oh, if you'd seen the hatred in her eyes when she said his name, you'd have had no doubt. It seems this fellow ran the local Hitler Youth before the war. The woman claims this Drechsler fellow blinded her son. Beat him with a horsewhip.'

But Booth wasn't listening. A local man named Drechsler?

He walked across the room, opened the SS man's file and withdrew the photos within.

The bottom fell from his world.

11

For the second time in a week, Ilse found herself digging a grave in the garden. She cried as she dug. The tears welled up suddenly from somewhere deep within her and she could no more stop them than she could have stopped water seeping from a leaking pail.

She had been too late to stop Johannes. It had taken her all of twenty seconds to get outside and into the garden, screaming Johannes's name as she went, but by the time she could run to the spot where she had seen Piotr emerge from the trees, Johannes was already walking back from the woods, wiping the blood from his knife blade with a leaf.

Ilse had rushed past him, hands trembling. Piotr lay where he'd fallen, face up, his hare lip splayed. Blood welled from a horizontal slit in his chest just above his heart.

That was for whom she was digging the grave. The blisters on her hands bled as she scratched at the earth with the shovel, but she paid no mind to the pain.

She stopped as she sensed her brother behind her.

Johannes nodded towards the grave. 'That hole's nowhere near deep enough, you know,' he said, as Ilse grasped Piotr's ankles and dragged him towards the narrow trench.

'Leave me alone, Johannes. Go back to the house. Or go to hell, for all I care. But leave me be. I've had enough of you.'

Johannes came close and stood in front of her. 'Are you crying, sister?' he said, mumbling through a mouthful of apple. 'Whatever for? Those tears can't possibly be for that, can they?' he said, gesturing towards Piotr's corpse. 'A filthy Polack. And a diseased one, too. What was that phrase Rüdiger always used? You know, when he was pontificating from the end of the dinner table. *Untermensch*. That was it. God, I can see him now, waving that huge cigar around and patting his fat belly.'

'Why did you kill him? He meant no harm.'

'He saw my tattoo.' Still bare-chested, Johannes raised his left arm and pointed to the small gothic letters tattooed on the underside of his arm. 'I saw his eyes. He knew what it was. They are hunting Germans with these tattoos.'

'You had no right to kill him.'

'No right?' Johannes laughed. 'If you'd ever bothered to take a walk down to your husband's fucking mine, you would have seen a dozen corpses like that every day, I promise you that. But you didn't, did you, Ilse? You stayed in your house and pretended the world was still a fresh and innocent place.' Johannes spat on the floor and his eyes dripped with contempt. 'Take a good look at the boy's body, Ilse. That's your fucking *Lebensraum* right there.'

He waited for Ilse to respond. When she said nothing, he tossed his apple core into Piotr's grave and went.

Ilse did the best she could with the grave, but it was a poor effort. It was obvious to anyone what the rectangle of freshly dug earth represented. And Johannes was right. It wasn't deep enough. She was hampered by the blisters on her hands.

She didn't go back inside the house afterwards. She sat beside the grave and dried her tears while she considered her predicament.

Her brother was mad. She believed the worst now. That photo of him with the saw, it wasn't a fake. The money didn't matter anymore, Ilse decided. She would take her chances in Germany.

She sat there in the garden for the rest of the day. When the sun began to set, Johannes came outside.

'You need to get ready.'

'I'm not going.'

'What?'

'I don't want to go anywhere with you, Johannes.'

Johannes took a step forward. His scarred hand grasped her arm. The pain made Ilse cry out.

'The travel documents are for a husband and wife, so you have got to come. You're coming as far as the Spanish border, at least. After that, you can do whatever the fuck you want.'

'I won't go. Do you hear? I won't —'

Johannes struck her across the face, knocking her to the ground. A second later, she felt the blade of Johannes's knife pressing into her throat.

'You are coming, Ilse. If you don't, I will kill you.'

Ilse said nothing. One look at Johanne's eyes and she knew he was in deadly earnest.

He stood over her as she packed her belongings, his knife tucked into his belt again, but with his fingers resting on the handle.

They left an hour after sundown. When Ilse went to lock the door of the farmhouse, Johannes began laughing.

'Even if you were to come back here, what is there inside to steal? Leave it open,' he said when she continued to work the key inside the stiff lock.

She left it open in the end. She didn't want to arouse his suspicion. She had already decided how she would get away from him. She would claim she needed to pee, then she would run away into the darkness and hide herself. She would wait until it was daylight and make her way back to the house. Johannes would not be able to hang around for long.

When they set off, Johannes insisted she walked in front. He was using her as bait, she realised. If there were attackers lurking in the darkness, Ilse would meet them first. And then Johannes would deal with them.

They crossed the silent fields and woodland paths, with only the silvery light of the moon to guide them. That didn't matter. They both knew these tracks.

When they arrived at the address, Ilse withdrew the key Doctor Seiler had given them.

'No,' Johannes said, looking around him at the darkness, his scarred hand wrapped around the hilt of his knife. 'We will wait outside, sister.'

'We were told to wait in the cellar.'

'And leave myself trapped? Do you think me so stupid?' Johannes took her by the arm and pulled her towards the bushes.

12

It was mid-afternoon when Payne drove out to the townhouse where the Red Cross nurses were billeted. He had to ask directions of soldiers a couple of times and they gave him sly grins when they heard his destination.

When he arrived, he asked to speak to the Belgian nurse. The women on the porch frowned, but when Payne said he was a policeman one of them went inside and returned a few minutes later with the Belgian woman, who was wearing a man's dressing gown and towelling her wet hair. When she saw Payne, she smiled at her workmates to show them it was fine and drew Payne away towards his car. She seemed to suspect why he was there.

'The other day, at the camp, when I spoke to O'Donnell about the travel permits,' Payne said. 'Was he telling me the truth? It's important.'

The nurse looked over her shoulder before answering. She shook her head.

'Not all the documents are properly processed. There is a man, a German man. He has come to Mr O'Donnell three times now. Each time O'Donnell has had the documents drawn up but there has been no record made of them. He does everything in private. I only came across him doing it one night when I was looking for something in his office.'

'Did you not think it suspicious?'

'I assumed it was only people bribing their way to the head of the queue. There's normally quite a wait for travel permits. You don't think these people have done anything wrong, do you?'

'And who is this German man?'

'The doctor, Seiler I think his name is. He was at the camp today and I saw O'Donnell give him something.'

'That happened today?'

She nodded.

Payne thanked the nurse before he ran back to his car to drive to the Red Cross camp. It was dark now and the camp was preparing itself for bed. The light was still on in O'Donnell's office. Payne knocked before he pushed the door open. O'Donnell's face fell when he saw who his visitor was.

'What the hell do you want?'

'On my last visit I asked whether you ran background checks on everyone to whom you issue travel documents. I want to ask you that question again.'

O'Donnell folded his arms. 'You've obviously heard something or other, Detective Inspector. So out with it.'

Payne pulled the photo of Konrad Jaeger from his pocket. 'Do you remember doing the documents for this fellow? He's wanted for war crimes. And you helped secure him the documents. Now, you may be right if you say that I have no jurisdiction here. But I'm sure the lawyers working down in Nuremburg will be interested when I tell them a Red Cross official is helping war criminals to escape. And they *do* have jurisdiction.'

'That's a lie.' O'Donnell spoke with genuine anger but there was a trace of uncertainty to his bluster now. He kept licking his lips and blinking.

'When did you last do travel documents for Seiler? Come on, man. People could die.'

O'Donnell bit his lip. 'Today.'

'Did you give them to Seiler?'

He nodded his head. 'He brought me the photos yesterday. But he told me they were for a man and woman that needed medical treatment abroad. He's the one that's been helping war criminals, not me. You remember that.'

'And where did Suttpen fit into all of this?'

'He supplied the houses. These people needed places to meet and sort out their business.'

Payne drove to the *Rathaus* and found out where Seiler lived. When he pulled up outside the townhouse, he saw the earth in front of the building had been churned by deep tyre tracks, as if a heavy vehicle had driven across it recently.

He jumped out of his utility and rushed up the steps. He knocked on the door, but there was no answer, although lights blazed within the house.

He knocked again then kicked at the lock of the door. On his fourth try, the wood around the lock splintered and the door opened.

Seiler lay on the floor of the living room in a pool of blood, his throat slit from ear to ear. Payne stepped around the mess of blood. The daughter lay dead in the kitchen. Her throat was cut, too.

The killer was tidying up all the loose ends. He was preparing to move on. Payne had to catch him now. Payne knew he would be using one of the houses Suttpen and Lockwood had secured for the man. He would drive to each in turn until he found which one.

Payne ran back to his car.

13

Booth was in his jeep, driving out of town. His face felt numb, but it had nothing to do with the wind that was driving against it.

He knew the truth now: Ursula wasn't who she'd said she was. He muttered her real name as he drove towards the house: Ilse Hoffman.

He'd known something was wrong as soon as he saw the photograph inside the file on the SS man Freddy was hunting, that Johannes Drechsler. The black-and-white image that stared up from the page was the spitting image of Ursu … of this Ilse bitch. The queasy feeling of dread growing in the pit of Booth's stomach had increased when he read details of Drechsler's service record. He'd been in the 3rd SS Division, the *Totenkopf*, one of the Waffen-SS's elite units. And then his career had been crushed by disciplinary problems. One moment he'd been the top of the pile. The next he was transferred to the SS-Sturmbrigade 'Dirlewanger'.

Dirlewanger.

For a split second Booth had wondered why the name was so familiar. Then he remembered Ilse asking him about them, in the kitchen, the day he'd taken Piotr to the house.

It was the account of Drechsler's service in the Dirlewangers that occupied most of the document. Drechsler's unit had machine-gunned women and children. They had locked civilians in barns and burned them alive. Throats had been slit, heads crushed, limbs lopped off. They had been pitiless rapists. The Poles had found dozens of mass graves amid the ruins of

Warsaw in the sector where the Dirlewangers had been operative.

A separate file contained details of Drechsler's Nazi affiliations and his family connections. His brother-in-law, Rüdiger Hoffman, had been a known Nazi and 'coordinator' of a mine in conquered Polish territory. He had married Drechsler's sister.

That was when Booth had realised there were more photos beneath the documents. With a trembling hand, Booth had pulled out a photo of Ilse Hoffman, dressed in furs, gripping the arm of her husband on the stairs of some huge building against a spot-lit background of swastika banners. She stared directly at the camera, hips angled to display the curves of her body to best effect. She was instantly recognisable but utterly alien at the same time: her eyes had a dark shine to them; her face was a mask of hauteur.

That was why Booth was driving out to her house now, the house of lies. His anger was cold and hard; he focused on it alone.

As the jeep advanced through the darkness, Booth considered how he would greet her, this changeling bitch. First of all he had thought he would strike her in the face, but he decided against that. That would be what a Nazi would do. There was no reason to behave so brutally. He would look her in the face and spit in her eye. He would let her see the contempt he felt for her. Then he would arrest her.

He drove his jeep right up to the house, beeping the horn. In the trees, two wild dogs were worrying at something on the ground. They growled when Booth got out of the car. Booth shouted at them, feeling suddenly furious. He kicked the kitchen door, expecting it to be locked, but it flew open.

He realised why when he examined the interior of the house. Everything was gone. All the food. All her clothes. The two battered suitcases.

The bitch had done a runner.

Then he noticed the boot marks on the flagstones, the muddy prints that belonged to a man's feet. The brother. It had to be. But where would they go? They would never get past the roadblocks, the patrols.

Then he noticed the bottle of Korn on the table and the sheet of paper beneath it. He looked at the address written on it in pencil. He saw that it belonged to a rural property. Perhaps they had journeyed across country. That meant there was still time to catch them.

When Booth went back outside he noticed the dogs were fighting. He jumped into his jeep and turned on the headlights.

And stopped.

The beams of light had revealed a pale shape protruding from the ground. That seemed to be what the dogs were fighting over.

Booth took a flashlight and walked towards the two animals.

One of them fled. The other, the larger one, stood its ground. It growled at Booth as he approached and stared at him with feral eyes. Booth made calming noises but the dog's stance did not change. It lowered its head, teeth bared.

But Booth hardly noticed now. He was staring at the thin pale arm the dog had been gnawing, the bulge of freshly-dug earth. Someone was buried here. The animals had gnawed the flesh from the fingers.

Booth unbuttoned the pouch that held his sidearm and shot the animal in the face. The sound sent birds flapping from the tops of the trees.

Booth scraped away the earth. His fingers increased in speed when he saw the face that was emerging, saw how the dark earth had filled the mouth and now revealed the huge black rent in the centre of the corpse's features, just below the nose.

Captain Booth realised that he was staring down at Piotr.

He screamed and fell to his knees.

It took Booth ten minutes to recover. He considered digging up Piotr's body to rescue it from further indignities, but he realised he didn't have time. He wanted to find Ilse Hoffman. She had killed Piotr and left him as carrion for wild animals. He would give Piotr the burial he deserved later on. At the moment he needed to ensure that justice was done.

The first thing he did was walk to the edge of the wood where the other dog still lurked and shot it. Now there were two animal corpses for any new predators to chew on.

Then he drove out to the road and headed towards the address he'd seen on the paper.

14

Ilse and Johannes were crouching in the bushes opposite the house, waiting, until they saw the vehicle arrive. The lorry's headlights formed twin pools of white light as they swept across the front of the building.

The driver jumped out of his cab and Ilse realised she knew him. It was that wretched driver from the Red Cross camp, Joost. So he was in on it. Yes, that made sense. He knew all the Tommies that guarded the road. They were used to him rumbling back and forth picking up supplies and taking people from one transit camp to the next. What could be more natural than for him to offer a couple heading in the same direction a lift?

Joost went inside the house. Johannes waited for at least five minutes, anxiously peering into the darkness. Once Ilse fancied she saw someone else moving amid the trees. Then Johannes dragged her to her feet and pushed her towards the cellar door.

Joost turned when they pushed the door open. He looked at them from behind his glasses in that curious way he had of looking at people, almost as if he saw straight through them. He didn't smile. He licked his dry lips twice and nodded towards the Red Cross travel permits on the table. Johannes scooped his up and tucked it deep within his tunic. Ilse put hers in the bodice of her dress.

Joost was unwrapping a leather pouch from which he extracted glass vials and some hypodermic syringes.

'What the hell do you think you're doing?' Johannes said.

'Don't you want your vaccinations?' Joost said, and for the first time Ilse realised his German was perfect. He spoke with a slight accent, was from Hamburg, maybe. He was no more South African than she was, she realised.

'Vaccinations?' Johannes said.

'I believe Doctor Seiler mentioned them to your companion. You are travelling to South America. Doctor Seiler told me to give you shots for Hepatitis, Diphtheria, Typhoid, Tuberculosis and Rabies. It would be a shame to have survived so terrible a war only to fall victim to a fatal and yet easily preventable disease. And you have paid a great deal of money for them.'

Johannes shook his head irritably and began to roll his sleeve up. 'Who are you to be administering vaccinations?' he said. 'Are you a doctor, too?'

'Something like that.'

The light swung from the ceiling, glinting in the glass of the bottle.

15

When Silas Payne drew up in front of the house and saw the Red Cross lorry outside he knew he'd found the right property. Pale light shone from around the edges of the cellar door.

He parked and began to creep towards the door. He wanted to find some window, some vantage point where —

A figure moved out of the darkness. Payne jumped before he saw that it was Captain Booth. His face seemed different somehow, lit as it was from below by the orange light of his cigarette.

'He's inside. The man you are looking for. Your killer. His victims are with him,' Booth said, with a curious lack of inflection in his tone.

'What the hell are you doing out here, then?'

'Because I want the people inside to die. I know who they are. I know the killer's name, by the way. It's Otto Flense. I stood over there in the trees and watched his victims go down the steps there with him. He's probably wrapping his ligature round their necks right now.'

Payne began to walk towards the cellar door.

Booth stepped into his way, blocking his path.

'What are you doing? Let me pass.'

'Isn't that what you want? Justice. Then let the bastard alone. Those people in there deserve to die.'

'That's not your decision to make, damn you.'

Payne moved forward. Booth fumbled the sidearm from his holster and pointed it at the policeman.

Payne stood very still, watching Booth, seeking eye contact.

'You don't want to do this, Captain Booth.'

The barrel of the pistol trembled.

'They have killed my friend. So what better way to repay them than to let that psychopath have his way with them? We're going to stand out here and let Flense finish. Then you can arrest him.'

'Captain Booth, I am not going to stand aside and allow these people to be murdered, even if they are murderers themselves. So you're going to have to shoot me or get out of my way.'

Payne took one measured step forward, then another. Booth hesitated. The pistol barrel trembled.

'Stay where you are, Payne.'

'No.'

Payne took another step forward and Booth cried out, 'Damn you!', lowered the pistol and threw himself at Payne, trying to push him back.

The two men struggled and then the pistol suddenly bucked in Booth's hand and Payne's ears rang and he fell back onto his buttocks.

Silas Payne groaned and sat up. Then he saw that Captain Booth lay on the floor, gasping, with his hands clasped over his stomach, trying to staunch the flow of blood welling through his fingers.

Payne knelt beside Booth and tried to unbutton his battle-blouse. Booth was shaking and his face was already pale.

'I've blown a bloody hole in my guts,' he said, wincing.

Payne took his coat and rolled it up, placing it beneath Booth's head.

And then the cellar door rattled.

Payne froze. Someone inside was trying to open it. The handle moved, the door rattled again and blows began to sound on the wood.

Payne rose and looked at the door. A tremendous blow shook it and the wood around the lock began to break and splinter. More blows sounded. Payne picked up the pistol from the ground.

The door opened. Dim light within outlined a man's figure.

'Stay where you are, Flense, or I'll shoot,' Payne said, positioning himself at the top of the stairs and raising the pistol.

'What the fuck are you saying?' the man said in German.

'I know you speak English. I saw the records.'

Flense still spoke in German. 'Do you know, I've just about had enough of this fucking nonsense for one night. Get out of my way or I swear I will cut your eyes out.'

As the man spoke he began to shuffle up the stairs towards Payne.

Payne brandished the revolver. 'I won't let you —'

Something heavy flew up the stairs and hit Payne on the shoulder. He stumbled backwards and the man charged at him.

'Stop!' Payne shouted, knowing the warning was pointless, as the moonlight caught the wild, murderous look in his attacker's eyes. The knife blade rose and…

The pistol barked in Payne's hand and the man seemed to hit an invisible wall. The bullet stopped him dead and he collapsed.

Payne rose and walked towards him, keeping the pistol trained on his head.

The bullet had caught the man in the centre of his chest, right above the sternum.

He made weak movements as blood poured from his wound, but his eyes held Payne's as he whispered low curses, teeth bared in his gaunt face so that he seemed more animal than man. Hatred and rage flared for a moment and then the light faded from his eyes. A hideous rattle sounded in his throat: he was gone.

Payne raced down the stairs to the cellar.

A woman lay face up on a table. She was breathing, but her skin was pale. A single droplet of blood was meandering across the inside of her bared forearm.

A man was lying on the floor beside her, face down. The hair on the back of his head was matted with blood and there was blood on the floor beside him. It looked as if there'd been a struggle in the cellar: a chair was overturned and another had been smashed.

Payne checked their vital signs and found that both their hearts were beating strongly. He ran towards the road and began waving his flashlight in the direction of the nearest army checkpoint, flashing a single repeated message: SOS.

After he had done this for several minutes, he returned to the place where Booth was lying, caught hold of his hand and held it. Stomach wound, he thought. It was the worst place to get hit. Booth was losing a lot of blood. Several times he had tried to speak, but it caused him too much pain to continue.

It took ten minutes for the soldiers to arrive and another ten before the ambulance drew up. By then Booth was unconscious.

The ambulance took Booth and the two people from the cellar away on stretchers. Payne called out to one of the stretcher bearers, 'Make sure those two are placed under guard. They might try to escape.'

Afterwards he stood outside the house, staring up at the moon. He was trembling. He'd made a point of avoiding physical confrontation throughout his career and now within the space of thirty seconds he had separately shot two men.

Shooting Captain Booth had been an accident. It was one of the few times Payne had been unable to put his reasoning skills to good use. This failure would plague him; he knew that already. His hand was still trembling, a sense memory of the recoil as the pistol fired.

The killer lay on the floor where Payne had shot him. The soldiers had covered him with a tarpaulin. Payne lifted it and examined his face. It had been a lucky shot: a quick, clean death. The man's face still held an expression of surprise, the features frozen in the precise moment when the bullet had struck and for that one split second his brain had registered that the shot was mortal.

How old was he? It was difficult to tell, he was so battered and scarred. Payne examined the starburst scar on the man's jaw and wondered what had caused it. He stayed at the crime scene for two hours, overseeing the collection of evidence and trying to piece together what had happened.

There had definitely been a fight in the room. That must have been between the killer and the male captive. The woman did not have a mark on her.

Payne tried to reconstruct the scene in his mind.

Flense would have injected the woman first. That stood to reason. And then what? The woman would have passed out. Did the male victim become suspicious? Had he attacked

Flense? Yes, that must have been what had happened. The male had been beaten unconscious. Payne returned to the police station, brewed tea and drank it slowly, staring at the embers of the flame.

An hour later a soldier knocked at the door.

'Pardon me, sir. Captain Shelley, the medical officer, asked me to bring these over to you. When they were putting the young lady to bed at the hospital they found these tucked inside her clothes. There was another one on the dead man.'

Payne recognised the cardboard documents: they were Red Cross travel permits.

He thanked the soldier. Then he said, 'You've made sure the two casualties are under guard, haven't you?'

The soldier nodded.

Payne went inside and opened the first travel document. The woman's face stared back at him. Payne wondered who she was, what it was she was trying to run from. He held the photo up to the window and tried to detect something in the woman's features that might betray why she needed to escape.

There was nothing: she looked utterly nondescript, pretty even, in a worn, weary kind of way.

Perhaps the man's photo would show more.

Payne opened the document … and ran across the room towards the door, waving his hands at the soldier who was turning his jeep around.

'Is there a problem, sir?' the driver said, halting his jeep with a squeal of brakes.

'The male victim, where did you take him?'

'To the hospital, sir. But what on earth's the matter?'

'The man on this card, the man that was trying to escape Germany. *This* is the man I shot.'

They drove straight to the hospital, but when Payne saw there was no guard in the corridor outside the male prisoner's room he was certain of what he would find when he opened the door. He pushed at it, found it blocked from the inside. He had to find someone to help to break it down.

Only the guard was inside, lying stretched out on the floor. A thin trickle of blood ran down his forehead. The cord from the window blind was wrapped tightly around his neck. His eyes and tongue bulged horribly. His battle-dress blouse and trousers were missing.

The window was open.

16

Ilse awoke in a hospital bed. For a moment she lay completely still, enjoying the luxurious sensation of the clean linen against her skin. Then she began to remember what had happened and wonder where she was and how she came to be there. She remembered that Johannes had been arguing with Joost, the lorry driver, in the cellar of a house. Joost wanted to vaccinate Johannes but Johannes had become suspicious. He had insisted that Joost inject Ilse first. He had threatened the man with a knife. Ilse remembered allowing Joost to roll up her sleeve, the prick of the needle. And then … nothing. She couldn't remember a thing after that. It was all a blank.

She sat up in bed and realised a man in a civilian suit was sitting on the chair beside the bed. The man poured her a glass of water. Ilse drank it, handed back the glass.

'Who are you?' she said, looking up at his long, angular face.

'My name is Payne. I'm a British policeman. What happened in that cellar?'

'My name is Ilse. Ilse Hoffman, née Drechsler.'

'I know. That isn't what I asked you.'

'The man from the Red Cross, the lorry driver. He was going to vaccinate me. He wanted to inject my brother first but Johannes wouldn't let him. He made the man inject me instead.'

She trembled as the mention of her brother's name brought her memories crashing back. 'My God. Johannes. He killed the boy. The Polish boy.'

The policeman knew that, too. His expression did not change, but he nodded. 'He's been buried now. Did you know a man named Captain Booth?'

Ilse nodded.

'I'm afraid he's been flown back to England. He suffered an accident.'

'Accident?'

'He was shot. In the stomach.'

'Did my brother do it?'

The policeman looked towards the window. 'No. Your brother is dead. I shot him.'

Ilse felt nothing initially. Then relief swept through her.

'Will Captain Booth survive?'

Payne hesitated before answering and his eyes became briefly distant. 'Yes, he'll live. He might not recover completely, though.'

On the next day, Ilse was woken by a military nurse with a cold, abrupt manner. The nurse bullied her out of bed, gave her a plain shift to wear and clumpy boots with no laces.

'Where am I going?' Ilse said.

'To an internment camp. At first. They'll decide what to do with you when you get there.'

Ilse followed the nurse outside towards the waiting lorry, watching her laceless boots stir dust as she walked past the British soldiers, her head bowed.

Epilogue

Little Otto was nearing the end of the winding path now. His feet ached, but the mountain air was so crisp and pure he felt he could walk all day. He turned and looked back at the green plains of southern France. This would be one of his last opportunities to see them before the path wound down into a valley. But his spirits were soaring. He was looking forward to seeing Spain.

Two hours later he paused to eat some cheese and salt beef. He had made sure that he was well-provisioned.

Evening came as Little Otto spotted the huntsman's cabin at the far end of the valley. A light snapped on in the window.

Little Otto paused and watched it twinkling as shadows crept down the foothills. He wouldn't be alone tonight. That was lucky. It had been a while now.

He rummaged in the bottom of his bag, looking for his scalpels.

A NOTE TO THE READER

Dear Reader,

Thank you for finishing *Werewolf*. I used about thirty different books while researching Werewolf. Rather than list them all, I will only mention those that I found particularly helpful or inspiring.

The Last Nazis — SS Werewolf Guerrilla Resistance in Europe 1944-1947 by Perry Biddiscombe and Christian Ingrao's *The SS Dirlewanger: The History of the Black Hunters* were both obvious sources of inspiration. *A Strange Enemy People: Germans Under the British, 1945-50* by Patricia Meehan was an excellent source of information on British policy during the occupation, while Richard Bessel's *Germany 1945 — From War to Peace* painted a vivid picture of just how chaotic the situation was in Germany in the months after the German capitulation. My father also gave me an original copy of a booklet entitled *Why We Are Here* that was distributed among the soldiers of 30 Corps when the occupation began and which was invaluable as a tool to think myself into the mindset of British troops back then.

Finally, I must mention *Death in the City of Light* by David King, which tells the real life story of Marcel Petiot, a serial killer who terrorised Paris during and after the German occupation of the city. It was never my intention to write a second novel with a serial killer as the principal antagonist (in fact early drafts of *Werewolf* had a totally different focus) but I found Petiot so horrifying that, without realising at first, my baddie began to morph into something quite different from what I had originally intended. Now, much of Otto Flense's modus operandi (such as the mask of human skin, the use of a false escape line to lure victims and the treasure trove of suitcases) is based directly on Petiot's.

You can find out more on my blog: **www.matthewpritchard.co.uk.** I would also appreciate it enormously if you would review my book anywhere you think appropriate: reviews on **Goodreads** and **Amazon** would be especially appreciated.

Matthew Pritchard

22681077R00170

Printed in Great Britain
by Amazon